About the Author

Veronique Racine is a small organic farmer, life coach, fitness freak and huge science-fiction fan. She likes to imagine how the world will turn out if we continue with our ways… this is what she writes about most.

The Wanderer's Quest

Veronique Racine

The Wanderer's Quest

Olympia Publishers
London

www.olympiapublishers.com
OLYMPIA PAPERBACK EDITION

Copyright © Veronique Racine 2023

The right of Veronique Racine to be identified as author of
this work has been asserted in accordance with sections 77 and 78 of
the Copyright, Designs and Patents Act 1988.

All Rights Reserved

No reproduction, copy or transmission of this publication
may be made without written permission.
No paragraph of this publication may be reproduced,
copied or transmitted save with the written permission of the publisher,
or in accordance with the provisions
of the Copyright Act 1956 (as amended).

Any person who commits any unauthorized act in relation to
this publication may be liable to criminal
prosecution and civil claims for damage.

A CIP catalogue record for this title is
available from the British Library.

ISBN: 978-1-80439-164-8

This is a work of fiction.
Names, characters, places and incidents originate from the writer's
imagination. Any resemblance to actual persons, living or dead, is
purely coincidental.

First Published in 2023

Olympia Publishers
Tallis House
2 Tallis Street
London
EC4Y 0AB

Printed in Great Britain

Dedication

To my friend, Mike: he should know why this book is dedicated to him, but he's so busy, he forgot.

Acknowledgements

Special thanks to everyone who ever read me and encouraged me to continue.

Chapter 1

The Mark of the Damned

A wisp of wind stirred his hair, making his fingers tighten on the hilt of the knife that never left his person, never when he was awake, and certainly never when he slept. It did not wake him, but made his sleep, already restless, a little more chaotic.

He would claim he did not remember the time of before, that he lived in the now only, the now without apparent sense or purpose.

But his mind tormented him when he could not defend himself, reminding him of all that had been, all that had been lost.

His eyes revved up under his lids as the images forced themselves on his diminished conscience: he could see his first memories, when the world had seemed huge and full of promise, when people so far away appeared, their smiling faces and voices coming from a tiny box held in the hand.

He remembered when this big world turned small, when the people hid their smiles under white or multicolored masks, when demanding a hug seemed out of place and forbidden… when the dying started. Then the world didn't seem so big any more.

Confined between four walls, time seemed to stop, to seem eternal, a twilight of uncertainty he felt mostly through his parents' anxiety, and the restrictions to his life that seemed pointless and superfluous.

Until it became horribly real. Talk of friends gone forever, that near unbearable tension in the air, fear running rampant in the streets until it seemed as though it could be felt and seen, a living entity, chasing all those who dared defy the orders set by the government. The point of no return: he recalled it with unbearable clarity in his state of restless slumber. His father had found him shedding tears after learning one of his friends had died from the pandemic plague, and he had looked at him straight in the eyes.

"We do not know what God's plan is for us. It is not for us to know, my son. But we must believe, with all our hearts, that whatever happens, does for a reason. Especially in darkness... our duty is to believe." That was the moment it became clear to him: only belief could carry them through this ordeal, and true belief would reveal those who were worthy from those who were not.

Events that had taken years to unfold flashed before his eyes in instants; surviving the worst of the plague, managing to maintain a level of civilization where all those around turned back to a more primitive state, so much so that their city became known as The Beacon, the light in the darkness of post-civilization.

But such success always attracted the attention of the wrong people, always brought in the leeches and those desperate to profit and not build... and soon all able-bodied men had to defend their Citadel against all forms of attacks.

For a long time, it did seem that everything happened for a reason. Good and bad, it seemed that if you accepted and believed, the world made sense.

Until the Horde came. The Horde lay siege to their city, blocking all escape routes, attacking relentlessly, with no regard for the lives lost in the damned assaults. It seemed their bloodlust and drive to kill was infinite, unstoppable, inexplicable.

The Horde's leader sent his men to their deaths without remorse, only seeking to weaken his enemy, destroy the morale and see his plan through.

It was a mystery to the boy that had become a man, when he lay on his knees, watching his city being sacked to ruins, the women and children screaming in terror as the Horde's soldiers rampaged with the utmost savagery, how their belief could have failed them.

He expected nothing other than death from the Horde's warriors, he wanted nothing other than death when he heard his wife screaming, his son wailing... and then silence. He was wounded, bleeding, perhaps dying already when he was taken, pushed and prodded, to the Horde's commander. All the men thus captured were thrown on their knees in front of the Horde's commander, a tall man shrouded by a veil that was so common in the outer lands, in fear that the virus would return and destroy what was left of humanity.

The commander looked at them each in turn, spitefully and scornfully, before speaking in a low guttural tone.

"You have a chance, one, to survive. You have proven your worth as soldiers. Join us... or die."

"There is no escape, you are beaten, your city is lost. Those who refuse will be used as slaves, unto death, branded... with the Mark of the Damned," the commander continued, letting the weight of his words sink in.

There was no escape, no possible reprieve, no miracle. They were condemned. Death, or death. Physical death, or the death of every moral principle they had ever held dear. Only a handful of the men did not surrender to the commander's wishes. The rest received their brand; one deep cut, crescent-shaped, on the left cheek, one burn mark in the form of an arrow, crossing over the crescent, to complete the mark.

He bore him without a whisper of complaint.

He only wished to collapse and be left to die of exposure as they were pushed and prodded out of the city, bound to each other by heavy, rusted-over chains. But the pain was not yet over.

The procession came to an abrupt halt just out of the city; they had a perfect view of the ramparts that had once stood proud, invincible or so it had seemed at the time.

Shouts, whimpers, sobs; their attention was drawn upwards, where the elders of the city were being pushed forward, to the edge of the walls, by their own sons, those who had given in to the Horde's commander.

The commander was there himself, looking down at his prisoners, his slaves, his new fledgling soldiers

"No escape. No reprieve. The Horde is unstoppable!"

A whimper of pain and anguish did escape his lips as he saw his parents fall to their deaths. A flutter drew him from his dream and the knife flew in his hand, ready to find a target and end a life.

Just a small desert wheatear looking for food, nothing to worry about. He barely relaxed; the bird's nervous manners reminded him of himself.

Always on the look-out for danger, always on the edge of death, living day by day, night by night. Was there true purpose in that existence?

To have such thoughts would cause him a headache he could not afford. The day was coming to an end, the heat of the desert replaced by the brisk coldness of night.

Time to get moving. The night was not necessarily safer than the day, but the shadows made it easier to pass unnoticed. And that meant a better chance to stay alive for yet another day.

He watched dusk becoming dark, then swirled with the apocalypse lights, the night hues that meant death to the unwary when they came down on the earth with gray ashes. The way of the world now. Time to get moving.

Night would not last forever. He knew the paths by heart it would seem, where to go, what dangers lurked in the seemingly open, desert barren land. Nothing was ever what it seemed. More people than could be expected dwelled in the shadows.

For although the Horde governed the world with an iron fist of terror, many still survived in the fringes, their skills needed to continue the trade of more advanced civilization.

The old cities had been deserted for the most part, for fear that the terrible plague that had swept the earth still dwelled there. But the fringes' people overcame that fear to scavenge the cities for spare parts needed to repair automobiles or other systems, search for bullets and blades that could be sold to the Horde's agents, thus earning their nicknames of "Scavengers".

And those people were always on the look-out for the big score… like someone bearing the mark, someone who should not have been free but was.

His face was always shrouded by a mask and a hood; one could never be too careful. No one could know he was still alive, or that life would not remain his for very long. Nonetheless, he too had to survive. He hunted what he could to eat but animals did not thrive as much as could have been expected in this post-apocalyptic world.

The Horde kept a tight grip on all food production, terrorizing the farmers to ensure that all their yields would be given to their agents and those alone.

The black market existed but he needed something to trade

for whatever scraps he could get. And that meant venturing in the crumbling cities himself.

The proud emblems of the past, now decrepit and derelict, a danger to all those who dared defy the unspoken rule; to let the past where it was and focus on the future only. He studied his 'prey' carefully; he had been observing the old city for many days, trying to figure out how many scavengers dwelled inside.

They were as quick as mice, disappearing in the night, eyes always watching. This was their domain, he was the intruder. No matter the old fear of the disease, the Scavengers were what he really had to watch out for.

Despite his jaded demeanor and glum outlook on life in general, as he slipped into the city, he felt the thrill, the rush of adrenaline; one could not escape it.

The countdown was on; he gave himself three turns of his hourglass before having to leave. The Scavengers would not stay blind to his presence much longer than that… if he was really lucky. Nothing was more unnerving than being in enemy territory, trapped inside the hood of a car, sweating and swearing under one's breath as one tried to wedge a carburetor out while making the least noise possible.

Rust had made the screws impossible to turn, they had to be sawed or broken off, which meant an insane amount of noise he could not afford. But he could not leave the doomed city empty-handed either.

There is a kind of awareness, a sixth sense of sorts, when you are in danger, when you are where you are not welcome and from which you should run away from at full speed. You can start feeling when you are not welcome any more, when you are running out of luck, when you have been discovered, or you will be. He knew he should have run, left the carburetor where it was, and come back another day. But his client was getting impatient, uncaring of the danger he was exposing his 'tool' to with his haste to get the sought-after part.

His three hours were not up... but his time was.

A soft shuffle, scrapings of a metallic nature; he did not panic, he breathed in deeply, and emerged from the car to face his opponents.

Four of them, shrouded in shadows, circling around him like predators. They were silent and solemn, they were in the right, protecting their territory. He was fair game. If not, he hoped his opponents were prepared to meet their Maker.

He could see the telltale signs of guns, pistols, on the Scavengers' bodies, but he knew they would use their blades, their swords. Bullets were rare, scarce, reserved for the Horde, and so noisy.

There were those who revered the old cities, and all feared them; but the unspoken rule respected by all was that silence was to be observed. Out of respect for the giants of the past, out of fear of bringing back the calamities that had toppled the world... those who lived in the old citadels lived and died in silence.

They attacked swiftly, sure of themselves, four against one, how could this go in any other way than the obvious, than what was expected?

They had no idea who they were up against.

All his training as a Citadel soldier, all the hardships he had suffered through as the Horde's slave, surviving to this point in his life made him a redoubtable opponent. When attacking a lone target, coordination was necessary to ensure a smooth, successful attack. Blunt, brute force only resulted in confusion and someone who did not let himself be impressed by the odds in his disfavor, someone who neither feared death nor welcomed it, could use this to his advantage.

And so the fight began. The swordsmanship wasn't exactly important, the will to triumph was what won or lost an engagement. That and the ability to recognize the others' weaknesses, the cool-headedness necessary to rake in that advantage at the opportue moment. The first rule of any fight: never lose sight of the bigger picture.

He ducked and dodged the first strike and quickly identified the best fighter, the one he had to get rid of first to gain the upper hand in the battle, to strike fear in the others' hearts.

For fear won battles much faster than skill alone.

He had the speed and knowhow and slipped between two of the Scavengers to strike directly at the best swordsman.

But he was parried because he was faced with the best warrior. Speed was his best defense and while the Scavenger turned to attack, he ducked and struck at one of the fools scrambling to get to him.

A lucky hit, a masterful swordplay: he was showered with blood as the corpse collapsed on the ground, convulsing as its life force left the body. And when he turned around to face his opponents again, he saw that glint in their eyes. Fear, unbridled. They were not dealing with the usual malnourished thieves. They were faced with a real threat to their lives.

He didn't give them the time to adapt. Now was his chance, his one opportunity to turn the battle to his advantage. He was used to those situations, but the human factor was always a wild card. Anyone could turn the tide, a slip, a fall, one miscalculated step, and the life he did not care for would be over.

Unless theirs was called to the executioner's block first.

His blade struck an arm, slicing through flesh, bringing blood and a muffled cry of pain to his enemy's lips. They wanted to regroup and think of another attack strategy but he didn't give them the time. He could not afford it.

He thrust his sword through a man's back, uncaring of the un-sportsmanship of that action; there was no honor among thieves, among enemies, just the bitter struggle of survival.

The best warrior attacked at that moment, just as his sword was stuck in the other's body; he managed to duck but the blade nicked his hood and face mask, making it fall on his shoulder.

There was a moment of stupor as the Scavenger recognized the mark and sputtered in astonishment: "The Damned!"

He felt the panic himself. Recognized, branded, he could see the greed in the man's eyes even as he slit his throat. Panting hard, he turned to his last opponent, who of course had taken the opportunity to run, fueled by the thought of untold rewards.

This shameful, hateful brand that made him a target as soon as it was unveiled. The mark of slavery and defeat, the mark of the damned. And damned he would remain.

He could feel a thousand eyes on him. Somehow the word was given. And the hunt was on.

Chapter 2

Deadly Maze

He had to scramble to get out of the city, but he knew better than to go for the obvious paths, the main arteries. That was murder for him; the Scavengers controlled their city. They knew every escape path.

He had to think it through, not react with his most primal nature. Fear would kill him faster than his enemies would.

Not make a break for the city walls as quickly as possible but rather the opposite, go deep in the city, fool them... and hopefully, find an escape within that crumbling labyrinth...

He didn't even hesitate. The path was made, he had to follow it through, whatever the cost to himself. Death lurked in every corner and perhaps his time had come.

It didn't bother him. The fact that he still had a chance to live was what made it difficult to think rationally.

Facing certain death was easy. To think that one bad decision on his part meant his life or death had a paralyzing effect even he wasn't completely immune to.

But it didn't stop him from running off as soundlessly as he could. He had an advantage. Damned captures were worth much more alive than dead...

The plan. He couldn't lose sight of it. Escape the Scavengers, remain free, get as far away as he could from that doomed place, lest he wanted to draw the whole of the Horde on him.

But something was interfering with that great survival plan. He needed supplies, he needed tools, he was running on empty.

In other terms, he had come here to win, not to lose, and he didn't want to come out of this empty-handed, hunted and tracked like an animal.

He wanted that carburetor… and the excitement of the hunt for him could work to his advantage. If he kept a cool head.

He stopped running and found a small niche between crumbled walls to hide in. For a long while, all he heard was the pounding of his blood in his temples. Much to his shame.

Scared like this, how could he ever dream of gaining the upper hand, of actually coming out of this the victor?

Control. Slow those heartbeats. Remember that death was the final outcome for everyone on Earth, and death was far better than falling in the wrong hands again. Finally, he was able to hear what was happening around him. Scuffles of feet, near soundless whisperings; time to make himself scarce. They were closing in on his position… or sniffing around, unable to find him, having lost his obvious trace.

It convinced him he was right. Be bold, be daring, remain fearless. Recuperate what he had come for. Come out of this the winner… or not at all. The decision taken, he found that his heart stopped its unsteady beating. He was ready to face whatever the Scavengers had in store for him.

He had a few surprises of his own for them, if the inevitable happened.

As he had suspected, the way was opened, unhindered, back to the truck he had been working on. The Scavengers figured he was running scared, as anyone sane of body and mind should be. They didn't know him very well. They didn't know the consequences of bearing that hateful mark.

Just as he came into view of the truck, he stopped dead in his hurried tracks. He could sense it: someone was already there.

He was puzzled no end by the sight of the clothed figure. Dressed like the desert people, complete with rad shield to face the sandstorms that swept those immensities from time to time, carrying the poisons released in the atmosphere by the meltdown of too many power plants.

Even more so when, with a loud clunk and a muffled grunt of triumph, that person pulled out his carburetor.

And saw him standing there like a statue.

There was an instant of stunned stupefaction on both ends, but it could not last. The Desert Raider reached for his weapon, a rusted-over but still perfectly deadly AK-47.

The click of the safe, being removed, seemed incredibly loud to their ears, a sure beacon attracting the wrong attention, but both were too engrossed by their own confrontation to allow their eyes to deviate from the enemy that was the closest to them.

The standstill could not last, yet both were loath to provoke the other, to precipitate the inevitable.

Finally, one had to make the step, show their true colors, attack or run. And neither had the intention to run.

If body language could scream anything, it was: Go away! The Desert Raider seemed a little panicked and desperate, but that made him all the more dangerous. Him?

The darkness made it a little hard to see the eyes, but he could have sworn he was faced with a woman. Not that this made him relax in any way; women were just as deadly as men, just as cruel, relentless and vindictive. If she wanted that carburetor, it was to survive, and survival justified such leeway in one's conduct. Assuming one had a code of honor to begin with.

"Don't move," she said as he shifted to find his balance, her tone harsh and merciless. She wasn't shooting. She didn't want to alert the Scavengers. She knew she stood a better chance reasoning with him, or killing him, than to face the whole of the city's population.

"Give me that and we'll call it a day," he answered. Being stubborn had kept him alive all these years, he wasn't about to give it up and turn scared. Death came only once... in one's life.

"Come and get it if you dare," the woman answered through clenched teeth.

She wanted a silent exit out of this mess... as did he. But both wanted what the other had. Victory, success, something to show for what they had risked.

The stand-off could not last, yet they were unable to break it on their own. Too many chances of actually surviving had a strange paralyzing effect. So of course, someone came and ended it for them.

They both heard the whistle and ducked at the same time; the spear struck the ground with deadly precision, just centimeters from where the Desert Raider stood a second before.

Of course the Scavengers targeted her first because she held the obvious weapon. She was the most dangerous enemy, she would draw them in... which was fine for him if he could recuperate what he had come for.

Time to move. Be daring and crazy. Nothing to lose but life and limbs.

The Scavenger was calling his friends, ready to reap in the profits, hunt down the intruders. He didn't react in time to the mad dash to the car and the spear missed by a long shot.

She uttered a hoarse cry of surprise when he tried to grab her loot bag away from her; the weapon she was holding was pointed right in his direction and she depressed the trigger instinctively.

A dry click, nothing else. He didn't even have the time to cringe or feel a flutter of fear at the thought that he had avoided certain death by pure chance. Incredibly, he felt anger rather than anything else.

"What good is a gun without bullets?" he hissed at her, pushing the barrel away from his face, ready to tear her loot bag away and escape before the Scavengers were all over them.

The weapon's butt smacked against his temple in a swift movement that left his ear ringing and his consciousness teetering on the verge of failure. He shouldn't have dismissed her so easily. Anyone who survived in the wild had tricks up their sleeves.

"Has its uses," she said breathlessly before squeezing out of the car, wary of any possible reprisals from the Scavengers' part.

He tried to catch her but he was seeing double and he couldn't control himself, evaluate the distance properly or even make his fingers curl around anything.

Her receding image disappeared completely, fading to black, as he battled the dizziness caused by the blow. The ringing wouldn't stop. He collapsed on the worn-out, dusty car seat, wishing adrenaline would allow him to push through this wound and weakness.

Of course, the moment he managed to regain control, to see past the blur... was the moment he realized what horrible trouble he was in.

The Scavengers had gathered around the car, wary of a possible trap, ready to wait it out until their prey realized there was no escape possible.

Not even through death.

He emerged from the car, as unafraid as possible. Viewing this as the final test, on his way to the other world, or nothingness.

What did it matter, as they were nothing but ashes anyway?

"Who goes first?" he put to the bedraggled band, who looked more puzzled by this defiance than anything else. Did they really imagine he would go quietly to his execution?

He pulled out his sword: that language, the Scavengers understood. Violence, murder, wanton destruction… and bounty. The favors of the Horde leaders.

They rushed toward him and he surprised himself by smiling; not even in a feral fashion. Relief.

He felt immense relief at the thought that he would not see another sunrise ever again, that his battle for survival was finally over.

He even considered not fighting back, letting them cut him asunder, but there was a small chance they would hold back and capture him. He could not take that chance. Take as many with him as he could, make them blood crazy, and then his death would be assured.

He started swinging as they closed in on him and then the improbable, the impossible happened.

A sound like thunder booming across the city limits, making them all come to a dead stop in surprise and incomprehension.

And one of the men fell face first on the dusty ground while the others were still stupefied.

One word, one order echoed throughout the city: "Run!" And he knew this order was addressed to him.

He started moving without even realizing what he was doing. This was not a providential save, but he had no clue what to make of it.

By the time the Scavengers reacted to this new threat with their usual savagery, he had cut a path through them and was on his way to the nearest exit, a breach through the walls he had noticed while scouting the city.

He heard a spear whistling in his direction and just had the time to jump sideways, colliding with the wall hard enough to make him see stars… just when he needed all his wits about him.

Another gunshot made him scramble forward even faster before he realized that it was working for him, keeping the enemies at bay, providing cover for him.

Still, he hated the thunderous noise, the reminder of the past that wasn't any more. It did not have its place in the new world.

Those weapons should not exist any more, like the world that had made them.

But in this particular case, he had to admit that the range and effectiveness came in handy.

He ran into the desert, expecting a spear or arrow in his back at any moment. There was another gunshot, loud, startling, and then silence.

He had to keep moving. The Scavengers had been pushed back but they would come back, wanting revenge for this affront.

He had not survived all those years on the fringes of what passed for 'civilization' without developing skills in tracking and hunting. Only one person could have come to his rescue like that, although he did not have a clue why she would risk anything for him, or help him in any way.

He intended to find out.

One wasn't supposed to look a gift horse in the mouth, doubt or question miracles or motives, but he had more than one reason to want to see her again. Apart from the timely rescue, she still held the carburetor that was his.

He had no intention of being gallant or giving. This world was unforgiving and he followed the given example. One could not be nice and survive. This was an impossibility. Everyone for him or herself.

She was gifted, he had to grant her that. Able to cover her tracks and give him a headache trying to feel where she had gone, as the minute details he could look for had been for the most part erased by the rising wind of the coming day.

Maybe it was the threat of the Scavengers that made him more panicked, less observant; the rising sun was weighing on him. He had to hide.

Then again, so did she.

The fire was small, inconspicuous, barely enough to keep the cold of the night at bay. In the small cavern, the smoke it made was almost enough to be intoxicating; what wood and dried plants she had gathered produced a bad smell that got to the head through the lungs.

Still, she wouldn't have gone without it. It gave a sentiment of security, of home, that always brought a wave of nostalgia she couldn't quite control. False security, she knew, but sometimes, that was the only thing that allowed her to go through the endless nights.

Never relax, always keep one eye open, but sometimes, fatigue took over, that feeling of living life for nothing, of just wanting to sleep forever without worry took over. And led to inattention, to that sense of danger, waking up from half-slumber to find herself looking up at an unsheathed blade.

"Not so cocky without your guns?" the man said a little disdainfully.

"I saved your life," she said in a breath, recognizing him. By the light of the fire, she could see his disfiguring scar.

"I am forever grateful, he answered. I might let you live as well."

She waited tensely; one slash and that would be the end of

her. At the same time, her fingers inched toward her salvation, the way to turn this stand-off to her advantage again. At least even the odds... if only he didn't see it, if only he could be blind to this... the shadows were everywhere in the cavern...

"Where is it?" he asked, exposing the source of his apparent generosity.

"I sold it, what do you think?" she answered softly. "Hot item like that, I'd keep it around? You must think I am stupid. "

"Not making that mistake," he answered; she could feel the weight of his stern stare on her. One false move and that would be the end.

"I'm not playing," he said warningly.

"Okay, okay, I give up. Promise you'll let me go and I'll tell you where I stashed it."

He knew there was something about her tone... he couldn't trust a word she said. Not that this was news in any way... what was she planning? What except a mad dash for freedom, liberty and gaining back the upper hand? But where would the threat come from?

The atmosphere in the small cave was so thick with tension that it seemed to choke out the fire. It became more feeble and weak with each passing second, making the shadows become alive...

But neither of them could take their eyes off each other for a moment. They both knew what they were, killers, opportunists, with little to no conscience, only out to save their own skin. This could not end well.

"Just tell me," he said and the words seemed to be blasphemous. No one could talk their way out of this situation. It could only turn bloody.

"Right here in my bag," she said, nodding at an old duffel

bag right next to her leg.

Two choices. Ask her to throw it to him or tell her to move away. He stared at her eyes but he couldn't tell what would please her the most, what she wanted him to do. She had a trick up her sleeve… but he could just kill her. Be done with it.

There was no reason to be gallant, human, not in this broken world. No reason to spare her, as she wasn't innocent. If such a thing still existed.

"Why did you help me?" he put to her and for a long moment, she just looked at him as though she hadn't understood him.

"That scar on your cheek," she said finally, actually lowering her eyes a second to look at it. "Anyone who has it deserves a little help."

Not the answer he expected and it made him feel more exposed somehow; she seemed to be telling the truth about that particular action of hers. "But not enough to hand me that auto part without a fight?" he put to her.

She actually chuckled. "Nah… people need this. They trust me to get it to them. Not without a fight, no."

"What's stopping me from just slashing your throat?" he answered.

She glanced up at his face again; her eyes were so weary and tired, but still with a glint of amusement. "I'm supposed to have that answer? Go ahead, I can't stop you."

There was something so abasing about killing freely, especially when one had been in the scope of others for so long. To be lenient was to be weak, but what he really wanted was to get what was his back and never cross her path again.

"What people, besides yourself?" he said, if only to buy some more time, evaluate her character a bit more, try and guess what he could expect from her.

"People who have no love for the Horde," she said in a whisper, as though she was loath to say that hateful name aloud, for fear of reprisals or simply because it brought back very unpleasant memories boiling to the surface.

He let out a dry chuckle. "Wonderful answer. Who loves the Horde, apart from its leader?

"…Tell me more if you want to live."

He didn't like the change in her face, from resigned back to calculating, but what game was he playing? One slash and he would be free of these doubts and worries. There was no point being humane, it was only weakness that would lead to inevitable death. "Frankly, if survival is your life mission, best you don't know anything more. These people are crazy… crazy to think they can take on the Horde… But they pay for premium parts, so who will complain?"

"So what are you doing with them?" he inquired almost idly. This had to be the most conversation he had had in the past year. His voice sounded rusty even to him.

"Had to get away from the rads," she said after a long moment of silence, spent squinting at him in the darkness. "Getting worse, it's spreading, on foot, I'd've died. I owe them that much."

"Good prices and the likes," he said with a hint of sarcasm.

She chuckled and shrugged. "Are you going to kill me? Because this is getting uncomfortable."

"No need to kill you if you give me what I want."

"No need to give anything when you can take," she retorted, apparently a little blasé with the whole stand-off.

He lowered his blade, a tad, a bit, hesitating a little. Just what she was waiting for. She threw herself backwards to avoid his blade, as he only had to thrust forward to impale her; she rolled on herself, grabbing her bag as she did, and pulled out a pistol before he could do more than take a step forward.

Changing the balance of power and threat in her favor.

She didn't shoot him right away though; that didn't mean he could relax, only that his problems with her were far from over.

"Another dud? Will it work or blow back in your face?" he said with more scorn than he felt. But there was not a trace of fear in his voice.

She laughed a little. "Only one way to find out, right?"

For a long moment, it looked as though she would have no qualms, she would shoot him point blank, no remorse or question asked.

"Get out of here," she ordered finally.

"Will this one work?" he retorted, not willing to let it go. What he wanted, even he wasn't sure. The part, of course, victory, closure, triumph, proof that he could outwit anyone. He would face it to the end, the bitter end if need be. He would not back down.

"You really want to find out then? Take this, get out while you still can," she warned. What could you do against a man who did not fear death except kill him? When bluff didn't work, you had to prove your mettle, your ruthlessness, or be forever considered a wimp, a sentimental, weak, lenient fool.

She was none of those things, but even as she held his gaze, to convince him she meant deadly business, her eyes tracked to that scar. The scar that was causing such an uproar she had trouble containing it.

And, his senses being just as attuned and sharp as hers, he noticed that lapse right away.

"Who?" he put to her in a murmur.

"Who was given that scar, who did you know that had to bear it? Unto death, I am supposing," he continued softly.

She grunted in exasperation at her own weakness. "Sit down!" she ordered. "This is not over… but I bet you're hungry."

Not exactly what he was expecting but they were both treading on dangerous slippery ground. He sat down, keeping a close eye on her.

"You have food?" he asked; he was feeling weakened by the privations of the past days and weeks.

She sighed and chuckled. "A bit left, getting stale, why not share?" She moved slowly to get her bag, as they were both as jumpy and tense as possible.

He waited until she had bitten into the bread - which was extremely stale and tasteless - to risk a bite himself. She hadn't killed him outright but that didn't mean she wasn't playing a game of some sort.

She handed him some moldy figs and a canteen of dust-tasting water. All in all, the best meal he had had in a long time.

"My father," she finally said after he finished the canteen.

"What did he do to deserve the mark?" he asked.

"What's your name?" she replied.

"What does it matter?" he retorted. "Who cares about a name? What's yours?"

"Raydr," she said, a glint of malice in her eyes, as this was more of a description than anything else.

"Madan," he answered, flashing a smile that seemed out of place on his privation-hardened features.

She chuckled. "Funny."

He shook his head. "No not really."

"Before it happened, 'IT', he had just been transferred to the consulate… some city, I don't remember, it's been so long… He knew it would be bad, and when it started to get even worse, he did everything he could to get us out of there… away from the rad stations. He knew it would be horrible, and he wasn't wrong."

"That's not how he was marked, or why," Madan said, wishing he had more water. His throat was dry.

"Of course not," she agreed wearily.

He settled down a little more comfortably, if rocks and dust could be called comfortable. She glanced at him from the corner of her eye and sighed.

"We settled in a town, it had kept some tech. My father helped organize things, and for a while, it looked as though everything would be okay… until they came."

"The Horde?" he put to her.

"I don't think they were called that then," she said slowly, as though searching through her memory for the answer. "Just a band of thieves and murderers… intent on pillage and looting and slavery… you know the kind."

"I know the kind," he confirmed.

"My father hid my brother and I when they attacked, and we survived… but he was gone when we finally came out."

"Gone but not dead."

"Not dead, she confirmed with a small, bitter smile. Unfortunately not dead… No one would tell us anything, barely enough of them left to tell us what had happened. But I knew he was alive, just this feeling… I had to find him, save him."

"Did you?" he inquired idly. His head was heavy, why was he so sleepy?

"I found him. I didn't save him," she said, her tone turning harsh. "No one could, after what they had done to him. They broke him. They destroyed him. He would have been better off dying that day."

"Yeah," Madan agreed heavily. How many times had he thought and wished the same?

"No happy ending in this world, no hope, no compassion… no pity," she concluded, looking at him with a strange telltale intensity.

And he understood what was wrong with him, just before the poison finished taking effect and he fell like a brick on the pebbly ground.

Chapter 3

Fool's Crusade

The sun was setting again when he emerged from the slumber caused by the poison she had put in the water she had given him. He couldn't believe how foolish he had been; it was embarrassing to say the least. Dangerous. Suicidal. Everyone was an enemy, there was no truce possible, no in-between. Whatever good there had been in this world, it had long ago been snuffed out by the vileness of mankind.

How could one mention of another marked, another Damned soul have made him forget that?

And yet she had not been lying. Proof of which, she had left him alive, only using her subterfuge to escape.

That didn't mean he would be caught twice. That didn't mean he would let her get away with it.

It wasn't only the insult or the stolen part, it was the principle of it. He had to get back at her. He wasn't sure he could explain it himself; if he let this pass, he would lose his edge, his self-control, his invincibility. Or maybe he was simply pissed off.

Very pissed off to have been shown a weakness of his; and the only way to repair this lack on his part was to take it out on her.

Of course, the road ahead would not be easy: she had left a long time ago and he had a lot of catching up to do.

The day's wind had erased every trace of the direction she

had taken but he knew he'd find her. His instinct was never wrong.

No matter how much time it'd take, he would find her… and repay her in full.

Following someone's trail was not that difficult, in a desertic world that offered little to no oasis of life. There were only so many places she could go to for supplies and she had said too much of the truth. That was her mistake.

There were rumors of a new group, contenders to the Horde's title, amassing from the south, building an army on the hatred generated by the Horde commander's population control techniques.

And although they would have liked to keep their location a secret, it was not too hard to track them down either.

They were a suspicious bunch, however, and getting into their encampment just to get back at that woman seemed a little far-fetched a revenge, even for him.

But he had set his mind to it, so he would not back down: this stubbornness was what had allowed him to survive the mark all these years.

First to gain their trust and learn of her whereabouts: she was his target, not their doomed rebellion.

There wasn't a doubt in his mind that they would fail miserably. He had fought the Horde's soldiers, and as long as the commander was still alive, they would be unstoppable.

Only fools and madmen would stand in their way.

As he was neither, he wasn't about to make the same mistake as those idiots.

But he would make them tell him where she was, where she had gone… and then he would leave them to their inevitable fate.

To infiltrate such a group, you need to possess something

they wanted. He quickly made contact with one of their suppliers, who was not against an extra hand, especially after he proved his worth in a small test of combat skill.

And so he accompanied them in a raid on a nearby city. They were numerous and feared not the Scavengers, preferring to massacre their enemies than to slip in and out unnoticed.

He was amazed and appalled by their gall, even as he helped them achieve their objective; they truly thought, believed that they would witness, herald, a new order to the world. A herald made of the blood of innocents… or as innocents did not exist in this world, people unconcerned by such grand visions of their existence, people content with surviving only.

There was a perverse pleasure to being the leader, to being the stronger, to imposing pain and suffering on others, without them being able to retaliate.

He had never been in that position, he had always struggled to survive, to come out on top, to keep fighting to live. And this facility was sickening to him.

Maybe the Scavengers were scum, maybe they didn't deserve to breathe the air… but who were they to make that decision for them?

He was careful not to let the disgust show. Their victory was bringing him closer to his goal and that was all that mattered.

And with everything they recuperated from their Scavengers' Cache, there was more than enough to please the fools and their 'visionary' leader.

He wasn't completely sure the 'cure' was better than the disease, in this particular case. The 'loot' gave them access to the Challengers' camp and he evaluated their defenses and the risk they posed from the inside. So easy to get in, they were not nearly careful enough. What if he were a spy for the Horde?

Their petty rebellion would have died an early death. Who did they think they were against?

Only the most barbaric savages left on the planet.

He was appalled by their incredible naivete, their idealism, backed up by the blood of others. From what he could hear of the whispers as they walked past, from what he could feel of their group as an ensemble, they had escaped the invading rads of the South and had never expected the situation to be so bad in the North. To survive, they had had to stick together against the forces of a nature made toxic and destructive and had thought this was the worst this broken world could throw at them.

And they intended to set things straight, back on the right path.

He really had to hurry in finding Raydr and having his revenge because the days of this bedraggled band were counted and headed toward the end at an accelerated pace. Madan followed his 'war chief' into the leader's hut, a yurt made of oily, smelly tarps that were patched up and had seen better days decades before.

The chief had taken a liking to him given his fighting skill and wanted him for a personal bodyguard, which was just fine with him, as long as it got him where he wanted to go. He had to stay inconspicuous, not draw too much attention to himself, and keep his eyes and ears open to find out where she had gone after delivering her sought-after auto part. So it was quite a surprise when the first thing he saw when he entered the yurt was Raydr, leaning over a map and pointing out strategic locations to a man with bad rad burns on his face and exposed skin. And an even worse surprise when she turned her head to look straight at them.

Straight at him.

The moment seemed to last an eternity - or was it only a

second?

Her eyes turned away from him, from his eyes, where they had wandered, as he was wearing his hood and his features were hidden by the desert guard, the cloth that hid his mark.

All she had to do was pull that mask and reveal him... she would recognize the mark in an instant. But she seemed preoccupied by the map she was showing the Rebel Leader and did not give him so much as another glance.

Madan and his 'leader' waited for the 'war meeting' to be over, both trying to listen in as much as they could, but for very different reasons. He could not fidget around, but that map... he could have sworn he recognized that map, what it showed, save for a few modifications made over time. His heart squeezed painfully in his chest. Home.

He hadn't thought about it, consciously, at the very least, in so much time. He had done so much to let it go, to forget it, to act as though this nomadic existence had been his life all along.

And yet one look at that map and his interest, his need to know, came rushing back, so strongly that he could hardly contain it. What had happened in all those years? What had they done to his conquered, defenseless home?

"As you can see, they reinforced the walls after the last rad storm. It caused heavy damage to the North Tower, and they haven't gotten around to that side yet. Their slaves were left exposed and they're suffering from exposure, making them less efficient workers," Raydr explained with cold, clinical precision.

"They don't know how to deal with rad storms yet?" the leader questioned.

"Oh I think they know. What I've been trying to tell you, sir: They don't give a damn. About anyone or anything."

"Ruthlessness is not a strength, Raydr. It'll be their

downfall," the leader said with confidence... and horrible naivete.

"We'll see, Zahim," Raydr said with barely concealed disbelief. "They've been in charge for more than twenty years. They must be doing something right."

Zahim chuckled harshly. Perhaps he was not as naive as he seemed.

"Violence is never right, taking is never right... And that's why we'll beat them... in their own home."

"Wasn't theirs to begin with, Zahim. They conquered it, like everything else here," Raydr said, a complete waste of breath on that dreamer.

"Then they made a lot of enemies, created resentment, and that will work in our favor," Zahim said with retching certitude.

"And if all else fails, we have you, don't we?" he said, winking at her. With his burnt skin and the suppurating boils around his head, he looked monstrous.

But no one cared about appearances any more. Looks didn't matter, the vision did. And this man's vision of a better life had fired up his followers' imagination, to the point that they were ready to die for him. And die they would.

Not that this was any of Madan's problem. He had come for one thing, one person, and he had her within his grasp.

Although leaving her in this mess was probably a bigger punishment than exacting his revenge on her... But it was the principle of revenge, however petty it could seem.

Plus, he was almost sure she would be smart enough to slip through everyone's fingers. She had done it with him, after all, and almost no one could claim as much.

"Oh, hey, Khasir, there you are," Zahim said, finally glancing in their direction. "Did you get everything we asked for?"

"Yes, we did, sir," Khasir answered readily. "More than you expected and imagined, actually. A very worthy raid."

"Good, great…" Zahim said, putting a friendly, bandaged hand on Khasir's shoulder (the raider shuddered in fear at the contact, but the rebel leader didn't seem to notice or care). "How many of them joined us?"

Khasir sputtered with uncertainty for a moment. "They, they were-" he hesitated.

"Devout followers of the Horde. Impossible to reason with," Madan intervened, making his voice deeper and hoarser in the hopes that Raydr, still looking at her map nearby, would not notice and recognize him.

Zahim sighed in disappointment, not even thinking about questioning or doubting his word. Was he naive or purposely blind to the truth and the obvious?

"It's crazy that these people can't see what's bad for them," he said in a breath. Pained breath. What was wrong with him? In close contact, he reeked of death.

"The important thing is that we have everything you wanted and more," Khasir said. "These people are not real soldiers. Not useful, treacherous."

"Told you as much," Raydr intervened. "You cannot trust anyone here. The Horde has a good system. Rewards or death."

"That works only when the good people let it work. We will show them that it doesn't have to be this way."

Raydr sighed inaudibly: Madan himself couldn't believe what he was hearing. Was such determination madness or folly? "And this'll happen before or after you die?" Raydr said, meaning her words to sting. And they did. Zahim looked particularly stricken by the reminder, and now everything made sense. Only a man on death's doorsteps could lead such a foolish quest.

"Before," Zahim answered finally. "My last contribution to this world."

"A great contribution," Khasir said with exaggerated reverence.

All he wanted was to get paid and get another job. The extent of his admiration for the 'cause'. All lies and deceit, nothing true, one propaganda replacing the other... But still Madan had trouble tearing his eyes away from the map of his city... and remembering the true reason behind his crazy infiltration of this demented group.

"Yes, exactly," Zahim answered as though he didn't see the greed in Khasir's eyes. "Worthy... Pay him, they deserve it. Good job out there... and... who is this fellow?"

First time he actually laid eyes on Madan and the Marked man suddenly felt so exposed. Seen and recognized by all. How had he thought he could pull it off? They were naive, but they weren't stupid... were they?

"He is mine," Khasir said, the greed omnipresent in his voice. If he hadn't wanted some cover and protection from Zahim's stare and Raydr's furtive glances, Madan would have hated that proprietary attitude and he would have put a term to it immediately. Never again would he belong to anyone. Death was far better an alternative than the degradation of slavery.

"He's your son?" Zahim asked with surprise. As they were both about the same age, the question seemed simply ludicrous. To both men.

"No, he is... employee. Muscle. Skilled fighter. I am lucky to have him. Very useful in a fight," Khasir said.

"Is that so? "Zahim said, eyeing Madan evaluatingly. Those

looks... How he never wanted to be looked at like this again! Like merchandise to be bought and traded. "We could always use more good fighters," Zahim said with such tact and subtlety.

"He is mine, debt of honor," Khasir assured with a quick look at Madan, to make sure he would not object.

The Rebel Leader glanced at the desert dweller to verify Khasir's claim in the matter.

Madan kept his eyes forward, un-reacting; no denial, no acceptance. He wasn't anyone's merchandise, anyone's property... but if only this awkward moment could pass... If only the two men could stop acting like preening overgrown idiots... If wishes filled a well, there would always be enough to drink...

"I belong to no one," he answered finally. "I follow Khasir for the money, nothing else. I have no interest in grand goals and ideals. A waste of time and lives."

Zahim smirked in obvious disappointment. "Well, if that's all you care for... of course that's all you'll get. Pay them! Do we need anything else from their kind, Ahmed?"

A clerk-like boy of maybe twenty raised his head from a pile of books that was at least as tall as he was. "We're lacking weapons and ammunitions," he said, which made Zahim groan.

Apparently this demand was a daily recurrence, if not an hourly one. The need for more weapons and ammo had to be forefront on their minds at all times. More weapons gave them a much better chance against the bloodthirsty soldiers of the Horde.

"No worries," Khasir said with apparent glee. "We brought you many and harvested many more for our own use. But we could be persuaded to be generous to the holy cause."

"For a modest additional fee," Zahim understood immediately.

"In this world, everything has a price," Khasir confirmed,

his smile hidden by the mask he wore at all times, a necessity in the desert, but also a relic of the disease that had changed the world forever. No one felt confident to be in a closed room without protecting their faces, mouths and noses. Especially not the scavengers and nomads.

Zahim, on the other hand, wasn't wearing anything special and neither were his people. Perhaps they had more pressing matters to deal with than the demons of the past.

"I know a city," Raydr said finally as the clerk counted gold coins carefully under Khasir's greed-filled stare.

"You know a city," Zahim snorted. "And you mention this now?"

"I'd hoped Khasir would bring enough back. I've been gone a long time. I thought you'd've figured a way by now. It's a stronghold. Attacking and beating them might be just as difficult as taking on the Horde's Citadel itself."

"Good practice, then," Zahim said with his obnoxious confidence. "We'd need ruthless soldiers to pull this off. Used to scavenging work… Maybe you should offer dear Khasir some hospitality… and a new mission," Raydr proposed reluctantly.

Khasir was busy laboriously counting his coins but his ears were always perked for any kind of new offer for remuneration. "At your service, madam," he said with a flourished bow.

"It'll be dangerous. Fair warning," she added.

"It's worth it?" Zahim queried gravely.

"The Horde itself would like to get their dirty paws on the content of those vaults," Raydr confirmed.

"You'll get double pay if you and your men pull this off," Zahim promised the scavenger leader.

Khasir's eyes grew wide with renewed greed at the promise of all these riches. The reward always justified the risks incurred, in his personal opinion. "I am here but to serve the cause," he assured.

"I'll make some plans." Raydr shrugged.

"You are welcome to stay the night, or as long as it takes for Raydr to make a plan. We need your men rested and ready for this fight," Zahim said.

"As you wish," Khasir said with obvious happiness. Free meals were not something you spat on, and neither were comfortable beds and the safety of numbers. Being more suspicious than his 'boss' by nature, Madan thought the whole thing was a little contrived... rehearsed. But he himself could not see the purpose behind this whole scene, the endgame... what could they want from them, other than what they claimed?

Then again, he couldn't see the purpose behind their grand quest, attacking the Horde... It disturbed him to realize that they had instilled a deep-rooted fear in him, a fatality... He simply did not believe the Horde could be beaten... not while its bloodthirsty leader still lived, in any case.

It was so strange to be among people again. Not a small raiding party, silent and glum before the attack, but a real feast. There were no festivities, but there was chatter and laughter, prompted by the free food and watered-down ale that had been generously distributed to all the members of Khasir's scavenging party and all Zahim's soldiers who happened to stop by for a bite. Madan stayed in the shadows as much as possible, observing the others, mostly the members of the Rebel Army, trying to figure them out, and of course, Raydr. Her most of all, trying to see her endgame, the truth from the lies. She was concentrating on some maps and drawing lines, unmindful of the general ruckus, focused by her task, absorbed by her thoughts.

Which city could she have been referring to?

Assuming she wasn't scamming their sacrosanct leader... Nothing about her would surprise him.

Zahim presided over the 'feast', barely eating.

He looked green and a little nauseous in front of all that food, and as well he should have been. If he only had a few months to live, the insidious killer, the rads, were wreaking havoc with his every internal function, making his life a living nightmare.

Eating, sleeping, standing, breathing a constant torture with only death as reward. His strength and resolve were admirable - but completely useless.

All he would do is lead his people to certain slaughter.

Madan was getting sleepy; he hadn't slept much in the past days, since joining Khasir's crew, because he had trouble trusting any single one of them... not to stab him in the back as soon as he let his guard down.

But that constant alertness had a price eventually, and he was beginning to feel it.

He couldn't forget his true purpose here.

Not be Khasir's good little attack dog, not become another one of Zahim's mindless drones... but get back at Raydr for poisoning him. He was aware that his vengeance seemed petty when seen in the scope of their 'Holy' war against the Horde.

But he didn't care. Himself first.

His ambitions, his desires, his petty need to see her at his mercy, like he had been. And he wasn't quite sure he would show the same restraint she had.

To leave an enemy alive was to risk them stabbing you in the back. She should have been aware of that.

So despite the almost overwhelming fatigue and general drowsiness, he did not miss when Raydr retired from the party, carrying her full load of papers, to go to her tent to sleep.

And he slipped out after her, silent and stealthy like a shadow in the dead of night. He knew where her tent was - he had asked around very discreetly - and he took a shortcut to get there first (most important rule of reconnaissance in enemy territory was to know the lay of the land like a native).

In any case, a guard had slowed her down, attempting to flirt with her - something she did not seem to appreciate in the least from her increasingly hissing tone.

That gave him the time to prepare his ambush and be ready for her. He unsheathed his blade silently and ducked inside the tent - and almost managed to dodge the two pairs of hands that were waiting for him to make that terrible mistake.

Almost only - they hit him on the head just as he was struggling, getting past the paralysis of having been figured out and fooled once more. He kicked one guard away just as the other hit him and he spent too many seconds reeling from the punch to be able to jerk himself free.

Blood flooded in his mouth; he had clamped down hard on his tongue. But he didn't care about that; what mattered was that they were stripping him of all weapons and preparing to beat him to death when Raydr came in herself.

"Just hold him, make sure he doesn't do something more stupid," she said, sounding irritated.

"Last time I underestimate you," Madan grunted between clenched teeth.

The guard he had kicked had punished him with a vicious roundhouse blow to the abdomen that left him half-winded.

"Just how stupid do you think I am?" she retorted.

"Last time," he insisted, spitting blood on the guard's shoe just to show his complete and utter disrespect. And spite.

"Definitely," she snorted. "Because I should have you put to death right here and now. "

"Why won't you? What's keeping you back?" he put to her - as was implied by her somewhat reluctant tone.

"Able-bodied man with fighting skills and all. Better put you to good use out there than execute you here," she explained, but it obviously wasn't her idea or plan.

"What if I refuse?" he said defiantly, spitting again.

The guard came within an inch of gutting him with his sword, from the looks of him.

But Raydr made an imperative hissing sound that stopped the brutish man cold.

"Let him go," she ordered finally, much to everyone's surprise, especially Madan's.

"You won't refuse because in combat, there's a chance to slip out and away. You've had that mark a long time. You're a survivor. And you're no fool, even if you can't judge people too well. So you won't give us the slip until it's certain we can't send resources after you."

"You know me so well," he said resentfully. Perhaps because she was right.

"Prove me wrong then," she retorted, going to light an oil lamp. She went back to studying her maps, the shadows playing on her face, making her look weary and tired.

And sad beyond belief, in spite of her tough-as-nails veneer.

"I thought they were dangerous fools," he said as the guards prodded him out.

A head nod was all it had taken to get them moving, she was truly someone important in the Rebels' hierarchy.

"They are. Believe me, they are. Didn't I tell you to stay as far away from them as possible?"

She dismissed them with a head nod that was worth a

thousand words.

Khasir was not too happy that his prized 'bodyguard' had decided to join the Rebels of his own 'free will', but as nothing truly bound them together, it wasn't as though he could do anything about it. Joining up was about the farthest thing from Madan's mind but as Raydr had said, he was a survivor, he knew how to wait for an opportunity.

Six whole years he had waited in the darkness of the mines, starved, beaten and brutalized whenever the guards felt like it. After the fall of his city, the death of everyone and everything he had ever loved and held dear in the world.

Sometimes he wondered why he hadn't given up there and then, when there was absolutely no light at the end of that dark hole that was the mines, when his life meant absolutely nothing to him.

He refused to believe that it was hope.

Hope was useless, a killer.

So, simply, it was surviving and waiting for a chance to get back at his captors. Revenge had kept him alive.

He wasn't dead, his wound hadn't killed him despite the poor conditions, therefore he would not die until he had gotten back at those who had enslaved him.

This in comparison, was nothing. Not even a hindrance to his plans.

Because Raydr was heading this expedition to this mysterious bountiful city. And now he had twice as many reasons to make her pay.

Chapter 4

Fool's Errand

It did not take them very long to get under way. A whole raiding party escorted by much too many Rebel soldiers.

Compared with the usual way he traveled, Madan felt incredibly uncomfortable, so loud, so visible!

And the fact that they traveled during the day did nothing to improve his disposition toward his noisy, flashy companions.

It felt as though they were painting a huge bullseye on their party, condemning it before they even had a chance to prove themselves.

Madan could tell Khasir and Raydr were just as bothered as him by the noise and lack of general stealth but they needed those men and those vehicles to bring the 'loot' back to the Rebels' camp.

A thousand eyes upon them, zeroing in on their position, on him… It was easier to feel fear this way than in the middle of a fight for his life, ten against one.

What he hated most about this 'mission' was being a mere pawn, a chess piece moved around by the 'higher powers'.

In this case, Raydr, who was seconded by one of Zahim's most trusted lieutenants, who went by the name of Elhalfu.

They called the shots, they made the decisions, who lived, who died, and for what reason.

He did not like that one bit.

He did not trust them one bit.

From the general direction they were going, a few old cities full of scavengers came to mind, but none of them seemed like the Holy Grail to him.

He spent the day riding in the back of the smelly trucks with the other foot soldiers, ignoring their boisterous boasting remarks, their belligerent comments, trying to find the right words to pry the truth out of Raydr once they would stop for the night.

Best play his role, as she had said.

Surviving was a full-time job especially when his fate was no longer really in his hands.

They finally stopped for the night under a luminescent sky that was not really reassuring. Madan would have loved the safety of a cavern compared to the arrogance of a camp - but he wasn't the one in charge.

Discretion was the name of the game when you were planning to steal someone's hard-acquired riches. Didn't anyone realize that in those Rebels?

Raydr should have; maybe she did.

She was sitting by herself near a small fire, looking at her plans. She had put up her tent herself, refusing everyone's help.

Lack of confidence or simply force of habit?

He was willing to bet she didn't know herself.

But the point was, she was alone, deep in planification thoughts, and she wouldn't hear him coming if he made a small detour and-

"Pray with us, brother?" a young man asked him, holding him back by grabbing his arm.

He was a teenager but his face was ravaged by rad burns; he also had many missing teeth, made all too visible by the wide smile he was gratifying the desert raider with. All in all, he seemed like a good person but Madan had no time for such things, especially not when the boy referred to something he particularly abhorred.

"Pray for what?" he said irritably.

"God's blessings on this holy expedition, the young soldier said as though it was self-evident. Be grateful for what we were given, what we have and what we will soon obtain, by God's grace."

"If we obtain anything, it will be through hard work, battle and death, sacrifice… not God's divine grace," Madan retorted through clenched teeth.

"God is everywhere, always with us, brother," another soldier said.

"He will grant us victory over the Horde, only He can," another insisted fervently.

"And what do you think they're doing right now?" Madan countered. "Praying to the same God to grant them victory over their enemies. I have better things to do than pray to someone who does not care or exist."

The young soldier holding his arm looked properly shocked. "How can you even say such things? They are Godless fiends."

Madan chuckled dryly. "I know for a fact that they are devout believers. Prayer time was the one time we could rest in peace, without fear of beatings and abuse from our jailers."

"How could you know such things?" another soldier asked with sudden suspicion.

"I have better things to do, I must go now. Have fun praying," Madan said with utmost spite.

"God is on our side," the boy said as Madan pried himself out of his grasp.

"God is on the side of whoever wins, because the winner will claim as much. 'God was on my side, therefore I crushed my enemies'. No truth in that, only the winner gets to claim as much."

"God is on our side!" the boy-soldier insisted.

"If you win, of course He was," Madan said sarcastically.

The men were getting agitated because of his sarcastic words and two of them sprang on their feet, looking ready to start a fight.

"God is with us against these monsters! They have poisoned the world and killed for decades and-"

"Yes! God let them!" Madan cut in spitefully.

He knew it was a pointless bicker, he knew he was just fueling their fire and provoking a useless fight but he couldn't help himself. He couldn't bear such naivete.

He could not tolerate anyone singing God's praises, His divine influence over the broken world they lived in.

God sided with the winner, like everything did.

"It was a test," the young man said with certitude, "God was testing our faith and resolve."

"And when you lose again, God will be testing you just a few years more. His will and all," Madan said acidly.

He had the knack to bring the fury out of people.

The peaceful, smiling boy was all but gone and his friends were just as enraged and ready for a fight.

"You do not mock GOD this way!" one of the men said through furiously clenched teeth.

"I would never mock God," Madan retorted. "He and I have unfinished business… I am merely mocking your view of His influence and care over the events of this cursed world. Our petty inconsequential lives do not matter to Him."

The camaraderie the soldiers had felt toward him had vanished like water in the burning afternoon sun.

Spite and hatred were on every face: his plan to get to Raydr unseen was completely ruined.

He was headed to a fight to the death with at least seven soldiers... and more would come as soon as they figured out he would not be beaten by so few men.

They were all on the sidelines, waiting eagerly, morbidly, to see what would happen next.

Geared up for a fight, they needed to express their belligerency on any outlet.

He was sure he could take down half of them without problem; so much for the great soldiers of the Holy Rebellion.

He was ready to fight to the bitter end.

"You will choke on your unholy words, dog!" the boy growled, reaching for his sword.

Madan was just itching to show him what a real survivor was, what the Horde had made of him: he was not afraid in the least.

"ENOUGH! "Raydr roared before they could clash.

It stopped the lunging boy in mid-motion and he looked just a little ashamed, while breathing hard and looking at Madan vengefully.

"What is this?" she accused. "Why are you fighting?"

"He insulted God! And he mocked God and our quest for Holy Vengeance, he insulted God's plan for us!"

"So what! So what if he did?" Raydr cut off before the boy could go on the rampage again. "He'll pay the price for his disbelief in the afterlife, won't he? God sees us, knows all! It's not your place to exercise his judgment on this man."

"But he mocked us-" The boy hesitated, looking at his

friends for support.

"I suggest you go pray, then you eat, then you rest. Remember, Zahim wanted him on this raid, he asked that Madan come specifically. Do not come in the way of his will. We are all tense; take it out on the real enemy," she suggested.

The men did not seem particularly pleased but just the mention of their sacrosanct leader was enough to calm their belligerent ardors.

"All right," the boy said. "But God sees all and forgets nothing," he warned.

"Exactly," she agreed. "Pray, eat, rest. Busy days ahead. You need your strength, all of you."

The men mumbled and nodded and went to their prayers and soon the desertic landscape was filled with their soft chants. Raydr blew out a very silent sigh and threw him an evil eye while beckoning him with a head jerk, away from the men, back to her lone tent.

"Sit down," she ordered. "Do you do it on purpose? Or is it just a talent of yours?"

"Do what on purpose?" he said in a grumble. He was angry and felt no inclination to be told how to be and what to believe in by someone else.

"Make it impossible for me to stay away from you… You've been watching me all day, do you think I haven't noticed? Did you do this on purpose so I couldn't help but to come to your rescue?"

"I had it covered," he retorted hotly.

She laughed dryly. "I was hoping to have this unpleasantness over with before having to confront you again. Maybe die and avoid it altogether," she chuckled. "So what is it you want, now that you are in dire need of my protection from these devout men?"

"You don't believe. Why do you humor them?"

"You don't believe, why don't you? What's the point of antagonizing them? Their beliefs make them strong, so use that." She shrugged.

"Not when they ask me to join," he retorted with a vengeful smirk.

She waved a dismissive hand. "Okay. What do you want? Don't waste my time," she warned.

"Only to know where we are going. This fabulous fabled city of yours, filled to the brink with riches and treasures," he said with obvious sarcasm.

"Weapons and ammo, actually. Not too fond of need-to-know, are you?"

"Not when I need to know," he replied.

"Okay, true… But you know this place as well as I do. You know where we are going, there's only one place where we could be heading, right?"

He took a second to think it through, and then looked at her with near horror. "If you are thinking, actually thinking about that place, then you are completely insane," he declared, shocked to the core.

"A fool's errand," she agreed softly. "But I know for a fact that it's loaded with guns and ammo the likes of which you can't have dreams about."

"And death for everyone who ventures inside," he mentioned, still under the shock of the revelation.

"I came out, didn't I? Was sick for two months, but I survived. No reason for these big strong strapping men to do worse. And some survive, live in there… thrive in there. Believe me, I know. They're the ones we'll have to beat. So I hope you have some moves left in you. We'll need everything you have and more, at HomeBase," she added with a sarcastic smile.

Probably just to see if he would shudder or maybe make a movement to ward off evil. He didn't give her that satisfaction.

"You're completely insane," he said instead.

"And I'm in charge, the usual absolute power corrupts absolutely. So don't pick fights with the praying kind. Their faith makes them easy to control. Direct. Use. Zahim figured that out a long time ago."

"Yes, so did the Horde's leader," Madan said with biting sarcasm.

"This planet isn't big enough for the two of them," she said in a sigh. "But if you have any sense left in you, you will keep your strength for when it really matters."

"Dying for your doomed cause?" he snorted.

"Giving us fools the slip before all hell breaks loose in there. Escaping with everything intact, running to face another challenge," she answered; her eyes were very weary as she looked at him. She actually seemed to be envying him.

"So I suggest you eat and rest. I strongly suggest it. Because I will be watching, I won't let you get away so easily," she added after clearing her throat.

Madan didn't even think of protesting. All was said and done: they were condemned to a horrible death

Perhaps it had been better not to know…

But he chased that thought from his head quickly: his thoughts quickly centered on how he would survive this folly.

All throughout the meal, he went over every rumor he had ever heard about the 'fabled' City of the Dead.

No one who ever went in came out.

Its guardians were monsters, shadows, deformed beings with

no morality or remorse. Cannibals, they killed and ate whoever dared venture into their lair.

And still they guarded the greatest weapon cache of all time… but only used spears and swords to attack and defend their underground citadel, that reeked of death for miles around, so much so that even birds dared not fly over the spoiled, charred, malignant ground.

It was whispered that in the troubled days, they had been a stronghold, a military superpower that had held fast as the world crumbled around them. Their defiance had angered God Himself and He had struck them down with a blinding, searing light of malignant destruction.

Since then, everyone who ventured on their territory became sick, lost hair and teeth, bled from the inside out, so powerful was the curse upon the charred, vitrified land.

Madan wasn't so far gone down the superstitious road not to recognize the signs of radiation poisoning, but he himself would have steered well-clear of this HomeBase had he not been forced to tag along.

And that was the whole problem, wasn't it?

He had no choice.

And they were not being forthcoming about their intentions either. Would Khasir have accepted to participate in the raid had he known what he was getting into?

Follow Raydr in the darkest, deepest levels of Hell, had he known what he was up against?

Since sleep would not come, could not come, Madan slipped silently through the camp, carefully avoiding the devout and faithful in case they held a grudge, to reach Khasir's side of the makeshift encampment.

The man was a leech, a profiteering looter with little to no conscience, but he paid his men well.

A sentry stopped Madan before he could get inside the tent, only allowing him in after Khasir, in a muffled sleepy groan, approved the intrusion.

"What is it you want?" Khasir asked, his hair tousled and looking about to fall back asleep at any moment.

A lure, a fake; Khasir was ready to pounce and defend himself should the need arise.

A man like him knew better than to let his guard down.

"I know where we're going," Madan said gravely.

Khasir laughed in delight and relaxed somewhat. "You actually made her sing? Congratulations, she told me nothing. Of course, I saw the way she looked at you-"

Madan raised a puzzled eyebrow at that. "You won't like it," he added after dismissing the man's rantings from his mind. She was watching him closely because she knew exactly what he wanted to do.

Escape this doomed expedition.

"She is leading us straight to Hell."

Everyone knew the stories and Khasir turned a shade paler as he registered the name of the place they had to raid, their target.

"Have they gone completely mad?" he whispered in shock

"I believe that is an understatement," Madan said spitefully. "They were not sane to begin with. But the question is, how far are they willing to go? Who and what they will use and discard to get what they want? And how important are you in their plan?"

"You think they won't respect the terms, they won't pay us?" Khasir worried, showing the scope of his concern.

"I think money won't be of much use to us when we're dead," Madan answered evenly.

Khasir thought about it for a long minute. He was a ruthless being, who was not afraid of much, as long as the reward was worth it. "I gave my word," he said finally. "They are paying us not only in moneys, but in equipment we need. It is worth the risk."

"Not much use if you are dead," Madan repeated.

"All jobs have risks," Khasir shrugged, recovering the color he had lost. Greed had the way to get inside the brains of men so naturally, robbing them of all common sense, corrupting souls with incredible ease.

Until even the certainty of a horrible death seemed like an acceptable bargain in exchange for a full purse.

"We all die some day," Khasir continued. Better to be paid handsomely for it than to die on your knees with nothing to show for in the afterlife, like a beggar…"

Of course, he made his own kind of sick sense.

"In any case, brother, did you not join their ranks? Why are you telling me all this? What are your true intentions here?"

Finding allies to create a diversion to get away from Raydr and her army of zealots, but Madan supposed not all truths were worth telling.

"I want you to be fully prepared for what is coming. If nothing else, I have come to respect you, and if we are to survive what is coming, what lurks in the depths of HomeBase, we must be prepared."

"Thank you, brother… It means a lot," Khasir said with a sincere nod. "But I am convinced that with God's will, we will triumph over these adversaries, as we did those before. I have that faith."

Madan knew better than to start another fight over ideology, but it seemed he would have to stand on the brink of Hellfire before making his escape.

With Raydr pulling the strings to who knew what avail, because Madan wasn't sure he bought her freedom fighter conversion, to Khasir's unquenchable greed, to the buffoons that made up this army, who was still sane?

No one.

Not even him, and he knew it.

And yet only extreme sanity could allow one to survive what was coming their way. What they were heading for at full available speed.

In the early morning hours of the next day, they reached the scorched earth, the limits of the HomeBase territory.

Vitrified sand, dead land where nothing grew or could grow in that cursed place.

Animals and birds avoided it like the plague: they were the smart ones.

Even the stirrings of the wind seemed different, more ominous somehow, ready to turn their puny bones to dust... if they strayed, if they overstayed their 'welcome'.

Everyone wrapped cloth around their mouths and noses, as though they were in the middle of a desert storm, as though this would somehow help to keep the danger and poison away.

The only effect this useless gesture had was to allow them all to quell their doubts and resume their walk forward, disregarding all the warning signs, focusing only on their fool's errand.

The day went by with uncharacteristic snailniness: the hostile territory, the fear, made the minutes stretch into hours and the hours into weeks.

It should have been an easy walk through the desert as the soil was hard and vitrified in most places, crunching under their feet and the vehicles' wheels, but still allowing for easy transportation.

Remnant of the cataclysm that had hit the region only a few decades before, the charred, burnt, melted land smelled of death, promised unimaginable tortures, and yet they pushed on with resoluteness borne of folly.

By nightfall, everyone had guessed what their ultimate destination was and there were whispers, murmurs and unrest even among the most devout and faithful.

So much so that by the time they had made camp for the night, spirits were getting high, dissent was rising: they could have a mutiny on their hands before long.

Another day under the burning sun, hearing the crunch of black glass under their feet would push them all over the edge of madness.

And Raydr knew it, felt it herself.

They hadn't had the time to really settle in and let the resentment flow loose with the whispered murmurs that she called a general meeting, beckoning everyone to listen to her under the multi-hued sky, another source of terror for the superstitious men.

"By now, you all know where we are going and I understand your fear," she began, looking at the assembly, staring everyone she could in the eye, so that they could see, and later tell, that there was no fear in her eyes.

Madan caught her stare at one time; one thing was certain, she had that conviction, she knew how to play her role. He was almost convinced... almost only.

All that really mattered was that she could inspire the men. although he still could not figure her out.

What was her true endgame? Her plan?

The reason behind her participation in this rebellion? A rebellion, an uprising she didn't even believe in.

Seemed to him she was in the same position as he was...

Biding her time until she could escape the madness. But that made no sense, since she was also Zahim's right hand... Or at the very least, one of his most trusted agents.

Nor was this any of his problem.

But understanding her motivations could lead to a better understanding of what exactly he was up against, and thus, increase his chances of survival.

And that was worth wasting a little of his time and mind at trying to figure out her unique psyche.

"HomeBase is renowned for all the wrong reasons, and with good reason, I can assure you. And what we will find in there will be ten times worse than you can imagine... But what we can recover in there, what they are hogging, hoarding, their treasure, is worth it, justifies the risk and the inevitable sacrifices that we will suffer. The weapons and the ammo we need to take down the Horde. Once and for all."

She let the words and the implications sink in. For more effect. She knew how to manipulate a crowd.

"When you stand against injustice, it always seems as though you have the weight of the entire world on your shoulders. Every wrong is suddenly yours to fix, every enemy is lurking at the gate, ready to take a shot at you, preventing you from going after the real bad guy. As though the universe, the Powers That Be, league against you to test your resolve and your worth. See how long you will stand without cracking. We will prove our worth. We have been proving our worth and resolve for years, and we are not about to stop, no matter the hurdles that are put in our way."

There were murmurs of agreement and grunts of renewed resolve; by invoking their strengths and the hardships they had already faced, she was winning them over easily.

"For a long time, there has been no decency, no order in this world. It has gone rotten, it has been rampant with corruption, the Old World poisoning the new… No more. The Horde is the past, trying to drown us all in the darkness our ancestors created…"

A heaviness settled on the group: even Madan couldn't deny the veracity of her words. The past, the Old World was chasing them, haunting them… and those who wanted to honor the old ways were a plague to all the unfortunate survivors.

"We need to bring order back, we need to be that light, exposing the darkness before it engulfs us all… and if that means facing the HomeBase monsters and then the Horde, I know you are ready. I know you are willing to give everything you have, your tears, your sweat, your blood, your lives… Everything you have and more. You take this responsibility with a light heart, because you know this sacrifice will not be in vain… My brothers, my sisters, remember this fight is holy, remember that it is always darkest before dawn…

"God is on the side of whoever wins, I heard that somewhere. Well that means He is on our side without a doubt, a single doubt. Whatever happens, you will fight to the last, you will earn your eternal rest in paradise.

"And your bonus pay," she added, glancing at Khasir.

Her lieutenant took over at that moment, a perfectly staged transition: they were certainly experts at controlling a crowd and eliciting the right responses.

"This fight is Holy, and we cannot fail! Follow our lead, put your trust in us, and we will lead you to victory!" he called out. "It is not the easy path, but it is the one true path, against the darkness, against the fiends that would turn us all to dogs! We cannot fail!"

Fuel added to the roaring fire, the men had forgotten all about their fear, so sure that they were on the right, the holy path.

Surely a delight for the two leaders, but Madan stayed away from the general euphoria.

People were so easily manipulated to give up what should have been the most precious to them, their lives.

On the other hand, given the current situation, what choice, real choice did they have?

And at the same time, he recognized that feeling, that elation. Defending his city, so long ago, his way of life, he had felt the same.

Part of a greater group, a greater ideology, a higher plane of existence, one that allowed such sacrifices not to be in vain.

Everything had come crashing down when they had been beaten and crushed and perhaps that was what made him so scornful and resentful.

It was a dream based on faith and when that faith was destroyed, all you were left with was the bitter disillusionment and disappointment.

Raydr let her lieutenant harangue the troops a bit more while she retreated in her tent.

Madan was two steps behind her, determined to get clear answers from her.

A pep talk was far from enough for him: he needed facts and real data to work with.

They were getting closer and closer to fight time and he did not go into a fight blindfolded.

"Make yourself at home, why don't you?" Raydr snorted after stowing her pistol.

She was a little jumpy herself or maybe justifiably careful.

"What are we up against?" he put to her, sitting on one of the cushions that composed the whole furniture in the tent.

"General assembly tomorrow morning. You're invited. Us leaders have to discuss the game plan," she said.

"You tell me now," he insisted.

He would see right through her lies much more easily without the others hovering around, protecting her at every turn and preventing him from asking the real questions that needed answering.

"Okay, let's sacrifice sleep. Useless anyway, especially on the eve of this... right when we need it the most."

She did look stressed and exhausted. Almost haunted. Perhaps this trek wasn't bringing back good memories for her either.

"Readiness and awareness are better than sleep in this situation," he said.

"If you say so." She shrugged, stifling a yawn.

"What do you know? And how do you know it?" he put to her.

"What I know... this, their lair, was a vast underground complex made to withstand anything thrown its way... but the rad bombs that did this did get the better of it... extensive damage, water damage in the lower levels, it's damp and humid and hot, a hellhole, burning for the skin... rads, I think, but I don't know how... or why. How many hostiles? The original 'crew' of this HomeBase, thirty years after the fall. Don't think they're old and finished. They're ruthless, savage... and more dangerous than whoever they spared and trained in their ways instead of eating. Because they like to eat unwary travelers, it's their favorite meal."

"But the rads don't kill them? Rads kill everything."

"I don't know how they survive, they're not supermen, they can bleed... but they are so unyielding, so savage and ruthless that they do seem to be invincible... Natural immunity? Gift of their gods? Miracles of past medicines? Who knows... We can expect formidable resistance from their part and we have to be ready for anything-"

"How do you even know them?"

"Irrelevant question," she dismissed. "Nothing to do with what we will attempt."

"Not to me. Very important to me," Madan insisted.

She looked very dissatisfied with his answer: obviously a subject she did not want to broach.

He could almost feel the fear (or was it shame?) pouring out of her in intensifying waves. Which made it all the more imperative that she answer the question. A weakness like that could get them all killed.

"Maybe, years ago, after finding my father, we - uh, I - crossed the rad zone and had the misfortune of camping too close to HomeBase. One night was all it took for them to find us- me, find me."

"Us?" he repeated pointedly. Two mistakes could not be ignored or attributed to chance.

"My brother and I," she admitted, her voice uneven.

"What happened?" he asked, twisting the knife in the wound, from the murderous expression she served him.

"I made it out, he didn't," she said briskly, resentfully. "Satisfied, or do you want more details? Maybe this way, you can share the nightmares too..."

"I'd love details," he said mercilessly.

"How many days were we trapped in their cages? How they

poked and prodded us, trying to determine if we were worth keeping for training and breeding, or just use us for food? What I had to do to get out of there? Where I sacrificed my brother to save my own hide, these details are of strategic importance to you?" she continued hissingly, obviously the wounds had never healed. Could never heal.

"You're sure he's dead?" he queried, almost glad to drive her crazy.

She looked far away, into her memory, and shuddered involuntarily. "I hope so," she said finally. "God, I hope so…"

"What can we-"

"Because once we're done with stealing their treasures, there will be nothing left of that hellish place."

"So this is revenge for you," he understood.

"Long overdue," she confirmed. "But as the old saying goes, one stone, two birds. Zahim will get what he wants and needs for his offensive. I get to exact the only justice there still is in this world. Eye for eye, Death for death. You want to pass judgment now? Teach me a lesson on forgiveness, maybe? To make sure I square things out with God?"

"No, your business is your own," he said.

"What about you? When this is said and done, Zahim will march on the Beacon. Your old Citadel. He'll kill and lay waste to everyone who resists and collaborated. Lots of your buddies in there? Defectors, traitors, collaborators, people who never had a choice when you failed to protect them… Don't you want to say hi?"

One thing was certain, she knew how to spread the unease around. Now he wished he hadn't stirred her dregs: he didn't want his own ghosts to come back full force in his fragile mind.

"I'll be long gone by the time Zahim draws his last breath

against the Horde," Madan answered finally, smirking smartly at her.

She snorted in good humor. "We'll see, won't we? We'll just have to see."

"You won't be there to see it," he answered hissingly. "So what is the PLAN?" he put to her, determined to get things back to business only.

As far as he could tell as she started laying it out, she was telling the truth. Honest about everything, down to the last detail of what she expected as resistance in the complex and outside of it.

She repeated the exact same details the next day, preparing the raid with the rest of the leaders of their war party.

It was no longer need-to-know, everyone had to know their place in the mission to ensure its success. Everyone had to be as ready and capable as possible.

They would attack and attempt to overpower the HomeBasers on their own turf.

They could not make a mistake or an omission, they could not fail nor falter. They were up against monsters of a different kind, a deadly kind very few had had the courage to stand up to.

"The only way to win is to draw them out. Now, they are already aware of our presence… they're evaluating our numbers, our weak points, assessing the strength of every individual… it is their way, they take great care of evaluating the individuals for their strengths and weaknesses, as they are always looking for new blood, slaves, breeders, soldiers… food. If we fail, this is what we will become to them. The weakest of us, food. The rest, slaves. Slaves of the basest kind… so it is in our best interest to give everything we have and more. Much more," she warned, looking at every face to be sure she had their complete attention.

"The bulk of the army will be the bait, they will draw them out and face their fury... You will have to hold fast, retreat only when it appears inevitable, play wounded... anything to keep them occupied. And believe me they will not go easy on you... During that time, Khasir and his men will retrieve what we need from their armories... and our special team will place special charges that will ensure that this aberration will be forever removed from the surface of this wretched Earth. They will be sent to a hellhole... worse than this one, I hope."

Her lieutenant glanced at Khasir with distaste. "Are you sure he can pull this off?"

"I can get the job done if you hold your end," Khasir retorted.

Raydr didn't even notice the puffing contest. Her mind was on the maps she had drawn and the memories they held for her. Bad memories from the look in her eyes, horrible memories that could keep someone awake forever.

Madan knew just the kind.

"We will leave some of the vehicles near the south entrance. If memory serves, there are side passages there that lead to the inside fortress... and this should allow quick extraction of their gear and ammo. The cavalry is not needed for this," she added, looking at her lieutenant pointedly. "Thieves, quick, shadowy thieves are needed for this... If the bait is alluring enough, they won't leave too many sentries. But if there is too much resistance, they might go back for weapons... so it's a gamble. Everything is in this world..."

"We will make this happen, do not worry," Khasir assured seriously. "Take the monsters away, give us a window of opportunity and everything inside will be ours."

"Good to know," Raydr said quietly, looking at her right-hand man pointedly. "Very good to know... Everyone must be synchronized and as determined as the rest."

She gazed intensely at the men around her, her stare staying on Madan just a bit longer than on the rest. "If we fail, we will never be a match against the Horde. Remember this, gentlemen; on this mission hangs the future of the Rebels. If we fail, it will be all over.

"All over…"

Madan held her stare, determined not to be impressed. All he saw was the weariness in her eyes; she had not slept a wink after he had left her tent.

She was much more afraid of facing the HomeBasers than she had let him believe. Her brother's demise, her revenge… all this was driving her but the fear was eating her alive, and that was another motivation he understood.

The need to destroy that fear, to take back control of the mind and body, and never let anyone have such power over oneself again.

"Do not make the mistake of believing this will go exactly as planned. It will be mayhem… they must be tricked into believing we are an easy prey… they are tough and ruthless but they are careful. They know their greatest strength lies in that hole that has kept them protected for decades. We have to be an irresistible bait, so that they will leave their hole to cut us down, reap us for their benefit…"

"We will look like a fine meal, have no worries, we are ready," her lieutenant assured.

She let out a tremulous breath, letting a little of the nervousness she felt show through her tough veneer.

"Then it's done. The die are cast… May God have mercy on our souls if we fail…"

"God will have to have mercy upon theirs first," her

lieutenant answered with smug self-assurance, as though he had no qualms to face the HomeBasers, only a fierce desire to kill.

Madan was pretty sure God would have a field day sifting through the souls - or lack thereof - of everyone who would fall when the battle would begin.

At best it would be a massacre.

At worst... perhaps it was best not to contemplate the worst right at this moment.

Cannibals were destined for the deepest, darkest layer of Hell, for they were traitors to their own species, preying on the weak, soiling their bodies and minds with the flesh of their own kind.

Even if he would have preferred not thinking about it before the battle, he had to admit that they would be facing monsters. The thought almost imposed itself on his mind.

Monsters, the kind mothers of future generations would gladly scare their children into submission by mentioning... if they were defeated in the first place.

They had to be eliminated, eradicated from the face of the Earth before anyone would ever dare to use them as boogeymen... a bad memory that would hopefully serve a worthwhile purpose.

Like the Horde... If they were defeated, their legend broken, their bloodthirst finally vanquished, these past years, living in their shadow would become nothing more than a bad dream.

Could it be done?

Could he allow himself a glimmer of hope, of belief?

Why were these thoughts assaulting him now, when he needed his wits to survive, when he needed to focus, when he needed to be intent on this foolish task only?

Had he been wrong to admit defeat, to choose survival over

justice, tuck tail and run, pretend the wounds of the past were not haunting him, had never stopped harassing him...

Had he been wrong to think of his own hide only, to abandon the fight, to let fear rule his actions and justify himself that this was the only sane way to live the remainder of this futile life?

The wait was always harder on the nerves than the actual battle. Madan knew that fact all too well, which didn't make those hours less harrowing, the jitters threatening to overcome his better judgment, make him prone to irrational actions.

On the outside, nothing showed at all.

He looked determined, ready for action, cool, even... perhaps a little bored... if someone could have heard the racing of his heart...

His senses were heightened to the point where it seemed as though he could hear, see and smell better than ever before.

It seemed he could taste the poison rads in the air, seeping into his lungs with every breath, penetrating his skin despite the clothes, the poisons wreaking havoc in the fragile balance that kept him alive...

And those monsters lived and thrived in those conditions... How had they survived for so long, what kept them alive when they should have been dead a long time ago?

Sacrificing, feeding on the blood of others, with the ruthless determination of those who had nothing to lose and nothing to preserve except their own miserable existence, their corrupt way of existing...

CHAPTER 5

Into the Darkness

Raydr had been right to prepare and warn them. The suddenness of the attack left them a little disorganized and stunned.

One moment, the desert that had taken over the dead and destroyed town that had housed HomeBase in the days long past was still and silent, not a soul stirring save for them.

The next, they were fighting for their lives in an indescribable melee.

Men screaming and dying, fighting with bravery or panicking and giving in to cowardice, but enough of them kept a cool head, remembered the plan, and allowed the scheme to go on as planned.

Perhaps not as cleanly and efficiently, with much more losses than they had expected, but enough to get them inside the compound virtually undetected.

Those HomeBasers that did spot them suffered an early demise, blown to bits by the same weapons they hoped to steal from them.

Somehow, Khasir and his men kept it together too; everything was therefore going according to 'plan' but the plan seemed bitter and futile when so many had already died for it.

Raydr led the charge relentlessly: her info was accurate and they found the entrance she had predicted would be there.

Soon, they were climbing down a damp, rusty ladder that

stretched far into the ground, each man and woman acutely aware of the ruckus they were making in the confined space.

Although a bloody battle was happening right over their heads, they all felt as though they were painting a huge target on their backs. They were bringing the monsters to them... or plunging straight into the mouth of darkness.

In spite of the preparation and maps Raydr had provided, they all relied on her, her experience and knowledge in these matters, her familiarity with the hostile terrain.

She bore the pressure with ease and confidence but Madan could still feel the panic pulsating out of her.

Nothing in her stance, demeanor or actions showed how terrified she really was: it was all in her eyes.

Sunken and dark in this place of shadows and death, they expressed the horror and fear of another era, where she did not have fifty strong soldiers with her to face the monsters.

Alone, she had faced them and survived... but she felt no confidence.

Fifty strong could be cut down so quickly, one ambush and they would be done for.

They had to be vigilant and ready for anything.

Finally, Raydr stopped at an empty intersection. "That way to the armory, where they keep their weapons," she said in a breathless whisper that seemed much too loud nonetheless. "Be careful, be alert... If there is too much resistance outside, they will come for their big guns, they will raid their own stash and catch you red-handed."

"Do not worry, we are ready," Khasir assured, and headed down the corridor she indicated at top, cautious speed.

Raydr turned to the eight soldiers left. "Let's go, gentlemen!" she ordered, starting down the other corridor before

Madan caught her arm and held her back.

"Someone has to set the charges!" she said in annoyance. "To blow this place to hell, once and for all!"

Answering the obvious question before he even asked it.

"I know the optimal spots and I've got the C-4, so move out of the way!" she ordered.

"I'm coming with you," Madan answered.

She frowned in confusion for a short instant. "This place has to be destroyed, now is not the time to give in to vendetta. They need to be destroyed."

"I believe you," he said. "But you might need someone to watch your back."

"Come on, then, time's running out," she said, nodding at her handpicked soldier to move ahead. "No time to waste."

As they ran in the dark, damp, rust-covered corridors, Madan wondered unproductively how honest she had been with him, with all of them. How long had she spent in this doomed and damned underground city to know it so well, every nook and cranny it would seem, to hate it with such intense ferocity?

He had already guessed revenge was her driving force but in that instant, he saw with crystal clarity that this was her purpose, the reason why she had suggested this target to Zahim.

Her intent had never been to help the Rebels, or rather, two birds with one stone.

She had always wanted to destroy HomeBase, she didn't care about grand goals and the good of humanity.

Strangely, this revelation helped steady his nerves. Revenge, he understood and approved.

But that didn't mean he could close his eyes: on the contrary, he had to be extra-vigilant. Because there was a good chance they could get out of this alive, if they were alert and ready for anything.

This was hostile territory, as hostile as his proud city had become under the Horde's rule...

The deeper they ran into the cramped hallways and manholes, the more the heat increased, making them sweat profusely.

The air was bad, making them a little dizzy, unsure of what they were hearing and seeing... was this place completely deserted, was this a hoax, the ants running out of their hill, a dream? Or rather an endless nightmare?

Or were they closing in on them, preparing their demise? Only Raydr kept her aplomb, her unshakable determination, having only one thought in mind. If at first, she whispered some reassuring messages sometimes, assuring them they were closing in on the target in this impenetrable maze, now she was trapped in her own world, her memories, nightmarish, from the looks of it, possessed by one overwhelming desire. Burn this wretched place to hell.

No one could stop her, would stop her - she was the spirit of vengeance itself.

Until a door they were headed toward creaked open with a sound that froze the very blood in their veins.

They all stopped dead in their tracks, fear overwhelming their better judgment. It was the first time they saw one up close, and they looked huge, glowing a strange sickly color that was somehow mesmerizing.

It was difficult to get past that paralysis, to remember that their friends and comrades-in-arm were fighting for their lives up on the surface, that the battle was not won, and was only the first step to winning the more important battle.

And yet they all stared, unmoving, at the female HomeBaser

as she stood there, transfixed and stunned by the sight of them herself.

Finally she snarled: no fear whatsoever in her attitude, only anger.

And that finally got Raydr moving.

She threw a knife at the woman, but started running toward her at full speed at the same time, as though she knew what would happen next already.

The HomeBaser caught the knife between her palms in a near impossible movement and sent it flying toward the intruders in a powerful, fluid movement.

Madan ducked but the man behind him didn't have the same reflexes and was hit in the neck, bringing him down on his knees, blood gushing from his severed carotid artery.

None of them noticed, really, as all eyes were on Raydr, attacking the woman with deadly precision, slashing at her legs to bring her down and then gutting her mercilessly, getting covered with blood and gore in the process.

She turned to her party of soldiers, wiping the gore from her face, breathing hard.

"They know we're here, we have to move… they're coming for us."

"We'll set the charges here and leave!" a soldier suggested.

"Let's be done with it!" another added. It was as though the walls were closing in on them, eyes watching everywhere, a malignant being emerging from slumber, dead set on taking them down.

They were the intruders, they didn't belong, and now they would be cast out, pursued relentlessly.

"We don't quit!" Raydr said fiercely. "You want to quit, go! Get out of here! Give me your charges and run, cowards!"

Her rabid determination allowed them to forgo the paralysis caused by the reversal of fortune. They knew it could happen, they could be discovered and tracked down, it was part of the job, the risks inherent to any military mission.

They were seasoned soldiers and being in the belly of the beast, the jaws having chomped down on them a long time ago, shouldn't have caused them such panic in the first place. Death awaited them all in the end, but they had to make their death purposeful.

But everyone reached a point of no return, a rupture point, a limit where training and endurance seemed not to matter any more. Madan himself could feel the walls closing in on him; there would be no escaping this hot, humid hellhole.

They were all condemned and they knew it.

But in that situation, there was no point crying over the unfairness of the universe.

Long ago, in those mines, he had been in the same predicament.

Beaten, battered, half-starved, against better in every way.

Well-fed, well-armed, vigilant, vicious... and yet, he had triumphed. Prevailed.

The attitude to have was always the same. Take as many of them as you can. Make your death, if not your life, actually mean something.

And this was the resoluteness to have today.

Not care about tomorrow - at this point, Madan couldn't even claim he cared about his own skin any more.

Kill them all... that was the one thing driving them, driving their bloodthirsty leader.

Raydr was unstoppable and she pushed them deeper into the complex, uncaring of anything other than accomplishing her mission, fulfilling her purpose here.

The air was getting fouler with every step, and the rusted-over walls seemed to glow preternaturally, a faint sickly greenish glow that would have made them lose their heads and sense of direction if their leader hadn't been on fire.

Driven to avenge the wrongs of the past, she never missed a step, she never hesitated at any bend, she knew exactly where she was going.

She was their guide and their example, they took strength from her determination. They did meet a few of the 'natives' and with each encounter, their confidence was renewed and augmented, as they ran from the invaders instead of confronting them.

Raydr and Madan were not fooled, and they did not consider this a good thing, unlike most of the soldiers with them.

The HomeBasers were cunning, that much was certain, and those who escaped went to warn more… preparing to rain down their vengeance upon the intruders.

They were running out of time and an ambush was always a possibility. Those few hundred meters seemed to last a thousand miles but they were in too deep, they couldn't back out now.

Go all the way and let the chips fall where they may… die trying, that was their only future and their sacred duty.

The HomeBasers were surely regrouping, knowing the fight would not be waged inside their own stronghold, but they had a good window of opportunity to make their plan work.

And that was the only thing their demented leader cared about.

The success of the mission.

It was so hot inside the cramped hallways that it seemed as though their sweat was hissing on their skin, stinging their eyes, making ghosts come alive where there was nothing. Or was there?

Spirits of those that had been damned to hell inside this complex seemed to call out at them, demanding justice, demanding retribution... making them even more confused, restless and jumpy.

Finally, Raydr stopped running and turned toward them, sweat glistening a glowing green on her face, making her appear even more evil than she truly was... or maybe just exposing her true nature.

"Here, we set them here," she said, designating a chamber to their right, a huge immense chamber filled with various rusted-over machinery and consoles, from which the worst of the impossible heat seemed to emanate.

Finally, was what most of them were thinking. Finally the doubts could be cast aside, they could go back to being the good faithful soldiers that they were.

Amidst the fear, the panic, the confusion, they could finally fill their purpose... and then attempt to save their skins.

They deployed inside the room, Raydr leading one group of men while Madan was in charge of the other. Apparently, she trusted more in him than in Zahim's men.

The consoles in the cathedral room were huge and covered with translucent slime and rust, but one could still feel the power coursing inside them, the malignant power that should not have existed any more, that should have never existed. Tapped by monsters that ate their own, it never should have been allowed to remain.

No doubt Raydr was insane but she was right about one thing: these monsters had to be eradicated once and for all. They needed to be stopped, killed, eradicated - scoured from the face of the Earth once and for all.

They set the charges efficiently, painfully aware of the time they were taking, that the masters of the domain were regrouping, coming for them... their time was running out.

In the suffocating heat, all shadows came alive and told a gruesome story of death... the true owners would come back and kill them all, brandishing their heads like horrible trophies and eating their remains... perhaps while some of them still lived.

Those desperate thoughts seemed to haunt them, gain power with each new minute they spent in the doomed complex, threatening to make them lose their means. Just when they needed them the most.

Madan pushed them on relentlessly; they could not afford that kind of unproductive weakness now.

No fear, no weakness, no regrets or remorse, only perfect efficiency could get them through this ordeal unharmed.

They were setting their last charges when an explosion blasted through the huge machine room, making them all fall to their knees, their brains reeling from the sound, their ears bleeding, deafened by the blast wave in such a confined space.

Just one explosion... and so, although they were all groggy, they were not dead. The chain reaction hadn't been sparked, they could still make it out.

Something had gone very wrong... but not wrong in the insurmountable sense.

They could still make it out and survive this... Coughing and staggering, their inner balance definitely affected by the blast wave, they made their way back in the gloom caused by the dust hanging in the air, the dust forcing its way through their lungs, making them fear they would lack air and fall unconscious.

They found that entrance half-clogged with debris but still

practicable. Some soldiers rushed out, uncaring of helping their fellow comrades, wanting only to save their own skins while they still could.

Closer to the center of the explosion, many hadn't been as lucky as they had been; they writhed in pain on the floor, afflicted with various wounds and ailments, needing outside help to survive. Camaraderie, caring… and all they could think about, for the most part, was their own skins.

"Where's Raydr?" Madan asked one of the men who was actually helping another soldier get past the debris.

The man was so focused Madan had to grab his arm to make him realize what was going on around him.

"Where is Raydr?" he asked loudly. If his ears were damaged, it was possible the soldier was completely deaf.

"Down there," he said, almost shouting. "She blew a charge to help us escape, give us a chance, they were all around us… we have to go, we don't have much time."

"Is she dead? Are you certain she is dead?" Madan insisted.

The man's eyes were the only visible part of him; wide in terror, Madan was sure he would not, could not tell any lie.

"I can't hear anything, or almost, but I swear I heard… I heard her screaming in pain… after everything settled."

"She's alive…" Madan said. He was sure of it.

And trapped in her worst nightmare, dying in the place she wanted to see eradicated forever. Dying without being sure it was really gone for good.

"But it's too late," the man argued, seeing that light in Madan's eyes. "The charges are set, the timer's on, we have fifteen minutes before this place becomes hell!"

"Go," Madan ordered. "Get out of here," he added, running in the opposite direction.

"It's useless! She'd tell you to run, save your life!" the soldier insisted before shaking his dizzy head and running off as fast as he could toward salvation.

Not death. Or so that man fervently hoped.

His warning was the last thing Madan heard before he dashed toward danger: that soldier had a point, but he wasn't going to let precious time be wasted by indecision.

Everyone for themselves, the golden rule of survival - so why was he plunging headfirst the other way, trying to save a woman, doomed and condemned, probably so badly wounded she couldn't move, a woman he pretty much hated?

He wasn't sure he could put it into so many words himself.

This was Raydr's nemesis: her greatest fear and enemy.

To die here, knowing they were destroyed, would be satisfaction enough... but to outlive them, triumph over the monsters that had haunted you for decades, see their ultimate downfall, that would be much sweeter.

They didn't have much time to escape before the inferno they had prepared would be unleashed and he quickly became anxious at the idea that he would not be able to find her in the Stygian darkness caused by the dust hanging in the air and the lack of adequate light.

But he should have known better: her instinct of survival was at least as strong as his own.

Although she was wounded, she had crawled out of what had fallen atop her and she was dragging herself along, gasping for breath and straining every inch she gained.

She must have known there was no way she could get out in time at that pathetic rate, but she would die trying, and that was something he recognized and respected.

Somehow, she was alert enough to hear him coming and she

raised a trembling hand - and weapon - in his direction, ready to pull the trigger.

He didn't have a clue how she recognized him in the darkness, but she did and gasped in fear and panic.

"Get out of here, go!" she said in a strangled voice. "Get out while you still can, everything will blow, gooooooo!"

"Come on," he said, grabbing her and raising her off the ground, making her groan in pain.

Her left side was wet and sticky: she was badly wounded and she knew it.

"I'm a deadweight, go, save yourself," she said weakly.

"Shut up and walk," he said pitilessly.

The anxiety was gnawing at him, however: given all the time it had taken to get down to the machine level, fifteen minutes was far from enough to get them out, what with having to carry more and more of her weight with every step.

"No, no, this way," she said when he started heading toward the entrance they had used before.

"You're sure?" he questioned, although they literally had not a second to waste.

"Yes," she said, hissing in pain as he made her hop over rubble with no consideration whatsoever for her poor state of being.

"Much quicker this way," she said hoarsely when they reached an undamaged area of the hallway.

"Why didn't we take this way coming in?" he accused, if only to keep her talking and prevent her from falling unconscious from the pain.

"Their living den, their fortress, their lair, stronghold," she said hissingly.

"And we're going now!" he put to her.

"No choice," she let out in a pain-filled breath.

And he couldn't argue with that one.

And if she could have that satisfaction, if he could help her get it, maybe there was a chance, a small tiny chance...

He couldn't and wouldn't admit he was a believer in the cause now, he could not abide Zahim's idealism... but did he really want to spend his life running from the Horde?

Did he really want them to own him, haunt him forever?

And that was why he was pushing into the rubble, in the clinging dust, looking for Raydr. Saving her... was like giving himself a chance to win against his own monsters.

And that was enough for him to forgo all sanity and caution.

Hopefully their living lair would be empty... since the battle was going on outside full force. They had a chance... and they had no choice.

In either case, their fate was sealed. Either death by the fiery hell they would unleash or death by their enemies, what was the difference?

Death was death, inevitable, unstoppable... but that didn't mean they had to give in to despair and not fight for life every step of the way.

His ears were starting to get better, sound coming back to them in waves, but what really assaulted him was the smell.

With each new step that he dragged Raydr forward, the smell became more feral, potent and gagging.

Their living den, their lair, their living area... it seemed worse to him than their prisons and torture chambers... even their kitchens, because this was the place where they felt the most safe, happy even. Telling each other stories, who knew? This was where they were the most human, and it smelled more monstrous to him because of it.

He could not allow himself the weakness of getting overcome because of it, not with Raydr sinking more and more into his arms with each passing step, no longer capable of supporting her weight.

Luckily her impression had been the right one. Everyone had been called to the battlefront, either outside or for those who had set the charges. The only people left in the den were the babies, which they heard whimpering in other rooms, or small children, who scampered away as soon as they came within hearing distance.

Shadows of real beings; Madan felt no sympathy toward them, only the tension and panic of having a chance to survive… and his future in good or disaster, being thrust in his incompetent hands.

They had to escape the cataclysm they were about to unleash… but he was getting so tired, so exhausted…

"Up here, up here," Raydr said urgently, her voice barely above a whisper.

He wasn't sure how he heard her but he looked the way she was pointing with a trembling finger.

Another vertical shaft with a rusted-over, humid ladder, glowing with translucent green algae. Or maybe he was seeing things that weren't there.

Madan looked inside; up and up and up…

Endlessly up… he felt dizzy all of a sudden.

They would never make it. Not with Raydr in such a pitiful state.

She knew it all too well and she opened her mouth to speak the obvious words: Leave me here, save yourself, I'm dead already.

He didn't give her the time because he might have given in

to the temptation and there was no way he'd leave her there after coming back to get her

They made it out together or they both died.

He started climbing, dragging her up as he did. He refused to let go of her hand as he climbed up, even though that made the whole process harder.

If he let go, she would let go.

If he held fast, crushing her hand to keep her conscious, she would give all she had to live one day more.

She was a survivor just like he was, a tough, relentless one, determined, insane… just at the end of her rope.

Perfectly understandable, given her wound and where she was, her nightmare, but all she needed was a push and a shove to go on to the bitter end.

Somehow, they managed to make good time.

Sweating profusely, swearing, groaning, grunting for a breath that seemed to elude the both of them, they were conquering that shaft, and maybe they would make it out of the HomeBase with a few seconds to spare.

They reached the top of the shaft and he had to let go of her to push against the rusted-over cover that was standing in the way of their freedom.

"Hurry," she said urgently, her weary voice barely above a whisper.

It was so rusted over and he was so tired after the long climb that pushing it aside took everything out of him and he saw black spots over his eyes for a few dizzying seconds.

But no time for weakness; he grabbed her hand again and had almost dragged her over the last rung when she was almost ripped out of his grip by a sudden unexpected weight.

He gasped and held fast at the last moment, grabbing on as

best he could, scraping himself against the shaft as he tried to keep her from falling to her death.

In an effort that seemed superhuman to him, draining everything out once more, he managed to steady himself, holding on in a death grip.

If she fell, he fell… but if he fell, she definitely went down.

He recovered the use of his wits and looked down, realizing what was happening: they had an unwanted passenger in tow.

A child from the looks of it, climbing up Raydr and trying by all means to send her plunging to her death.

She was groaning in pain and whimpering at the same time, also sobbing, incapable of doing anything other than holding onto him.

"Kick it! Kick it or we both die!" he growled: they had no time to lose!

"Forgive me, forgive me," Raydr was crying under her breath, looking more ready to let go than to defend her life.

Even fighting for both their lives, even with the exhaustion, the sweat in his eyes and the dust and the darkness of the shaft, Madan managed to catch a glimpse of the child's face.

Namely, its eyes.

Blue, deep blue, like the sky at high noon, like Raydr's.

It was so obvious now; what she had given up, what she had had to do, the price she had paid, the reason for her burning hatred… her intricate knowledge of the facility had come at a terrible cost.

And that was the way of the world. Pushing you to the limit, always challenging you to the core, to your very foundation…

"Kick it! NOW!" he ordered, and somehow his tone conveyed the message, forcing her to react, reminding her of her survival instinct, making her forget her moral qualms and the consequences of the gesture.

It almost tore them both from their precarious hold on the ladder and Raydr cried out in physical pain as well as mental anguish, as the kick had torn more out of her than she could have believed. Her wound acting up, her will to go on at an all-time low again - he had to drag her out of the shaft, as she wasn't really doing her part any more.

Dust swirled around them: it was a carnage in happening, a true warzone. Men screaming, deafening roars of weapons, explosions in the distance but they could still feel the heat of the blast waves, as though they were on ground zero.

Maelstrom, madness…

What had happened while they were in the belly of the beast?

The battle's hot spots were further away… and they could not care about any of it.

All Madan thought about was getting away from the explosion's zero-zone as quickly as possible.

They were completely out of time.

Only a miracle could save them now and since neither of them believed, they simply had no chance to survive.

Walking wouldn't do it; Raydr could barely lift a foot up any more.

Was it a sign?

The dust swirled, stinging their eyes… and revealing one of their trucks, untouched, standing there as though nothing had happened at all.

The bodies around it told a different story, one of death and desperate fighting on both sides; they sidestepped the bodies or simply stomped on them: no time.

They had to move. The explosion was sure to contain rads, considering the nature of the HomeBase.

The truck was filled to the brink with ammo and weapons but they didn't care about the 'loot'... all that mattered was the speed.

Madan dumped Raydr in the passenger seat unceremoniously; despite the pain, she was conscious enough to glance at him, eyes wide.

"Can you even drive?" she put to him in a gasping breath.

He wiped sweat and blood from his face, trying to figure it out. Good thing he had been observing the drivers recently, just idly, to pass the time.

"Does it matter?" he retorted breathlessly, muttering under his breath, hoping the damn truck would start!

A horse would have been so much more welcomed right now but once he managed to shift gears, he could only appreciate the speed with which they left the doomed area.

His driving was far from perfect and there were a few close calls that made Raydr cringe but once they were out of the ruined city, the desert driving was much smoother.

"Stop! Stop now! Cover your eyes, stop now!" Raydr ordered, looking as though she was in a trance of some sort.

He did as he was told without even thinking about it; he didn't have the time to cover his eyes as the desert behind them suddenly became a fireball of light and ash and darkness.

The end of a nightmare, ending in nightmare...

But somehow, neither of them felt reassured in the least.

"You can go now," Raydr said, her voice faint. "You should go now."

He gunned the engines and raced off as quickly as the truck could go on the vitrified desert while the mushrooming ash cloud grew behind them, ever growing...

Chapter 6

The Scent in the Wind

They had launched the attack in the early morning and so much time had passed in the bowels of HomeBase that it was now ominously close to the night. The expanding cloud of dust and rads coming from the explosion also darkened the skies to a point where it was hard to see anything, even with the truck's lights.

A storm was brewing on the horizon, clashing with the expanding explosive cloud, forming lightning of every color, even black. The worst storm possible, the forces of the damaged Nature combining with the worst that the technology of old had to offer.

A whirlwind of clouds in the sky, bright blinding flashes, stygian darkness spreading over the land.

This would be bad, horrible, cataclysmic.

They needed to find cover, they needed to hide… but the desert was bare in every direction, as far as he could see. Exposed, alone, they didn't stand a chance.

Madan didn't know if there were many HomeBasers left after that explosion, but he had the urge to get as far away from ground zero as he could.

As though he knew, could feel that whatever was left of that doomed race was after them.

Not the bulk of their army, but the two of them specifically.

Coming for them with revenge in their hearts. Determined to

make them pay for everything that had gone wrong.

And so he pushed the engines as quickly as he dared in the storm, uncaring of the pain he imposed on Raydr because of her wounds or the risks he was taking because of the darkness and poor conditions.

He had to get away. As far and as quickly as possible.

He thought she might have fallen unconscious, but when the first raindrops hit the windshield, she spoke up in a hoarse voice.

"It's a bad one," she told him. "You got to find some cover, otherwise the lightning will fry the electrical components."

"I know!" he grunted angrily.

Why spare parts were so valuable: Nature had a tendency to destroy everything that came from the old world.

Thunder rumbled even louder, and lightning, bright, glowing, rosy, shot through the sky, illuminating the landscape for a long moment, making strange shadows appear. It looked even more deadly and macabre than before.

"If we get hit by that lightning, we go up in a big ball of ammo," Raydr warned. Apparently, she still wanted to live.

"I KNOW!" he growled through clenched teeth.

All his attention was focused on his driving. They were running from something very bad and deadly... but revving into something even worse.

Apparently, they had used up all their luck.

Raydr was more awake now, in a panic, staring at the sky with fear. The gossamer of lights, endlessly renewed...

Coming straight for them.

The engine sputtered during that eternal moment that lasted a lifetime, time enough for both of them to fear the worst. The end of their journey, their flight, their lives. They would not survive the storm if they stayed in the open.

But in that moment of blinding light, Madan managed to see ahead - see how Raydr was gripping the edge of her seat, her knuckles white, as though this could somehow avert the worst, but mostly, a dark formation on the left.

Mountains. Therefore caves, the possibility of hideouts and continued life.

He veered abruptly, and they almost toppled over, as he was not a master at driving a truck.

Somehow, they stayed upright after skidding on two wheels for another eternal second… Madan was able to gun the engines at maximal speed, all too conscious that he had one chance to get there, one chance only to bring them to safety.

Salvation was so close… and yet slipping through his fingers.

The ride was so bumpy even he felt nauseous: it was a wonder Raydr hadn't fallen unconscious already.

But terror had a way to keep one awake even through the most difficult hardships.

The lightning was intensifying, the rain turning to ice pellets, hitting the windshield with such force that it seemed as though it would crack and split everywhere, exposing them to the unforgiving elements.

Somehow they made it to the mountain range with only two other close calls. The engines couldn't take much more of that electro-magnetic battering.

And it only took him a moment to find an adequate cave.

The truck could fit in snugly but the wind was driving the ice pellets in; they needed some more adequate protection.

Madan dragged Raydr in more deeply, cursing the darkness and wind under his breath, until he found a nice niche, dry and protected, where he could dump her while he went to look for supplies in the truck before everything got soaked through and through.

Nothing to make a fire with, but they would have choked to death with a fire in that enclosed cavern; he was content with an armload of blankets and a few electric lights, as well as some food and water.

He wished he could have relaxed a bit, but no such luck.

Raydr needed help; she had lost a lot of blood and was in bad shape.

Raydr was propped against the cavern wall when he came back, looking gray in the faint light that came from the incessant lightning coming from the outside. The thunder crashes were so strong they seemed to resonate in their very bones; Nature was unleashing its strongest forces against those who had destroyed it and continued to mock it.

Given they had just detonated a rad explosion, they felt they were one of Nature's targets.

He shone a light her way: she looked even worse this way, which was not surprising since by all accounts, she should have been dead.

"You should save those for when you will really need them," she admonished hoarsely.

She was writing herself off, a common method to remove fear in face of death. Consider yourself hopeless, remove the hope, just wish the pain would go away.

He didn't buy it for one second: her eyes were wide in fear when they weren't closed, wincing from the pain.

She was scared of dying, but she was even more terrified at the thought of suffering through that crippling pain longer than necessary… and still ending up dead.

But she wouldn't heal on her own. More pain was necessary

to ensure that she had a chance to recover.

"Let me take a look at that," he ordered as she was keeping an arm around her wound, protecting it as though that would somehow help.

"Are you a doctor now?" she hissed but without any real strength. "What do you know about-"

"Shut up, keep your energy, you'll need it," he countered, peeling the ragged clothes from her jagged wound. Already swelling, purple; he probed it delicately, making her inhale sharply, trying hard to keep the sobs in. Anyway, sobbing would only hurt more.

From her gasps, her whole left side was a bruise, painful to the touch, even though he was as gentle as he could be. "You have a broken rib and several others that were bruised," he finally declared, rummaging through the meager medical supplies he had recuperated from the truck.

He found some alcohol, but nothing that could soothe or numb the pain efficiently, or really prevent infection. But that was to be expected.

"I have one SHATTERED rib and several broken ones," she corrected hissingly. "With all the blood I lost, I probably punctured my spleen, so I will die for sure. No point doing anything."

"The spleen is on the other side," he argued, almost chuckling at her poor attempt to discourage him.

"How do you even know that, desert raider?" she grunted unhappily.

"My father was a doctor," he said and for the first time in so many years, a clear picture of his father imposed itself on his mind.

It almost brought tears to his eyes, for he had thought

without a doubt that he had forgotten what his father looked like. But no, those memories were in a corner of his mind after all... it left him shaken and yet, uplifted.

To remember the face of his father, to see how it mirrored his own... apart from the brand on his cheek, of course... Somehow gave him back the courage he thought he had lost forever. Courage, or maybe a purpose. It was so strange to feel this connection once more.

And of course, Raydr ruined it with a dry disbelieving chuckle. But she regretted it immediately, her body incapable of supporting even a sarcastic laugh.

"Well, doctor's son, I hope he taught you well. Enough to know what's the prognosis on that wound?"

She inhaled sharply as he tightened the makeshift bandage he had made out of a torn shirt of dubious cleanliness, and gasped in pain as he applied alcohol over everything.

He gave her an eloquent look. She knew it was bad. There was no need to sugarcoat it.

"You lost a lot of blood," he said. "If an infection sets in..."

"You should have left me there," she said, trying to position the blankets around her, to find a comfortable position. Lost cause there.

"You'll pull through," he countered.

"And then you will kill me yourself, is that it?" she grunted mirthlessly and regretted it immediately.

She couldn't afford humor, she couldn't afford anything right now.

He came to her aid, letting her settle down against him: she was shuddering under the blankets.

"So cold," she muttered softly, desperately. "I'm so cold."

She was cold, that much was certain, but that wasn't the only reason for the shudders. A lot had happened in that doomed complex, and the wound, as crippling as it was, was just the tip of the emotional-trauma iceberg.

Cold and hot at the same time; was an infection already brewing? He couldn't be sure but the next few days were sure to be harrowing for her.

He gave her a little food - stale bread and dried fruits - as well as water in a half-filled canteen.

After the day they had just had, eating was the farthest thing from his mind, but his body strongly disagreed with him. He started feeling better after a few mouthfuls, as though food was just what was needed to fill that hollowness in the pit of his stomach. But as long as it worked, who was he to disagree?

"You should eat," he told her as she continued shuddering in his arms.

"I'm nauseous enough as is," she said in a small hoarse voice. "Just the thought of food makes me want to vomit. Better keep it for you."

"Okay," he said, acknowledging the wisdom of her words.

"I don't think I'll be able to sleep," she admitted.

With the thunder echoing in their 'lair' so hard it made their teeth shudder, it was hard to believe anyone could sleep but Madan was getting drowsy - the efforts of the day catching up with him.

"Who was that child?" he asked when, from the feel of her, she believed he was asleep. (As she was relaxing a little more in his arms.)

"You know the answer," she said as though she had been stung, her tone cold yet broken at the same time. "The answer is, this is the last thing I ever want to talk about."

"It's poison in your mind," he said softly. "Poison that will stop you from healing."

"Good," she retorted, before falling unconscious, from the pain, the exhaustion, all of the above... or maybe just faking it to avoid facing the questions.

There was no way to tell if she would survive, much too early to tell... but she was a survivor, she had proven it enough times already.

After a very short while of listening to her breathing, trying to determine if there was something to worry about in that rasp, his eyes closed on their own and he fell asleep against the very uncomfortable cavern wall.

And dreamed of his Citadel falling into Zahim's hands, the Horde defeated by the Rebel Forces.

Strangely, the dream did not make him feel reassured in any way.

It was trading a monster for another.

Even the satisfaction of seeing the Horde's commander on his knees, begging for mercy while awaiting his just punishment, did little to soothe his tortured conscience. He woke up feeling more worried than refreshed.

Zahim was an idealistic fool, he couldn't be a threat. But he had so little time left to live...

Whoever would replace him, that was the worry, the question nagging at him.

He fell asleep again, because he woke up with a start, feeling that something was wrong. Raydr was no longer a weight on his chest and arms - had she crawled away during the night? Pretended her wound was worse than it really was?

Did she truly have a death wish?

He found her at the cavern's entrance, looking at the sunrise over the land that had been scoured clean by the preternatural storm that had raged the night before. The ground seemed to glow with the sunlight; it was a mesmerizing sight but he barely spared it a glance, preferring to focus on his wounded companion.

Before he could ask the obvious question, she turned to him, eyes wide in barely contained terror. "They're coming for us," she revealed apocalyptically.

He didn't even think of doubting her. He dragged her into the truck, abandoning the supplies he had left deeper in the cavern, just to get moving, get some distance between them and their pursuers.

There was an urgency in her tone, an imminence of danger and he had that strange impression he needed to heed her words right now, even though he wasn't sure how she could know these things.

She knew and that was enough for him.

He didn't even have the time to utter a short prayer as the engine chugged to life - their luck hadn't completely run out.

He sent the truck speeding over the muddy ground, the tires screeching and skidding before catching and rushing them forward. They came within an inch of staying stuck because of his reckless driving but the truck trundled ahead - thank God for small favors.

Finally, they were in the open desert, no one in sight, and he turned to her (half a second, he could not afford to lose control) to ask the question burning his lips. "Who?"

She was doing all she could to remain conscious with that near disastrous ride. "Some survived," she said breathlessly. "Their target for revenge, us not them. They caught our scent. The last to escape the HomeBase, those who wrecked their home. They will never stop. Not until we are dead…"

He accepted her words at face value, and checked the

rearview mirrors often, as though expecting them to spring up from the ether.

So far, nothing, just the glare of the Sun rising over the storm-bleached desert, promising a scorching, unbearable day.

"Where should I go?" he asked after ten tense minutes or so of driving. "What direction? Raydr! Stay with me! Where do I go, any plan?"

She snapped awake reluctantly when he shook her. "Where do I go?" he demanded. The original urgency was fading and now he felt a little ridiculous, speeding away from nothing like that.

"North," she finally answered, feeling nauseous with the ups and downs caused by all the puddles the storm had made. Madan seemed to hit every one with malicious intent.

"That'll take us opposite Zahim's encampment," he thought good to mention.

"That'll take *you*," she corrected.

"We're in this together," he retorted.

She glared at him from her hollowed-out-by-pain eyes. "Once the fuel is spent, I will be a huge hindrance and you will have to let me go. You should get rid of me right away, less fuel spent this way for nothing."

"Raydr, we are in this together," he insisted.

"I won't make it with a shattered rib," she replied.

"It's just broken," he said.

"Anyway, what does it matter to you? You wanted to kill me anyway, remember? I'm dead already, rejoice… or did you really want to do it yourself so badly?"

"For someone who is dying, you sure have a lot of energy to convince me you're a lost cause," he said.

"For someone who can't drive, you sure take your eyes off the terrain a lot," she quipped back with her usual bite.

"You'll be fine," he said after dipping into a pool caused by the rain of the night before, making her grunt with near nausea. "When we reach Zahim's camp, you'll have the best people work on you, it'll be nothing. Just a bad patch... why do you want to go the other way?"

"Zahim will have plenty on his back already," she said breathlessly. "The last thing he needs is these morons kamikazeing on the camp. "

"Altruistic to the last cell? It does not suit you," he told her, not buying a word of it.

"If you can get them away from Zahim and the Rebels, all the better. They will fight to their last cell, it'll be useless death and mayhem..." she explained softly.

"We can get them away. We can," he insisted, hoping it would sink in. "But where to?"

"North, there used to be a city. The disease took everyone there, as far as I know... no one risks it there, not Scavengers, not Desert Raiders, it's forgotten... even I walked away... now if you lure them there-"

"If *we* lure them there," he insisted.

"If you lure them there, with enough weapons on you, you can end it all, once and for all," she said, wheezing.

"Sure, one man against how many?" he snorted.

"Size doesn't matter," she replied, which made him chuckle, then laugh outright.

"In this case, I think it does," he answered.

"Well, that's your problem then," she said acidly.

"You had no choice," he said somberly, seriously. "Then or now, no choice at all. You know that?"

She looked up from her slump, eyes filled with physical pain, but mental anguish as well. "I have been telling myself that for the last eleven years," she said, her voice close to breaking. "And it never sunk in. Do you really think you can do better? Convince me of that lie? I saved my skin. It's what I do... until now, it's what I always did."

"So keep on," he suggested.

"Tired," she said in a broken sigh. "Useless. No fuel."

"Well, the fuel is not spent yet, so you're still on this ride. When it's all gone, we'll see if you still want to die."

"I will be dead. What I'll want is moot," she grunted in response.

He almost cracked a smile. There was definite resentment in her tone, a good sign. She was a survivor, despite herself even. Down to the last cell, she was a survivor.

And survivors kept on, no matter the odds in their disfavor.

The day stretched on interminably. They made good time even on the wet ground but Madan lived in fear of when the fuel would run out, leaving them stranded.

He kept a general northerly direction; as there were no roads to speak of, he had to backtrack sometimes when they met a patch of land that was simply unsuitable, like when they encountered a flash stream caused by the storm.

But surely, if they had trouble moving around, the same applied to their pursuers?

Raydr managed to fall asleep or unconscious and he couldn't spare her a thought or a glance, not when the road to follow was so chaotic.

He wanted to stay resolute, determined... but as much as he could be exhilarated by the speed of the machine, in the end, Nature always won. The truck sputtered to a stop, out of gas, leaving them in the middle of nowhere, with monsters closing in on them.

Raydr didn't even wake up; he wasn't sure if she was unconscious, sleeping, or worse. And he didn't have a clue what to do any more.

So he checked her pulse, because this was something simple, something he knew how to do, something that didn't mean life and death for them... well, maybe for Raydr.

She was sweating, her pulse racing, fluttering under his fingertips. Gangrene settling in, infection, death eating away at her?

Just another bane to add to their list.

He got out of the truck, under the boiling sun, seeing dark spots in his field of vision. Heat stroke, or just despair?

What to do now? Run?

Abandon her, save his skin, live in fear or the HomeBasers and the Horde? For the rest of his life... Live with that guilt on his mind and heart forever...

No, there had to be another way.

Raydr was in a bad way, yes; the next few days would be a test of her strength and character.

And she would get that chance to be tested ... his father had always said...

If nothing else seemed to work, you could still pray.

And sometimes that made true miracles happen.

He hoped it wouldn't come to that with her or with their situation because he wasn't sure he remembered how to pray.

Or that praying worked if those involved didn't believe.

He went in the back of the truck and rummaged through their supplies. Ammo, weapons, explosives, but nothing that could get them out of the mess they were in.

He came across food supplies and canteens full of water and brought them back to the front seat to get a little respite from the heat and eat in peace.

He had to come up with some sort of a game plan. And eating wasn't doing wonders for him on that aspect.

He checked Raydr again: she had stopped sweating, which was not a good sign.

Of course, she coughed and spilled half the water when he forced it down her throat. Waste of time and resources for the survivor he was, but he didn't say anything, only helped ease her back in her seat as she regained her breath, looking the worse for wear. Coughing her lungs out had not improved her condition and her eyes threw thunderbolts of hate at him as she took back control of her body once more.

She was awake now, that was something. And she hated him, that was a good sign…

"Out of gas? Why are you still here? Run, why don't you," she ordered.

"Without a vehicle, they'll catch up with us in no time," he answered, not wanting that debate right now. But really, what had he been expecting? What else would she say?

"Get out of here while you still can," she grunted angrily.

"Ready for water?" he put to her.

"No! I'll just waste it, I'm dying, I'm dead already. Just leave me here, maybe they'll think I got out on my own and they won't come after you."

"Since when did they turn stupid? They caught my scent, it's in the wind… they'll never give up now. We are in this together, whether you want to admit it or not."

He put the canteen to her lips and tilted it very gently, so she could get a small sip in. She gulped down very reluctantly, glaring at him throughout.

"Thank God for the Horde," she said bitingly after getting a sip in at last. "With your bedside manners, you would have made a horrible doctor."

It was such a pathetic attempt at making him angry that he couldn't help but chuckle, then laugh out loud, then laugh near uncontrollably.

There was no reason for this burst of uncontrolled hilarity, after all, they were in serious trouble, stranded, alone against who knew how many, and here she was trying to hurt his feelings so he'd turn against her and leave her to die alone.

He laughed until he thought his sides would explode until her furious glare.

"I don't see what's funny in this," she retorted as spitefully as she could, trying to find a comfortable position to sit in.

In her condition, comfortable was akin to impossible.

"Nothing. Nothing funny at all," he said, a gleam in his eyes.

He moved behind her chair, ignoring her puzzled expression: laughing, he had espied something in the tiny compartment there was behind the two seats.

Something vital... and kept in the last place he'd look.

Of course, it was smart to keep extra canisters of fuel next to the driver's seat; less distance to travel to refuel, faster and more expeditious... the last place he'd look.

And she had made him see it.

"Four of them," he told her, grinning despite himself. "Why didn't you tell me you guys actually thought ahead?"

"Because we didn't," she answered succinctly, but he could tell she was excited too; there was some color back in her cheeks. "This must be Fatine's truck, he's a thief and a hoarder," she said, almost chuckling.

"Let's take a second to thank him for his thievery... we are getting out of here," Madan said, this time definitely grinning.

A sliver of hope, mobility and speed returned to them and suddenly the world didn't seem glum any more.

Even Raydr sat up straighter when he came back to drive on, truck refueled and ready to roar over the desert.

A faint smile even fleeted on her lips as they started racing down the dunes, until the bumpy ride made her groan in pain again. The wounds were still there, nothing had changed, but now they had a tiny chance.

And that was enough to give them a second wind.

Eventually he had to rest. When night came, he stopped the truck, and helped Raydr out, satisfied that her wound hadn't leaked out of the field dressing he had made.

She was exhausted or maybe a bit feverish, but in a much better mood. She seemed to think they were in the clear, at least for now.

They had driven into a more forested area; the next day was sure to be a nightmare to find an adequate road to travel on… and even worse for Raydr as a wounded passenger.

He gathered wood to make a fire - the rations were better reheated, in his opinion. And a fire would dispel the gloom and shadows of the night.

Raydr was still hidden under the blankets where he had left her, risking one eye and one weapon out of the hideout to greet him.

The sight made him chuckle, especially since her hand was trembling so badly he wasn't sure she could shoot him at point blank range.

"Just me," he assured.

"I know," she grunted grumpily.

"Think you can eat something now?" he asked as he started the fire, the twigs crackling under the growing flame.

"If you're cooking, then noooooooooooo," she said, which made him laugh.

"That's funny?" she put to him.

"No... True," he answered, handing her some bread while he put water to boil.

She munched the bread half-heartedly - but at least there was half a heart in it, which meant she had gone over the worst of her self-destructive glumness.

"How many of them do you think are after us?" he put to her as he stirred the rice he had put on to cook for the next morning. With the fire so low, it would take hours to cook.

"Everyone's that left," she answered with extreme assurance. "I don't know how many, but more than we can handle, that's for sure."

She meant to be defeating and glum but he still smirked at her when she wasn't looking. She had said 'we', which meant she was no longer writing herself off.

If she had decided she was going to survive, then she would and her wound would be a minor hindrance only. Mind over matter and all. He hadn't a doubt about it even though she didn't seem to realize it at all.

He gave her a canteen of water; she was gazing at the fire, eyes lost in the flames, in her darkest thoughts, from the looks of her.

"In HomeBase, who was it?" he asked.

"You want to kill me now, ask those questions," she snapped, but her voice lacked her usual bite when someone asked her a personal question.

"I had a son," he revealed as he sat down next to her. "And a wife. Awan... Maira... They were both taken from me by the Horde."

"Well, he was never mine," she said but her trembling voice belied her harsh words. "Only theirs. He was theirs."

"Whoever is left alive... We will make them pay, Raydr."

"Since when are you an optimist?" she snorted, if only to hide the gleam of tears in her eyes.

"I'm not," he assured as he lay down to sleep.

The next day, Raydr looked a lot better and even the tough ride through the forest - he had to backtrack often as there was no road to speak of and the route was often blocked by overgrowth and fallen trees - did not seem to dampen her spirits. Positive Thinking made wonders for healing, especially on someone as used to pain and suffering as Raydr.

They reached a more mountainous area by nightfall and Madan was quite glad to turn off the engine and enjoy a bit of silence.

Raydr didn't exactly look happy when he tore her out of the seat and set her down on the ground while he prepared a small fire.

She looked a lot more worried than the night before, but perhaps that was because she was more alert. Still in crippling pain but capable of using her brain actively once again.

"Why are we stopping? We lost a lot of time," she said finally when he came back with some wood.

"I'm exhausted, it's getting dark," he answered, lighting the kindling.

"Yeah but we didn't progress much, we need to-"

"If you wanted to drive, if you think you can do better, by all means-" he said just a little hotly.

"I think we should travel tonight... maybe I can drive," she said.

"I wouldn't risk it, it's too dangerous... and staying alert with that wound of yours? You want to kill us?"

"They are catching up, Madan. I can feel it. We need to get to the city before they catch up with us, we need to set traps, prepare-"

"In case you haven't noticed, I am doing the best I can," he retorted, pulling her bandage away just a tad roughly to make a point.

She inhaled sharply and clenched her teeth against the pain, but did not give him the satisfaction of a yelp of suffering. Not wanting to concede a victory - she was in no condition to drive.

"I know you are," she answered his last statement when she could finally do it without a quivering voice.

He finished cleaning her wound without looking at her; better than the day before but not as healed as he had hoped it would be. The swelling had gone down and was now centered around the broken rib.

An excellent sign but she was far from being in good enough shape to defend herself or fight for her life.

"I know you are doing the best you can but we have to be ready… they outnumber us. Something bad…"

"You can try to be ready for anything but in the end, you will always be surprised, always meet your match when you least expect it," he told her.

"Wonderful words of useless wisdom," she countered sarcastically - so he tightened the bandage a bit roughly just to remind her that she was not in any shape to argue with him.

She did groan in pain and glared at him vengefully.

"Still true," he said softly.

"Okay then, fine. Tomorrow I'll drive too. You save your strength to drive at night, okay? We need as much distance between us and them as possible, trust me on that please."

"Still think we should have let Zahim's army deal with them. Make them useful for once," he told her.

"They have the Horde to deal with… with a little luck, that'll be taken care of when we get back to them," she said.

He laughed. "You don't believe a word of that. You don't think they stand a chance against the Horde without you there to advise Zahim."

She hesitated, proving him right. He chuckled at her gall, but he couldn't say he really disagreed with that assessment.

"Good night," she said tartly, making him laugh more, which seemed to enrage her even more.

What were Zahim and the Rebels without her?

He supposed those boys were finding that out right now…

The night wasn't very restful for him.

He was trapped in a nightmare that he couldn't control or end.

In it, the HomeBasers were on their trail, sniffing the air everywhere they had stopped for a minute, for him, to see if there was a way ahead, or just a quick rest to eat or drink, or get water from a clean stream.

Their scent was in the air, and the HomeBasers were zeroing in on them, they knew their every step… and they were closing in on them.

He couldn't chase the feeling away even when he woke up. They had his scent and would never let go of it… Raydr's paranoia washing down on him?

Or was he simply becoming insane?

It seemed like complete madness and yet he could not deny that it felt so true.

He packed Raydr into the truck, looking over his shoulder many times as he did, worried, certain that they would come out of the shadows like vengeful ghosts, intent on death, their deaths.

How many of them were left, out there, in hot pursuit? Dozens, hundreds? The whole damn tribe? And why was he letting it get to his head?

He had never been afraid of odds before, only the Horde managed to make him feel fear… and only because of his past experience with them.

Nothing in HomeBase had affected him adversely, he had seen the same kind of horrors there everywhere, so why was it inside his head, gaining strength with each passing second?

Why was his heart racing at the thought of them breathing down his neck?

"It's what they do," Raydr said softly. "They get inside your head."

She still looked gray and would have needed a few more hours of sleep but she looked much better than in the past few days.

"I don't know what you're talking about," he countered, not wanting to hear it.

"They are in your head now… The farther they are from you, the less effect it has. The voices and images will come… it'll get worse as they gain ground on us. So be ready, be warned… I had hoped it wouldn't influence you."

"Influenced by what, what are you talking about? How can they be affecting, influencing me?" he grunted.

"I can't explain it with… words… a sort of… hive mind, I guess. Ants, bees… but without that single leader to guide them… Just chaos, and it's contagious. You spend time in their lair and you come out changed. Different. Linked to them, or them to you."

"That's insane and ridiculous," he refuted.

"I know," she chuckled. "Completely insane, absolutely ridiculous. Like this life we're living isn't completely insane. They get in your mind, they take root there… the further you get away from them, the more normal you feel. But they're always there, lurking…"

"Well, we will make sure it ends… now!" he said; he wasn't going to live with those monsters in his head!

She looked at him, not with disbelief but some hope. She had been living with this connection for years and obviously she had given up the idea of ever being rid of them.

"How?" she queried.

"We will kill them all," he answered with fierce determination.

She had a fleeting smile; maybe she actually believed they had a chance to make it happen.

He was dead serious about it. His mind was the one thing the Horde had never possessed, the only thing that had remained his, battered and bruised, mistreated and abused and dazed by pain… It had remained his and his alone, and he would never give it up… or accept squatters in there.

The Horde had tried to crush his spirit, reduce it to nothingness, but never had they crawled in to try to claim it as theirs.

The HomeBasers had to be wiped from the face of the Earth, wretched as it had become, once and for all.

His newfound resolution helped put his fears to rest, and got him through the day - they had to reach the city and set their traps.

They would end the HomeBasers or die trying.

And strangely, Raydr seemed to get all the better for it. Still wounded and weak but in much better spirits.

She drove in the afternoon, to allow him to rest; he did so as best as he could. Sleeping through that bumpy ride was akin to a miracle, especially with his heart racing, feeling the HomeBasers coming closer, ever closer...

He drove as much as he could in the dusk and coming night, stopping only when he was sure he couldn't keep his vigilance up and he'd put them in more trouble than actually serve the cause of gaining more ground on their enemies.

The panic, the urgency was there, the creatures were coming... and the night wasn't exactly restful.

The dreams were omnipresent; the HomeBasers were trying to ruin their morale to make them weaker, make the ultimate kill easier.

Fighting that sensation, their influence, while trying to make up a game plan, was putting a much greater strain on them than they were willing to admit and the more time passed, the more they became irritable.

They were two against so many more, what were their real chances? Weapons aplenty but still, the odds were not in their favor.

And the route was difficult, unsure, the roads washed away or obstructed, no clear direction to follow or timetable until they reached their destination.

"How much further, do you even know?" Madan put to her the next night when they stopped to eat and rest.

The aurora-like lights were bright in the sky and he could have kept on but he was almost sure they were going in the wrong direction and she was completely lost.

"It looked a lot different then," she admitted, groaning as he set her down a little roughly.

Make the fire, prepare the meal, mundane tasks that usually helped him relax... but now seemed useless, a waste of his time.

He should have been eradicating his enemies, not cooking jerky to make it palatable!

"And that was what, eleven years ago?" he asked her.

"Eight years ago," she sighed. "I was on foot... took me a lot of time... my bandage is leaking."

"Take care of it yourself, I am busy," he replied tartly. She had no idea where they were or what direction to take, just vague notions that would get them killed. He should have listened to himself and gone toward Zahim's camp. Then they would have had a real chance to survive.

She chuckled a bit desperately. "Thank you, doctor. Your bedside manners amaze me."

He snorted and left to find more wood. He definitely needed to unwind a little, he was so wound up, ready to bite her head off.

He needed some peace and quiet to get his mind together again.

Unwind somehow... and he couldn't do that with the constant threat on their heads... Inside his head, never relenting, never giving him a moment's respite. He needed to take back control of himself and with Raydr watching him, all he felt was like going crazy and taking it all out on her.

Of course, gathering wood while pestering against her bad decisions, he wasn't exactly calming down.

But why was he so nervous? Why couldn't he keep this nervousness under control?

He was carrying a full load of wood and still muttering under his breath, not even sure what he was saying to himself, so there was no way he could have heard Raydr's groan of panic... and yet he knew she was in trouble.

Big trouble.

And by magic, it would seem, all the doubts seemed to

evaporate - finally something concrete to do!

Incredibly dangerous, facing horrible ways of dying, who knew how many enemies, but the distraction was more than welcome.

He yearned for that kind of action; something to do, someone to kill.

Definitely that would soothe his nerves. Someone to eradicate once and for all.

His gut feeling did not disappoint.

A HomeBaser, alone, from what Madan could gather or 'feel'... and he was choking Raydr, holding her up in the air by the neck, interrogating her from the sounds of it although Madan could not understand the words.

He didn't care what the man was saying, all that mattered was getting him out of the way, getting him dead.

The HomeBaser turned around just when he was a few feet away. Without hesitation, the monster threw Raydr on him, in an attempt to destabilize him and gain a few seconds to win the upper hand in the fight.

But Madan was prepared and dodged Raydr, who crashed heavily on the ground, with no consideration whatsoever for her wounds.

Finally, a face-to-face encounter with the people who thought they could control him, bring him down, kill him in his own mind and make him their slave. Finally, a duel that would redistribute the pain to those who really deserved it.

The HomeBaser thought the fight was already won and that was his mistake.

He didn't expect to meet such resistance, such will to survive, determination to live. He thought his anger and hatred at having lost his home and power could not be matched... but it was pale in comparison to Madan's rage.

The HomeBaser had a gun and tried to bring it to bear on his enemy; two shots were fired in the air, useless, before the fight was over.

Years of wielding a sword to survive had made Madan proficient at its use. Give no mercy, expect none.

And sometimes, that was the way of the world.

Raydr gasped in pain and fear when he turned her over; covered in blood and gore, he was a grisly sight indeed.

But as soon as she recognized him, the terror turned to relief and she almost looked ready to cry. Or maybe it was because of the wound.

"I hope it didn't rip the stitches or cause more damage," he grumbled, but strangely, he did not feel anger or impatience any more.

He no longer felt the need to run, the helplessness of being a tracked animal.

"He was a scout," Raydr said, gasping as he set her against a rock. "He was the closest to us. The rest are-" she inhaled sharply as he probed around her broken rib - definitely, the rough treatment had had some unfortunate consequences.

"They're farther away, yeah, I can… feel it," he admitted reluctantly. "They're coming, but we have… some time," he said, blowing out a sigh.

"Yeah some… some time, not much," she agreed.

"So it's not perfect, their psychic link?" he put to her as he cleaned the wound again.

"I'm no expert," she retorted, hissing in pain.

He chuckled mirthlessly; covered in blood and gore as he was, he looked pretty horrible but she didn't even notice. The blinding pain in her side took up most of her attention.

"Closest thing we have," he said; the obvious truth.

She blew out a pain-filled sigh. "The closest you are to them, the more powerful it is. Overwhelming, like you can't think for yourself any more."

"But it is possible to resist it, resist them? You escaped them after all," he reminded her.

"Yeah, you can resist it, especially if they're not concentrating. The whole bunch together, it's terrible. Takes every ounce of will you have… Like you don't exist any more… I escaped… at night, they were sleeping. Most warriors on a raiding party."

"Smart girl," he commented.

She was in a lot of pain but she took a second to glance at him in puzzlement as he bandaged her up again. "What do you mean?"

"What I said… there… maybe next time, you'll be able to help… we have some time now."

"Some," she agreed, still unsure whether or not he had been sarcastic.

The next day, they made good time although they were using up the last of their fuel supply. They were not worried any more; Raydr started recognizing the terrain; according to her, they were a day away from the city in question, on foot.

They stopped for a midday break, both needing some respite from the constant movement. They were much more relaxed now that the threat of the scout was off their heads. Not breathing in relief, far from, but breathing a little bit easier nonetheless.

"Can it be used against them?" Madan asked as they ate slowly, enjoying the stale bread and dried jerky and fruits as much as they could.

"Used what against who?" Raydr asked in incomprehension.

She was almost dozing off.

"Their mind link to us. Can we use it against them? Make them feel more confident than they should be?"

"You mean mask our thoughts, our emotional state?" she finally understood.

"You escaped from them. At night, most people away... but they have guards, they always have guards. Tell me how you did it, how you fooled them."

She took a long moment to answer, gathering painful memories. "I was in turmoil, I wasn't sure of anything. Abandoning my brother, the- the- uh-" she couldn't bring herself to say the word, but he understood her- "I wasn't thinking much. I had my plan, fear, turmoil... I don't know," she admitted finally.

"So it helped you escape, the turmoil?"

"I had this planned for a long time. Since the beginning, it had been my plan... Can we consciously influence them? Not a clue, not a single clue."

Then I suppose we will have to find out the hard way," Madan said with grim determination.

They ran out of gas two hours later but as the city ruins were now in sight, they were both in good spirits, even Raydr who dragged herself with more determination than strength.

They reached their 'battleground' safely, a dead ruin of a city that had been badly battered by the most violent storms Nature could produce. They didn't have time to explore much: Madan found a building that seemed in okay shape and left her there, while he returned to the truck to begin carrying their weapons back to their 'lair'.

He shuttled the heavy boxes forward, tiring, exhausting work... making him wish the gas has lasted just a few more kilometers, to make their preparation job much easier.

When he came back from the first 'run', Raydr showed him a functional cart she had found. Obviously, she hated being reduced to inactivity by a wound… and he was quite happy about it.

Not only was it a sign of healing, but her foresight made his job a lot easier.

He was half-way through emptying the truck when night fell: he knew their enemies were coming closer but he definitely needed the rest.

Raydr was tending the fire and preparing dinner when he crashed heavily on the floor. She had begun cataloging the contents of the boxes he had brought back, inventorying their weapons to be able to make a plan of action.

"How much time do you think we have before they catch up?" he put to her after drinking deeply from his canteen.

"Two days, maybe three, they are on their way," she answered offhandedly.

He nodded, as this was his vague, unsettling impression as well.

Sooner than they'd want, barely enough time to organize their defense… but if they had too much time to think it over…

Best be done with it, one way or another.

"There's a good amount of C-4," she said. "It must have lost some of its bang, but I can make triggers and we can ambush part of the city … Lead them into an ambush," she added, ladling some rice for him, wincing as it pulled on her wound.

"Don't overstress," he admonished. "You are no good to me dead."

"We will be dead, both dead, if I don't do my part. Now shut up and eat," she retorted.

He nodded and gobbled a spoonful; she made a good point.

Die trying was a much better attitude than just plain dying.

"Lots of C-4, huh?" he put to her.

"Yeah, it's an explosive, if you don't know. We have enough to level this city," she said, easing down in a sitting position to eat, trying to escape his scrutiny.

"Yeah, I know what it is… we have lots, good… but did you really have to waste some in our dinner?"

She frowned in confusion, not understanding him. Until he showed her the burnt rice and started laughing - of course she didn't find it funny at all.

"It's an old recipe," she defended.

"Hmm," he approved. "As old as the world to burn dinner, of course," he laughed, exhausted but in much better humor than he had been in weeks.

Poised to fight the last of bloodthirsty monsters with only a crippled ally to help him, and he impossibly felt good. Almost at peace.

Of course, a few seconds later he was sound asleep.

The focus for him was getting their supplies in as quickly as he could, before their enemies could lay their hands on them and use the weapons against them. They needed every possible odd in their favor, as they were already in their disfavor.

That made for harrowing trips to and from their useless truck and if at first, he enjoyed the simplicity of the task, after lugging the cart to the city five times, he began to grumble about the gas that could have lasted all the way to the city, help them a bit instead of putting them in this difficult situation.

One liter more and he could have been helping Raydr with their offensive, where his wits and energy were really needed.

She was doing all she could but was severely limited by her incapacity to move around and map the city to use it as a battleground.

A third person would have been really useful right now… but he didn't have enough energy left to complain.

He crashed down next to the fire she had built with old wood he had recuperated from old furniture in the building.

He downed a whole canteen and felt a bit dizzy because of it. The whole world was spinning and Raydr was looking at him critically from behind the detonator she was making.

"You should rest a bit," she admonished.

"Same. You should rest a bit or you will pull the stitches," he retorted, seeing as her bandage was wet.

"No time," she replied tartly.

"Same," he countered smartly.

At last they agreed on something.

"Maybe you can bury the rest," she suggested.

"They could find it, can we take that chance?" he argued.

"They're frenzied, even if they come across the truck, all they want is us… if they see no obvious weapons, they will hurry to us instead. They know we're here… when they're close, they will be tasting us already."

"What a beautiful turn of phrase," he shuddered involuntarily, only because he knew she was telling the truth.

Dinner was what they could expect to become if they didn't manage to fend off these monsters' attack.

"Bury… Okay," he sighed, just imagining that tiresome work.

At least they had a few functional shovels, that would help get the task done.

"Good… and then we'll be able to set up the trap, the explosives… I'll have them ready by then. If you can help me with the city layout, that would really help… I'm going with memory only and a lot has changed in eight years..." She snorted in disappointment when she heard snoring.

The exertion had vanquished him after all... and since he was actually taking her advice, she couldn't be mad at him.

He was sore all over when he finished burying their 'loot'. If at first, he had tried to hide the mounds, make them less obvious, make them appear like natural dunes, he quickly gave up the idea because it took up too much time and effort.

Some tasks seemed insurmountable for just one man and woman to accomplish and he felt as though they had taken much too much on their shoulders.

But of course, the choice had been made for them, they hadn't really had a say. Was that destiny? Choosing to face the HomeBasers alone, their destiny?

Their folly, their madness... or simply their lack of options...

He couldn't even think straight any more... and he knew part of it came from the fear that was invading him again.

'They' were coming closer.

Catching up with them. Their time was already running out.

"Done?" Raydr queried without sympathy whatsoever when he crashed down next to the fire, having had the brilliant idea of loading the cart for one last trip, as otherwise it would have been a waste of a voyage.

Sweat-soaked and completely exhausted, pulling it through the soft dunes made by the wind, how he had regretted his 'great' idea.

He grunted an approximate answer. All he wanted to do was sleep, not be bothered by more impossible-to-solve problems, not be confronted with dilemmas, as Raydr was about to do from her worried expression.

"Don't worry, don't worry," she reassured him. "They won't bother to dig it up, it's safe. Unless they kill us, then they probably... but it won't matter any more."

"Great bedside manners yourself," he muttered under his breath, not feeling reassured in the least.

"What's for dinner?" he put to her, hoping she would get the message. A few minutes of peace before the next bane.

"C-4," she said and he looked at her wryly a moment before bursting into laughter. For a moment there, he had actually believed her.

"C-4 detonators," she answered seriously. "I didn't have the time to make dinner."

He grumbled in dissatisfaction and groaned as he tried to get back up, which made her chuckle - not too hard, as it was much too early for her to laugh. A real torture with her broken rib.

"Come on, I'm not that heartless," she laughed. "In the pot."

He was starving and so any food could have tasted good but she hadn't burned it and it was so satisfying that he almost forgot his pains and worries.

Almost only - and Raydr's busy fretting reminded him of their real problem... they were far from safe.

He couldn't let the fatigue of the day overwhelm him.

Their enemies were coming, the 'respite' was almost over.

Raydr settled down some time after, looking preoccupied.

With all the physical work he had had to do, he hadn't given a single thought to how he would defeat the mental attack of the HomeBasers. And that was a mistake he could not afford to make again.

This battle would be waged on two fronts, both the mental and the physical aspect at the same time. There would be no mercy, no quarters. Eradicate them or die trying.

Just thinking about it, he felt a flutter of fear. He wasn't sure he had the time to rest any more. He wasn't sure his worried mind would allow him to rest any more.

"Do you... do you think-?" he began, not sure how to put it into words, how not to appear scared and weak.

There was no use to pretending, to parade, but if he admitted it aloud... he was admitting to himself that he was terrified then.

And that they were two people against dozens or more. And they had something to lose whereas their enemies did not.

Seen that way, it was almost inconceivable to think they had a chance to make it out as the victors.

"Sleep," she ordered, settling down carefully on the covers to spare her wounded side.

"But if we don't prepare-" he argued.

"We have time. Time enough to sleep. For now. I suggest you take it," she said adamantly and strangely, the gnawing worry evaporated.

He trusted her; she knew best.

In the morning they both felt it. The day was going to be scorching which would not help to move around. And their time was rapidly running out on them.

Their enemies were closing in on them, no mercy allowed or considered.

They were both in pitiful shape for their own reasons but the urgency of their predicament took precedence over their bodily woes.

Death waited for them on the other side - so what did it matter if his muscles were stiff and unresponsive, like every day working in the mines as a slave for the Horde?

Pain could be mastered or ignored; death on the other hand, had a definite finality to it.

He had to pull Raydr around to spare her ribs, which wasn't exactly easy in the streets filled with rubble, debris and sand from the frequent storms, but she made up for the inconvenience once they reached the city area she had chosen as their 'ambush ground'. She knew her way around explosives and she was a master at organizing an attack and defense strategy.

But would it be enough?

Strangely, as he followed her orders under the burning sun, Madan began to think that it was up to him, to them both.

They were their own enemies, as much as the monsters coming their way.

And perhaps that was the way to defeat the HomeBasers' mental gridlock.

By realizing that the effect the HomeBasers had on them was what they allowed them to have. By repressing their anger, fear, guilt, they were giving the HomeBasers the power over them.

And maybe if they faced it, if they forgave themselves for what they had had to do, what tore at their souls every single minute of every day, they would realize that the HomeBasers' power over them would disappear as though it had never existed in the first place.

Easier thought than done. He hadn't a clue how to unlock those secrets of his mind.

Forgive himself?

It seemed somehow... he'd rather die.

This theorizing was sapping his strength, and he needed every ounce of it in the here and now.

"It all depends how we make them come to us," Raydr said as she drew an approximation of the city in the sand. "They're smart, but desperate, feverish and vengeful now. Going for the kill. They might not be as careful as they should be."

"We need to herd them, bait them to your ambush," he understood. "And for that, you need a good vantage point... to blow them to hell when they fall in the trap."

"Yeah... exactly, and here, we have the perfect vantage point," Raydr said, making a line around what represented a tall narrow metallic tower whose old purpose was completely lost on them.

All that mattered, in any case, was the here and now.

"It's exposed but the best chance we have to watch over the area," Raydr continued.

"You'll be fine," he assured.

"As long as the structure is sound, there shouldn't be a problem," she said. "I'll watch from above until the time is right, the conditions for the optimal kill... but to be the bait... that won't be an easy task."

"Don't worry about me, I can make it," he assured. "Lure them to the square, play scared. Be scared, in fact, make them feel my fear, make them believe it."

"Believe me, that shouldn't be the hard part," she retorted.

"Then track to the tower as quickly as I can... you blow it when the time is right. You don't give me a single thought, just them. Blow them all to hell."

She chuckled a bit desperately. "You are my ticket out of here. If you die... without you, I can't move. I'd be killing myself."

"I thought that's what you wanted, you didn't care about surviving this, surviving at all, any more," he reminded.

She blew out a sigh. "What can I say?" she chuckled again. "Old habits die hard, don't they?"

He smiled fleetingly. "That they do. Yes they do..."

And that was a good thing as well...

They went over their flimsy plan a dozen times at the very least, they discussed every crazy idea they could have and placed their weapons at strategic locations, trying to be as prepared as they could be.

And then all that was left was to wait.

Waiting was torture on the nerves; one advantage of the psychic link, or whatever the HomeBasers had on them, was that they could feel the wait would not be long.

So they were able to keep their cool, and took up their positions long before their enemies came rolling in.

They rode strange machines, like great big motorcycles, made for only one person, but they were piled up, six or seven on them, which must have made their speed much slower, explaining why they had taken so much time to catch up.

Madan closed his eyes, trying to calm the fluttering of his heart. When he had left Raydr on the top of the tower, he had turned back. Only once.

"Don't hesitate," he had said seriously. "If they catch me, I'm dead, you're dead, we're both dead. Better take them with us."

"I won't hesitate, Madan," she said. No good lucks; they were useless in any case.

Luck came to the ones who won the fight… and the victors of this battle were yet to be determined.

Once in place, Madan tried to control his breathing, control the fluttering of fear in his stomach.

Anticipation, tension. He had to be strong, he couldn't let their mental magic get the better of him.

This was it, his proving ground.

All his life had been a succession of proving grounds, each more demanding than the next…

They wanted him weak and begging for mercy, he would be sure to surprise them.

Show them they had picked the wrong target, that he was too much for them to handle. Strangely, all he could see in his mind was not the here and now. He kept getting flashes of the day the Horde had attacked the Citadel.

The day his life had changed forever.

The fear in his wife's eyes as he rushed outside, the last glimpse he had had of his son, playing in his crib, all those memories he had suppressed for so long… coming back to the surface, rushing up like an unstoppable wave.

The sorrow was overwhelming him, the dead, the dying, the mistakes, the pain, the loss, oh the loss, heartbreaking!

Until he could hardly breathe any more.

The punishment for surviving… a constant torture without end, how he had wished to die, to be no more, to no longer feel anything any more.

Everything he had ever held dear, turned to waste, to ashes, slipping through his fingers, lost forever…

He fought the emotion, the fear and the rush of tears that wanted to spill uselessly from his eyes… Useless, weakening tears.

After a moment of fighting it with all his might, the hold began to lose its potency.

Was that the key to their power, their mental gridlock?

Making them relive their worst nightmares?

Making them see all their mistakes, all the people they had lost, the people that had mattered the most to them?

Consciously, he pushed the mental onslaught away, and thought of the mushrooming cloud, the explosion of HomeBase, the death of all their friends, all their people, trying as hard as he could to twist the knife in the wound, give them a taste of their own medicine.

Their loss, their shame, their mistakes, their regrets…

And much to his relief, although he felt a bit dizzy from this mental effort, he was able to get past his own painful memories to concentrate on their assault, their plan, their one and only chance of survival.

He hoped Raydr would have the same insight as he did but he could not worry about her right now.

Because they had arrived.

CHAPTER 7

Battleground

They rode strange vehicles that looked like motorcycles but bulkier somehow... and although there was seat for only one, they rode three or four on them, plus additional weapons, probably one of the reasons why they hadn't caught up with them sooner.

Some looked burned and close to death, others looked feral and ready to kill, but every single one of them was intent on revenge.

And their hatred now assaulted him, making him feel puny, dead already, incapable of even standing up to them.

But that emotion was easier to push away. He had lived in that state since the Horde had ripped him from his home...

The good memories, the loss, that was what affected him the most.

But loss was passing, inherent to their condition... and now it was time to redistribute the pain.

He closed his eyes and let them come nearer, letting them invade his mind with their alien presence to feel them rather than need to see them.

To know when the time was right to put their plan into motion.

With his eyes closed, he emptied his mind, thinking of all the decisions, good or bad, that had led to this moment. Every battle, won or lost, that had led to this fateful one…

Two people against an army.

He thought about how chance meetings provoked ripples that grew and grew until they shaped one's future… shaped the world's future.

How the tiniest choice could have such wondrous or disastrous results.

Was this battle only borne of chance, nothing else?

Or a greater power at work, pulling their strings until they finally faced their demons?

But why would that higher power care? About their puny, inconsequential existences?

His father's words imposed themselves on his mind again, and he didn't try to chase them away, but rather tried to understand the whole scope of them, the wisdom behind them.

"Our duty is to believe. Even in the darkest times, especially in the darkest moments, our duty is to believe, and our belief gives us strength. The strength to bring the light again…"

His eyes snapped open. They were close enough now.

He wasn't sure he believed, he wasn't sure he had the strength to bring that light, to make it exist again, but one thing was certain: it was time to move.

He let out a salvo that cut down a few of them: he was running off before even seeing the results of his attack.

What mattered wasn't to kill as many as he could now, but to make them mad, to make them lose their caution and fall headfirst into their trap.

Make them furious, make them bloodthirsty, insult their honor by showing them one lone man could keep them in check.

Make them lose what little was left of their sanity.

From the roars of pure rage he heard amidst the small

weapons fired after him, that first part of the plan was going great.

Now came the trickier part.

Staying alive until he got them to the ambush… and then somehow surviving the ambush itself.

He hoped Raydr was alert and ready - but on that point, he did have faith.

The adrenaline was running high in her veins, like in his, and all bodily woes were forgotten, in favor of the here and now.

She was ready to blow them all to hell.

He ran past the first marker and plunged to the ground as a small missile exploded the wall right in front of him, showering him with debris.

Raydr had warned him they had the best weapons available, and the loot they had taken from them should have been proof enough, but he had expected them to want a more personal revenge for the affront they had endured.

Blowing him to bits? Where was the revenge in that?

He flipped from his stomach to his back, emptying his clip on those closest to him, which made them scramble for cover, allowing him to get back on his feet.

Breathless, he sprinted, not even feeling his legs.

He had to make it!

He fired his entire clip as he felt they were gaining on him and taking aim again: now the weapons' cache they had placed around the city would come in handy.

But he hadn't expected them to be in such hot pursuit, to go at it so recklessly, as though…

Maybe Raydr had been smarter than him, maybe she had managed to hide her presence somehow, and they thought he was the only one left.

Receptacle of their complete hatred, he bore the entire assault on his shoulders.

He couldn't let the fear of failing overwhelm him; this was exactly what they wanted to happen.

Except that he had to stop for a few seconds to pick up those weapons and that left him vulnerable, especially with their rocket launchers.

And he stayed a second too long.

The blast wave knocked him off his feet; he was showered with stinging debris and left breathless, pinned down under a slab of wall that had crumbled with the explosion.

Dust everywhere, he could barely breathe, and more buildings were collapsing, the only reasons why the HomeBasers weren't on him already, ripping him to shreds.

He couldn't get a decent breath in, he was hurt and his ears were ringing badly, making him dizzy. But the panic was the worst, overwhelming him completely.

He couldn't be weak like this, he couldn't fail!

He tried to wriggle out from under it but nothing seemed to work, it was so heavy, he needed to breathe!

And the buildings kept falling, making so much dust... but soon it would settle and the HomeBasers would come calling for their victim.

He tried to push the cement chunk off him, putting all his strength at it, until he saw dark spots in his field of vision.

It did not budge one centimeter.

No despair, just try to get a breath in: with oxygen in his body, he could accomplish anything.

Or so he hoped.

He felt so weak and wasted, his great plan reduced to rubble... like the one he was stuck under, pinned like a bug.

He tried moving his hands and felt one of the weapons he had been looking for, the weapons that had perhaps cost him the whole assault.

But they were too close, he had almost no control over his fingers, too much weight, too much pain, he wouldn't make it, they were closing in on him, closing in for the kill!

Three shots, fired in rapid succession, made him jump up, even pinned down like he was.

Raydr had come to his rescue, but had exposed her position, her presence.

And the HomeBasers' attitude changed immediately. He felt it as though he could see it with his own eyes and that panic gave him the strength to push and wriggle out from under the wall chunks.

Their enemies were now converging on her, away from the ambush, their anger and hatred finding a new outlet.

They must have felt that they were being fooled, that something was happening, and they wanted their revenge more than anything else.

With an effort of will that seemed to take everything from him, making him see dark spots dancing in his field of vision, he got up, numbering bruises by the dozens.

Luckily, nothing seemed to be broken, and that meant he had to go on the warpath again.

How he wished he could have a psychic link to Raydr's head, to tell her to blow it all to hell right now, before the HomeBasers escaped the optimal blast radius.

But he must have had one, because he knew she was dead set on completing the plan, allowing him to run out of danger before blowing up the charges.

That woman was impossibly stubborn.

Their enemies had no qualms, no consideration for each other... they should have been as ruthless with each other.

But they weren't, they couldn't be, and so he had to scramble to fulfill his part.

Distract the HomeBasers and get them to die in their ambush.

He started shooting just to draw attention and it worked; he had to get loud.

Break their unified bond and spirit, get them confused and divided, influence them instead of being influenced.

Projecting fear was not too hard but he needed more than fear to get them to forget about the shooter... relay that they had some sort of plan, an ace up their sleeve and by going for the one with the good vantage point, they were actually falling into that trap.

He hadn't a clue if it was working until another rocket blasted walls in front of him, making him duck breathlessly, the stinging debris hitting his back and arms... and it hurt.

He ran faster, drawing them in, uncaring about his life or death, if he could just end them, end them once and for all.

"Now or never, Raydr," he muttered under his breath; he couldn't waste any time or energy shouting it to her and wishing it would get through her thick skull.

She did not disappoint.

Soon he wasn't worried about the HomeBasers on his tail any more... but the path of the explosion, coming his way, and somehow staying alive...

They had set markers for the boundaries of their trap, Raydr's calculations of how powerful the explosion would be and just as the blast wave propelled him forward without ceremony or kindness, he recognized one of them.

In the clear - ish.

Not that the blast wave seemed to care about their calculations.

He landed heavily, almost knocking himself out. His ears were ringing, there was a wave of fire and dust expanding before him… he just had the time to cover his face that it washed over him.

The heat was intense but he knew he couldn't stay put, he knew he had to move, he was in very real danger coming from the nearby buildings, those that still stood precariously after the explosion.

The HomeBasers had forgotten all about him; with revenge on their hearts, those that had survived were converging on Raydr's position, having identified her as the real enemy.

He was considered lost, dead, swallowed by the dust and fire.

Up to him to prove that they were lacking judgment once again.

They were rabid, relentless, completely insane… dangerous.

They would fight and kill to their last breath… Luckily, he was prepared for that.

He hoped he was prepared for that.

Fervently.

Storming the tower where Raydr was hiding, all they wanted was to kill and exact their revenge on the one who had caused their race's demise. Uncaring of their wounds, they had already climbed pretty high up when he arrived and he wasn't sure he had the skill to shoot them down.

Which meant he had to scramble up himself and take as many of them down as he could, hoping he would catch them all before they reached Raydr.

Unfortunately, as he climbed, more survivors came after him, sandwiching him between two layers of desperate, intent on killing, madmen.

And from the sounds of shooting he was hearing coming from up above, they had already reached the top and Raydr was in trouble.

He didn't panic, no time to panic; she was used to taking care of herself, wounded or not, she would take as many of them down as she could.

She excelled at the art of surviving, taking care of herself… he had to be just like her, focus on the present moment.

Time to kill.

He wasn't sure what he felt any more, if he was feeling it, or if it was the HomeBasers' effect on him, and he couldn't say he cared any more.

His intelligence, his will to survive, he had to keep that intact to keep his edge over his enemies, but it was drowned by bloodlust, by kill or be killed.

He couldn't let them overtake him, he had to remain himself somehow.

But amidst the carnage, the killing, left, right, up, down, everyone that came his way, every single thought became moot. Irrelevant, inconsequential.

He was climbing up and killing everything in his way, acting like a wild animal with a single idea in mind.

Revenge. Get to the top and kill more.

He didn't even know how he stayed alive, how he managed to strike first and parry to make it, leaving a trail of bodies in his wake. It was a complete blur in his mind.

Was he really in control or carried forward by the upward motion, losing all thread back to reality?

He had to scramble over a pile of corpses, still warm, some still moaning, to get to the top of the tower. Raydr was a very good shot, and that was why she had managed to survive all this time.

No one left behind him: somehow, they had thinned themselves out.

A neat pile of bodies at the base of the tower was all that was left of the HomeBasers' formidable force and as he reached the top of the tower and saw the devastation, the loss, the fuming city that had engulfed so many of them, he was no longer dominated by the same emotions.

Bloodlust and rage were still there, but they did not dominate his mindframe any more. He was overwhelmed by a strange, sapping longing, the sudden need to lay down and die.

Abandon everything, just give up, everything was over...

Just over...

His father falling to his death from the wall that had been his city's pride, all their efforts reduced to nothingness...

Just lay down and die.

"Madan!" Raydr's strangled voice snapped him out of the feeling in an instant.

He perceived the HomeBasers' presence before seeing anything and ducked, avoiding a fatal blow.

Back to surviving: the battle was far from over.

Raydr fired her weapon again but only to slow the advance of the other HomeBasers, make them cower and duck protectively to give him a chance to recover his wits and take care of the enemy in front of him.

Give him a chance to take back the reins of his thoughts, take back control of his mind.

They were the last of their race now, and so, entrusted with all the vengeful spirit of their species. Madan barely had the time to realize that the longing for death he had been feeling came from them, not him, before he was in the middle of a fight for his life.

Again.

The odds had been reduced in their favor but nothing was won in advance.

Anything would have made a good weapon at this point, because Raydr, as good a shot as she was, could not risk a shot without risking hitting him. So the HomeBaser was all his.

As such, he was reduced to parrying blows, dodging and backing up on the narrow catwalks that composed the top of the tower.

The HomeBaser was trying to push him against the edge: the emptiness made a formidable weapon.

Madan couldn't get a blow in, the others were converging, he couldn't find the time to draw his trusted sword, until he was against the side railing, with only the void to look forward to.

He was exhausted after his fight up the tower and it was crashing on him at precisely the wrong moment.

He was tired and breathless and of course, against better than him at the moment, the wrong moment.

Raydr fired many more shots, useless, or so it seemed, but her goal was to distract their remaining enemies, to break the mental hold they had on him.

Why should he be exhausted at the worst moment?

They were manipulating him for an easy kill, and he couldn't let that happen.

Her strategy worked to a point: two of them stayed on Madan to finish him off while the three others converged on her instead.

One of them threw some debris at her, a lucky shot really

that knocked her out of her hideout.

She landed heavily on the catwalk, uttering a groan of pain that made the men laugh and snicker in victory: one hurried to finish her off right away.

Exactly the moment she had been waiting for, to get an easy, clean shot.

Unfortunately, struck dead, he fell atop her and she had to struggle with the last of her strength to wriggle out from under him in time.

In time to shoot dead the other two, snarling as they rushed to finish her off.

More bodies to crush her and when she finally emerged from that human prison, she was breathless and dizzy, seeing double, using her remaining wits not to fall unconscious.

She had trouble interpreting what she was seeing: Madan managed to flip one of his opponents over his shoulder, making him fall to his death, but the other had a knife and was ready to strike.

She didn't hesitate and fired... but unfortunately, the bullet went right through the HomeBaser... Into Madan as well.

For an eternal second, it was as though time stood still, both men looking, dumbfounded, at the red blossoming on their chests, both slowly losing balance, falling over the railing.

Falling to their deaths.

Raydr wasn't sure how she did it, how she pushed her legs and body when she could barely breathe with her side on fire, with gravity being much faster and stronger than she was, but somehow, she caught Madan and held onto him as he plunged down.

She landed on her side - heavily - gripping his coat, arm and one hand in a deadlock.

The shock was jarring and the coat started ripping apart right away, making her gasp in fear and pain, and scramble to grab his other hand instead.

But he was so heavy, so limp and unresponsive, as though he was dead already, his mind having plunged into the abyss before his body could follow.

And maybe that was the whole problem, apart from her elbow and shoulder coming unhinged, trying to hold on to him.

And apart from his wound, of course…

But the last HomeBaser was falling, had fallen to his death… even she could feel that longing, just giving up and dying seemed so attractive in that moment.

"Please fight," she said through her clenched teeth, unable to draw a decent breath in, for fear of letting go of his hand for one wrong millisecond.

If she let herself go, she would let go. She couldn't keep this up, she could only let go…

But she refused to.

She had a few seconds of strength left in her: he was so heavy!

"Fight it, please," she choked out, the veins on her forehead, red from the exertion, standing out as though they wanted to burst from her head.

"Fight, fight, don't leave me," she added. Seconds left, ticking away so rapidly. She couldn't hold on, she wasn't strong enough to deadlift him, he was slipping out of her grip, completely unresponsive.

"Please fight," she said brokenly, knowing it was the end, that he was gone and nothing would bring him back any more.

Without him, she would die, but that wasn't what was shattering her to pieces. Useless tears sprang to her eyes and fell down on Madan's head.

"I can't be alone any more," she breathed out, ready to let him go; she was trembling all over, holding on through sheer will, reserves of strength she hadn't known she had.

But everything came to an end.

Always the same end.

It was a fog of pain the likes of which he had never experienced before.

Not just the fire of the bullet, burning through his flesh, but an overwhelming feeling of defeat, of loss, of despair.

All he saw in his mind's eye was not the now, not Raydr rushing to save him, grabbing him in extremis; the past.

His parents thrown from the high wall of the Citadel, the ultimate symbol of defeat.

The feeling of loss was as overpowering now as it had been then; nothing to do but die with them.

And all he wanted was to die. Not suffer through fifteen years of torture and abuse, physical pain and mental anguish, just to return to the very same position, the same moment, the same choice.

Live in pain… or abandon the fight and simply die.

Total crippling defeat, and there was no reason to go on.

In a way, it was as though he was already dead, so why even attempt to put up a final fight?

The fall seemed so sweet, weightlessness, flying, the void… and finally the ultimate release he had been looking for… for so long, it would seem.

Death was finally in his grasp: he had done all he could to stay alive, he had fought enough, given enough… and yet, something still seemed to hold him back.

How he wished he could have struggled against it, fought it, tore himself free from it…but even his father wouldn't let him have his peace.

There was no peace to be had, only more torment. Obstacles to overcome, to triumph over.

"Even in the darkest moments, especially in the darkest moments, our duty is to believe. To have faith, to keep on, to never give up."

Raydr's tears fell, not on his head, but on his face, as he was looking up, out of the daze induced by the last HomeBaser, falling to his death, trying to influence him unto the last second, get revenge over those who had destroyed them this way.

She was at the end of her strength, unable to hold him, giving up herself: so of course when he started climbing up on her, she gasped in pain and surprise, not even understanding what was going on.

It wasn't easy to hoist himself up, using her as a human ladder, and he was quite glad when he crashed beside her, having managed the feat of hoisting himself over the railing.

They were both in pitiful shape, exhausted, breathless… with a long climb down to look forward to.

But they were alive… and victorious.

"You're not alone any more," he told her in a whisper, and she did not retort anything sarcastic to that.

Perhaps she just didn't have the strength left in her.

They took a long time to climb down and, after making sure all the HomeBasers were in fact dead, they took rest to tend their wounds, eat, drink, and try to enjoy their improbable victory.

It wasn't a cold night but they huddled together nonetheless, both needing some human warmth after such devastation and death.

The night lights were making the sky bright, preternatural,

and they couldn't stop the shivers from taking possession of their spines from time to time. Blood loss or just disbelief at having survived such carnage?

They couldn't tell themselves.

"What do we do now?" Madan asked softly; he was exhausted because of his wound and the exertion but he couldn't find the calm, the inner peace to sleep.

"Tomorrow," Raydr answered drowsily, closer to sleep than he was. "Sleep… we have a tomorrow, so we can sleep tonight…"

He chuckled despite the pain in his chest. Enough worries for one day… they had deserved that rest.

The next morning, they were in worse shape, both suffering from their damning wounds; both out of breath and strength, they could barely move around. They should have stayed put and recuperated but they couldn't stand to stay in that city a second longer than they had to.

They had no means of transport to get out, except the vehicles the HomeBasers had used to track them.

They limped and struggled their way to where the HomeBasers had left them and took their time inspecting them to try and discover how they worked.

A mental challenge that proved more difficult because of their wounds. They constantly had to catch their breaths and bending down was a torture for both…

The sun was burning down on them, making it even more difficult to concentrate. Raydr straightened up and had to steady herself; the world was spinning around her nauseatingly.

"They don't seem to run on fuel," she said finally.

"Well, that's good, since we don't have any left," Madan retorted a little sarcastically.

"Right," she sighed.

"There's no fuel tanks anywhere," he added. "Just these large panels, what are they?"

"Like I know! Why ask me?" she replied.

"You were their prisoner for three years, no?" he retorted a little irritably.

"Two and a half, but… I was a prisoner? You think they let me near these things? If only I'd known they had these machines, I would have tried to escape long before, long before the…"

She stopped in mid-sentence, as it was still a difficult subject for her.

"Okay, but how do we make them work? We need to make them work? To get out of here, right?" he egged her on.

She groaned and hunkered down again to give the front of the machine another look again.

A motorcycle-like contraption with large luminescent panels on the back that gave it a sort of wing-like appearance, and reduced the transport capacity to one.

"A code… it needs a code to start up," she declared after tapping many panels and buttons.

"A code?" Madan repeated, not sure he had heard right.

Especially when Raydr started puffing out her breath on a clear panel in front of the driver seat. With much difficulty as she could barely breathe properly.

"What are you doing?" he put to her.

"Magic, I hope," she answered with a pale smile. "Bear with me…"

Smudges appeared on the screen, finger smudges of the most used numbers. Madan raised a questioning eyebrow at her as she started tapping numbers on the touchscreen.

"Five numbers," she cringed when the screen announced that

she only had three tries left before total system lockdown.

A safety protocol that was completely useless and a real hindrance to them as they had no clue what numbers to start with.

"How many combinations possible?"

She grumbled under her breath. "More than I ever learned to count... we have ... let's hope it's the same for every vehicle, we have four tries before the last one and then we are screwed... we go to each vehicle and we try until the last one, and we hope we get lucky, very lucky..."

"We will never guess it right," he argued. "No way."

"I better check... I hope it's a control code and not an individual combination or we are definitely screwed..."

She went to breathe on the next motorcycle's touchscreen to see if the smudges were in the same place. "Okay, looks like a general code. Numbers: 0-1-3-7-9... any possible combination, no clue which is the first or last one... your guess is as good as mine, but don't lockdown any of them just yet, and keep track of those you have tried. The best we can do for now."

"And when we will have exhausted all the tries but one?" he put to her.

"Then... we wish we knew how to pray, I guess," she said without humor.

He had to chuckle without humor at that... the universe had this tendency to put their inadequacies in their faces.

If they locked out every vehicle, they would have to walk... it would take months to reach Zahim's camp... which meant they would die, wounded as they were. Without food but mostly water, they would never make it.

"If only Mayzin were here," Raydr sighed when they had exhausted all possibilities but one on each motorcycle. "He'd know how to bypass this."

"Can we bypass it?" he put to her.

"If we were Mayzin, yes, but just us… we would be shooting ourselves in the foot here…"

"We're already dead if we can't get them to work," he reminded her.

"It's driving me crazy, so close, so far, so … dead," she grunted

"Not yet, not just yet," he said.

"Positive thoughts," she said with a snort. "They're sun-powered, I can feel it… why I wanted to drive at night, gain ground."

"So they would only work during the day?"

"I think so, anyway," she shrugged, a bad idea from the grimace she made.

"Well, if we just lock ourselves out, what difference does it make? Better get on with it, and face our lack of options after… right? "

Raydr groaned, not looking too happy with the idea herself. To be left with no hope when salvation was just a keystroke away…

And the worst did happen. Vehicle after vehicle, they didn't find the right code, they locked themselves out, until only one was left. Only one.

They both felt a little desperate.

"Do you want to do it?" Raydr asked him.

"Ladies first," he answered.

"I don't have the heart for it," she admitted after extending her hand. "I don't know, I prefer leaving it like that, still some hope left. Ridiculous, I know."

"Maybe… we wait until tomorrow," he said, sighing.

It was late and he felt tired, exhausted and a little miserable.

He was going over the facts over and over again in his mind, going insane with it.

If this one didn't start, they were doomed.

Dead already.

"Okay, sleep on it," Raydr said decisively. "Maybe we'll have a dream… maybe our good luck fairy will whisper the code in our ears… right?"

She was mocking as always but he heard the relief in her voice. She couldn't dash that last hope.

And of course, although he was dead tired, he could not sleep at all.

His wound was smarting of course, pulsating with every heartbeat but he was exhausted enough that he should have slept like a log.

Raydr's breath was steady and regular: she was healing faster than he was.

Or maybe her conscience was clear.

And his wasn't.

Her words stayed stuck in his head, running in an endless loop… Their good luck fairy would whisper the code in their dreams.

Such things didn't exist, of course, but wasn't there someone, someone you could turn to, when everyone else let you down, when all hope seemed lost?

So his father had always said: God helps those who help themselves.

A favorite of his, one he often used when patients complained when they hadn't followed his recommendations.

Hadn't he and Raydr helped themselves enough, as much as they possibly could? As much as humanly possible?

It was wrong to demand divine intervention, it was wrong to

wish for one, to claim he deserved one, and yet…

Grunting against the pain, Madan got up from the uncomfortable slouch he lay in and took a few steps out of their hideout, a building that was still sound despite the explosion they had set off.

He looked up at the sky, once again colored by bright lights, the preternatural sight that now awaited them at every sundown.

What mankind had made of the planet, what they were punished for every single day of their lives, the arrogance and carelessness of their ancestors.

And here he was, demanding a miracle because they were in a bad scrape. The very same arrogance…

He astounded himself… wasn't he used to relying on himself only, hadn't he always scorned the faithful?

Ever since escaping from the mines of the Horde, in any case.

For years, he had not given God a single thought (except curses perhaps) so why would God oblige? Forgive him for his arrogance, his hypocrisy?

Coming in like a beggar, asking for a magic fix to their problems.

He almost gave up before even giving it a try, feeling too ashamed of himself.

But they were really, really, really out of options.

Save for this one.

He closed his eyes and gathered his thoughts: his heart rate sped up, he felt terrified of even attempting this, of putting his pride and anger aside.

What could he expect except scorn and sarcasm, no, worse…

Silence.

Complete and utter, terrifying silence.

Why would God give him another chance?

Understand their plague, show them mercy?

He hadn't a clue. He saw no reason. He expected nothing but silence although his heart was hammering in his chest, wishing for some sign!

Just one sign!

He didn't even have the time to go through with an actual attempt at prayer.

His blood turned to ice in his veins… the fear…

The fear invading him was not his own.

The sign.

Stuck under the rubble for two days, more dead than alive, he was so thirsty… so close to salvation… Just run to the vehicles and flee. All thoughts of avenging his race gone from his head, all he wanted was to survive.

Madan was weak and wounded but his heart skipped a beat nonetheless, and a chill climbed up his spine, realizing that this was it.

The answer to his unspoken prayer.

He almost lost balance, he felt so dizzy and weak: was this what it felt like, to see a miracle with his own eyes?

He couldn't let the HomeBaser see him, hear him, feel him! The boy was scared, wounded, weak, frantic, there was a good chance… No time to get Raydr, wake her up to have all the odds in their favor…

If this was God's answer to their predicament, he was ready to do whatever was necessary to survive.

Including running (half-crouched) to follow the final survivor of the HomeBaser without being seen.

In spite of the extreme amount of pain this caused him.

He had to be close, because in the night, despite the

preternatural lights in the sky, how could he expect to see what numbers the man would punch on the touchscreen?

Salvation wasn't supposed to come on a platter.

Life had never been easy, and this was more than he could have ever expected from it, more than he had the right to ask from it.

He clenched his teeth against the pain: he had to fight a raging migraine as well as his bodily woes.

But it was worth it. This was hope incarnate.

A bastard that just refused to die was their best bet, their only bet at staying alive.

If he, somehow, stepped up to the challenge.

He managed to get within hearing distance: the boy was mumbling desperately in their strange language. Of course, there was only one motorcycle left able to work…

Wasn't that just another sign, everything happening for a reason, for once… in their favor?

Otherwise, their enemy would be long gone by now.

Madan hunkered down some more to be inconspicuous and stretched as much as his battered body allowed it.

The boy was too frantic to properly use his "psychic" ability to his advantage: he didn't realize one of his enemies was closing in on him. All he wanted was to escape.

He scrambled to another vehicle and his fingers danced over the touchscreen; he whimpered when he was refused again.

Definitely started with 0… but his vantage point was so poor.

Perhaps if they had had that starting point to begin with, they could have gotten lucky, unlocked the code. But now with only one vehicle left, he needed the whole combination.

Patience and faith had never been his strong suit.

0-3-1 he saw from the next try but the HomeBaser turned his

head at the wrong moment, forcing Madan to cower to avoid being seen. Losing his window of sight at precisely the wrong moment.

The boy was frantic and going at it with no sense or reason, no logical order, and he found himself next to the only functioning vehicle much more quickly than he should have, forcing Madan's hand.

He debated in his mind - for maybe half a second - whether or not it was best to attack now and torture the code out of the boy, or let him start the machine and then overpower him somehow, before he left with it.

The choice was very difficult, mind-wrecking in fact.

And he had no time, this hesitation had cost him the choice.

Madan rose from his crouch, in full view, perfect vantage point as the last HomeBaser survivor tapped in the code that had eluded them all day.

0-3-1-7-9

Raydr thought they only worked in the sunlight but that didn't appear to be true.

Or maybe they had some reserve power left, for the hybrid motorcycle powered up to life, humming like a huge insect in the darkness.

It didn't matter: Madan was already moving, pouncing on the boy before he could even mount the vehicle.

The boy was wounded, dying of hunger and thirst, but that didn't mean he wasn't a threat.

On the contrary, he would fight with the energy of despair, so close to freedom, to be held back…

He knew the type, he knew the power that came from having nothing to lose, having been in that situation more times than he could count.

But now he did have something to lose, and that was wreaking havoc within him.

Why was he thinking about Raydr, how if died now, here, she would be stranded, she'd find his corpse, and die herself?

If he couldn't beat this boy, they were both dead, and somehow, the thought was terrifying rather than strengthening.

But the battle had begun, there was no turning back now... there had never been.

They both evaluated each other in an instant, but an instant was all they needed to gather what was left of their strength, and attack each other with a savagery borne of despair - and necessity.

Both of them were in pitiful shape, what would determine the winner?

In spite of the 'divine intervention', Madan did not count on God's help to survive this.

Only himself.

They grappled and fell on the ground: the hard contact made stars explode in Madan's field of vision and the breath was knocked out of him forcibly.

He hadn't realized until that instant, adrenaline fueling him and all, how badly hurt he was. Fear had no place in a fight to the death, fear meant you were beaten already... He would have to prove that wrong because he was afraid. All he felt like doing was quitting, enough fighting, enough death, enough struggle...

He couldn't take it any more.

Not in his condition, not with his body wanting to quit on him. But he had never been one to give in to his body's demands.

They grappled again and this time, Madan did not only feel his enemy's strength but his weakness as well.

Which meant the victory in this fight was up for grabs, all he had to do was give it his all.

That realization gave him wings - or in this case, fists of steel.

He shut out the pain, knowing he was ripping stitches, wrecking the fragile repairs his body had made, and he couldn't have cared less.

Adrenaline replaced his blood and he felt nothing, save the joy of finally destroying the last thorn in his side, wrecking the last alien invader in his head.

The feelings of defeat faded as the HomeBaser boy lost consciousness: Madan had forgotten all about their psychic link and how easily they could influence his state of mind.

But it was over now… all over.

Satisfied that his adversary was down, he went to hunt for his weapon, feeling no inclination to choke the boy to death. He was breathing hard and the surge was coming down, pins and needles of pain invading his limbs. His shirt was stained with blood again.

The gunshot made him jump out of his skin. He whirled around to see the boy crashing to the ground, red blossoming on his chest.

"Never turn your back to them," Raydr, out of breath and exhausted, said softly.

She must have run all the way from their camp, arriving just in time to stop the HomeBaser boy before he threw a knife in Madan's back.

"Luckily I don't have to remember that… since he was the last one," Madan retorted, gasping from the pain that was now afire in his whole body.

Worth it, definitely, but nonetheless extremely painful.

"Thank you," he added.

"Thank me? Thank you, you mean… without you we'd be

stranded and dead right now."

He grinned half-heartedly. "A compliment? You must have fallen on your head... Let's get out of here."

He had no intention of staying in that doomed town a second more than he had to.

Of course they had to get their supplies and that meant a long trek to their sleeping area. Although they could both barely move their bodies, hope seemed to be buoying them and they found it much easier to move around.

By the morning, they were ready and eager to leave and their vehicle, being solar-powered, was brimming with the power to do just that.

Madan drove because he was the most wounded and sitting on the solar panels and holding on was more difficult than it seemed.

The cart had become a makeshift trailer for their supplies and they went off, finally leaving behind the HomeBasers and their curse.

Although the pace was slow, they both felt that they were getting somewhere, that their trials were somehow over and that they would reap what they had sown.

A little peace and quiet.

But of course, they were heading south, toward the rest of the war.

Towards chaos and death.... Peace was illusionary... this peace was just a hiccup in the ongoing battle of their lives... but they were more than willing to enjoy it, to give themselves a temporary respite.

Reality would catch up with them soon enough.

CHAPTER 8

To Face the Horde

The ride was chaotic sometimes and hard on their fragilized bodies but they were making good time, traveling back toward Zahim's encampment.

They hadn't a clue what had happened, what they would find once they reached the camp.

Many days had passed since their attack on the HomeBaser lair and so many things could have gone wrong… or right.

Zahim had been in such a hurry to attack the Citadel, prove his worth, make his mark on the world before his death.

Raydr didn't seem too worried; in fact, Madan felt more anxiety than she did.

If Zahim stormed the Citadel, the City of Light, if he was victorious?

That was what bothered him the most. Not that they would lose, but that the Rebels would actually destroy the Horde.

He felt ready to face them, he wanted to face them now.

Take back his heritage, his city, face his demons…

Maybe that was why Raydr seemed more at peace with herself now.

She had faced hers and had come out of it alive.

"What will you do once we reach Zahim's camp… assuming it's still there?" she asked him one night after they had checked and cleansed each other's wounds and eaten.

The night lights were bright in the sky and they were both tired but they didn't feel like sleeping just yet.

Conversation was hard while they traveled so they could only really communicate at night, if they were so inclined.

"What will you do?" he retorted, not certain of his answer. Or rather, strangely, her reaction to it. What would she think of his plan?

"I? I will... heal. Eat better, hopefully, and see what I can do to help," she answered.

"Your fight was with HomeBase. That's the reason you followed Zahim... right?"

"The main reason," she specified, "But what would I do now anyway? Move northward to avoid the Horde? The raids? From what I heard and gathered from the nomads and travelers, this place is blessed... The rads avoid it. Some kind of luck, why the Horde came crashing in to steal it in the first place, right? So if we can take them down, rid the world of them, all the better... right?"

"I guess," he said noncommittally.

"And if we win, maybe we can live, just live... before another two-bit dictator shows his ugly face."

He had to chuckle at that. "And what's living?" he put to her.

"Oh I wish I knew," she admitted, laughing softly. "Maybe I will get a chance to find out, what do you think?"

He shrugged, feeling a strange chill at the thought. Living?

"Maybe," he said.

"Good night, Madan," she said with a sigh, settling down in her covers.

He chuckled as he looked up at the sky. "That's not my name, you know."

"As though Raydr is my name," she answered. "Good night,

Mr. Unnamed, is that better? Get some sleep."

He laughed under his breath and settled down himself, although his chest hurt when he tried to lie down.

Living.

Had he ever really known what was living?

They reached the camp a few days later - or rather what had been the encampment for many weeks.

Now all that was left was the vestiges of it, places where the fires had been made, some waste and detritus, useless crates, abandoned before being burned...

Like the ghost of what had been.

They both felt a chill seeing this... would they ever again see those who had made this place vibrant, noisy, alive?

They were chasing ghosts... and all they would find would be corpses.

There had been storms here too and the wind and rain had erased the signs; it was hard to tell where they had gone, what direction they had taken.

At the same time, nothing could have been more self-evident.

They had to face the truth. And head for the Citadel.

They didn't have to consult each other, it was the next step.

Face the Horde.

The next few days were spent on the road, following the road to the Citadel, chasing after their comrades-in-arms, anticipating the next battle they would have to face, trying to heal their wounds as much as possible to be ready for that confrontation.

Because more pain and violence were definitely on the way.

"Something's gone wrong," Raydr said one night as they lay down to rest. "I know it, I feel it, I just... I know it. They're in trouble. Big trouble."

"Zahim can handle it," Madan answered.

"No, no, he's a diplomat, unrealistic, a dreamer... not a war leader, not a soldier. A great people person, a peace leader, but... this? This is beyond him. He can't face the Horde, it's not him. He has no idea what they're capable of, who you have to become to face them, beat them... not a clue."

Madan was almost amused by her worry, her analysis of the sacrosanct Rebel leader... so similar to his own.

"What would you have done if you had died at HomeBase? What would they have done without you then?"

She stopped fidgeting and looked at him directly. "I never expected to survive HomeBase," she admitted. "I never thought I'd ever worry about anything again."

He didn't know what to answer to that, so he just went to sit next to her. She wasn't crying but it must have been a struggle not to.

Death had a finality to it, an end. No more worries, no more troubles, no more anxiety gnawing at the soul.

The struggle, over, in good or bad.

Life was filled with those contradictions, those tests, and sometimes, it was easier to just give up and just forget all about it.

Hadn't he done the same for fifteen years?

Live as though he was dead already?

After some time, she relaxed and fell asleep. He lay back, trying to find a comfortable position to sleep in with her in his arms.

"They'll be okay," he whispered under his breath. "They will be, and if they're not... we're coming. We're coming to help them..."

He fell asleep at that moment, feeling strangely reassured. A choice had been made, maybe not completely conscious... but nonetheless, a defining choice.

That would shape his future. His life.

His choice: Never to run any more.

In the next few days, they began to see signs that Raydr's impression was right. Signs of a massive, hasty retreat. Abandoned corpses, faces she could almost recognize if not for the horrible wounds that had already begun to fester.

The bloated and charred soldiers were unrecognizable but the makeshift uniforms weren't, and told the story in much too cruel terms.

Madan could feel her anxiety rising, becoming overpowering, the weight of the loss overwhelming her, postponing her recovery.

She looked a lot grayer than just a few hours before, concern over the possible survivors clouding her judgment.

She had lost some of her tough, invincible, devil-may-care veneer but she didn't break down: he respected her all the more for it.

He knew exactly how that felt.

And finding the strength to keep on in those moments was more challenging than anyone could have imagined.

After two more days of rough traveling, they reached the remainder of the Rebel Army.

Now a bedraggled bunch fleeing desperately to avoid the wrath of the Horde. Many - most - were wounded, and all were panicked, wanting to run and hide and lick their wounds... like cornered animals, their reaction to Raydr and Madan's arrival was to shoot first but she was well-known, easy to recognize, and soon the threats and fear became a sort of celebration.

Madan was left out of it and he used the time to get the story straight from the few soldiers willing and eager to talk to him about it.

The doctors were overwhelmed by the sheer number of wounded but someone must have put in a good word for him because he was expedited through the lines and treated right away.

Not that they could do much more than what he had already done: clean the wounds, disinfect with alcohol and tell him to go easy on himself in the next few weeks.

Which, in all honesty, he had no intention of doing at all.

The story was the same: most defeats started and ended the same.

Of overconfidence and ill-preparation… Rushing into a battle that should have been planned for weeks, only to prove that the universe was on their side and that they could do no wrong. That with Justice to guide them, they could not lose.

Lost men, lost weapons, lost ammunition, lost confidence…

Their charismatic leader, lost, his naivete costing him the victory and most of his best soldiers.

Fearing their own shadow, disbanded, cornered, tracked, trapped…

Their Holy Ground ripped out from under their feet… but if usually Madan would have seen this as his cue to leave quietly and leave them to the mess they put themselves into… Now he saw this defeat with a whole other eye.

It took a long time for Raydr to be finally alone, longer still for him to be able to sneak into her tent without her 'guards' noticing; as she was the new 'unofficial' leader, they kept a good eye on her.

She was resting but not asleep: she seemed to be waiting for him.

"When do you move out?" he asked her, hunkering down.

"Tomorrow at first light… The Horde is marching out after us, to wipe us all out, erase the very memory of the attack Zahim is dead; we've lost so many weapons, half the men… the other half is wounded and demoralized. Most people want to find a nice rock to crawl under… and hope no one will stop to turn said rock over. When are you leaving?" she asked, her voice a little constricted, as though she feared the answer.

"When are you?" he retorted.

"I'm not," she answered with a sort of desperate chuckle, as though she couldn't believe it herself.

"Leadership went to your head," he said with a smile.

"They lost everything… everything… I can relate. And if not me, Haseeb will stay in charge and he's… he's- he's crazy, let's face it. Why do the crazy ones always survive?"

"It takes being crazy to survive," Madan answered softly.

"Yeah, lucky for you, you're crazy and sane… so when will you leave?"

"Maybe I am just crazy after all," he said, serving her a fleeting grin. "I think I might be staying after all."

She glanced up at him sharply, astonished. "Really?"

"I think we can win. I think we can surprise the Horde. When you are overconfident, you always make mistakes. They've made several already."

"Name one," she countered.

"They let most of the Rebels run. They could have organized and gone after them long before… so I think they were dealt a blow and they are licking wounds of their own."

"Wishful thinking," she dismissed.

"I also know the Citadel like the back of my hand. I know its secrets and weak spots… We can win this, Raydr," he insisted.

She looked at him, evaluating. "What are you proposing? A second assault, now? With our numbers down, gear missing? Wounded and dying, we crash on the Citadel's Walls again? Their army is marching on us, they're a few days away, some blow they've been dealt! Crippling, no doubt!"

"I need you with me," he said. "They think we are weak... so they send their army to finish us off. They take their time to instill more fear, make us push ourselves and lose our minds, not because they're strong, but because they're weakened. So we use this to divide. We divert, we separate, and we, WE conquer," he told her.

She chuckled in disbelief. "Oh my God, you are actually serious about this," she sighed in pain, shifting to straighten up a bit. "If you do this, if you even hint at this, Haseeb will oppose. And the soldiers trust him. He led the rout, he kept them safe."

"Lucky for me you're the leader," he answered.

She shook her head. "No, no, no... I can't make them accept this. If you are serious about this, Madan, you need to assume command. The only way anyone will follow you is if you are in charge. If the men choose to follow you."

"I'm no leader," he protested.

"Anyone who believes they were born to be leaders are fools," she retorted. "It takes time and effort, trial and error, there's always something to learn and to inspire the men, you have to be... the man with a plan. I'm not. I'm no leader and the second I tried to push this, Haseeb would declare me incompetent. He's always hated me, but I was always the better strategist. Zahim trusted me on this and Haseeb hopes to use me in the same way. The extent of his generosity."

"So what do we do? Are you with me? I only need you with me," Madan insisted.

She chuckled. "Me and a whole army, you mean."

"Only you. I only need you with me," he said, looking her straight in the eyes.

She looked away first. "Sleep. We both need to sleep. And I will see… if you are still here in the morning."

"I am not going anywhere," he said, hunkering down beside her and doing something he had been dying to do for a very long while.

Although her lips and breath were hot from fever and the infection coming from her wounds, the kiss was just as sweet as he thought it would be…

The next morning, Raydr called an assembly of the lieutenants that were left, Zahim's right- and left-hand men that had survived the doomed attack on the Citadel.

Haseeb was, of course, the most imposing of them all, half a head taller than Madan and sixty pounds heavier, barely bruised and looking fresh… and ready for a fight.

The kind who thought with his fists and used his head only to bash his enemies' skulls in.

Given his own wounds, Madan knew he wouldn't last very long against him, and a fight was all Haseeb would want to prevent him from assuming command of the Rebel army… or rather what was left of it.

The last thing they needed was to fight amongst themselves but this would inevitably happen, unless some miracle happened…

Madan had to prepare for the eventuality. Dealing with the rogue elements in your own group was sometimes worse than attacking your enemy. Because, with your enemy, you knew where you stood, there were no boundaries save surviving.

The bedraggled bunch that answered Raydr's summon did

not seem dangerous in the least; not a capable military force but scared, terrified, wanting to run and hide under a rock, any rock they could find... hoping no one would turn it over.

He knew exactly how they felt. What he was about to propose went against every fiber of survival that had served him so well since he had escaped the Horde's slave camps. "Thank you, all of you, for coming. I know we're running out of time, so this will be as brief as we can make it," Raydr said. She was standing and trying not to wobble to appear more decisive and in charge than she really was.

She put on a hell of a show, she was almost believable.

"Exactly, we don't have time for this," a man interrupted in panic before they could start. "They're coming for us! They are coming!"

One of his eyes was covered by a makeshift bandage; he had already lost a lot to this rebellion, which made his fear all the more understandable.

"And that's why I called you here," Raydr said firmly. "To address this problem and our options."

"We have none," Haseeb said, glancing at her almost defiantly.

No love lost between the two, that much was certain.

"That's what we will talk about," Raydr retorted.

"We don't have any options. Right now, their army is gaining on us, ready to wipe us all out. We have to go, far away, fast," Haseeb insisted. "I got us all out and I will lead us all to safety if you-"

"Run and hide, forget it ever happened, betray everything Zahim believed in, everything you believed in?" Raydr cut in as a murmur of desperate approval went through the men.

Running and hiding was all they wanted.

"You think the Horde will forget?" she put to Haseeb, seemingly unafraid of his bulk, of what he could do to her if he decided to rescind her authority completely. "You think they will let us run? Let us hide? Has your defeat made you forget everything?"

"We were massacred, Zahim is dead," Haseeb said resentfully. The dream is dead. Now we survive."

"That's a point of view," Raydr countered. "Let's hear another."

She looked at Madan insistently: now was the time to speak up, go against all sanity and better judgment.

He felt a wave of uncontrollable irrational fear; he was not a leader of men, he never wanted to be a leader. But in this particular instance, he felt it. He was the man for the job.

He stepped forward and looked at the men intensely. "They dealt us a crippling blow, no doubt. Zahim is dead, weapons, ammo, gone... But you're not dead, your mission is not over... Far from. It's just beginning. Right now, they're overconfident, sure of their invincibility... so it's time to strike."

"You're insane!" the man who had lost an eye said in a breath.

Haseeb chuckled under his breath. "Completely insane. Now is the time to regroup, run, gather our strength once more and-"

"And then what? How will it be different from last time? What have you learned? Won't you just run forever? But here, now, is a chance to make this wrong right again."

Haseeb sprang up, already insulted. "Who is this man, to dare speak? Khasir's right-hand man? Khasir ran with as many weapons as he and his vultures could carry... Before we even reached the Citadel. Who are you to talk?"

"He was born in the Citadel," Raydr said. "So you better

listen to what he has to say."

"The Citadel is very defendable, but with enough men, it's feasible. With enough men, we will break them," Haseeb argued.

"Didn't help you much last time," Madan countered acidly.

"We weren't prepared. Zahim rushed us into battle," Haseeb argued huffingly. "If I was-"

"Enough!" Raydr intervened. "Zahim is dead, you never liked him, don't insult the dead, they can't defend themselves. Now hear Madan out, if you know what's good for you."

"I see no reason to listen to this desert dog-"

"Enough!" Raydr growled. "You will listen because I say so. I have seen him in action, he is a survivor and more capable than any of you. We destroyed the remainder of the HomeBasers, two against hundreds. Match those odds... He was born to the Citadel, he was slave to the Horde, he bears the Mark of the Damned. He has survived more battles than you can have nightmares about. I move to elect Madan as unilateral leader of our army."

Even Madan was left speechless by her final phrase but in the stunned silence that followed her statement, he was able to slip a word in. His only chance to make his point. "Their forces will be divided; one part of their army sent to destroy and wipe us out. Only minimal reinforcements to guard the Citadel. We lead the army away, put on a show, send them on a pointless chase, while the bulk of our army regroups and collects the weapons Raydr and I hid from HomeBase. From then on, we march on the Citadel and, with their reduced forces, we will have a much better chance of overthrowing them, conquer the Citadel and use it to face their army when they come back. Divide to conquer is a time-tested method to triumph."

"Clever," Raydr approved. "Anybody has a better idea,

maybe?"

"It's feasible... and we have two choices here. Run and hide and die, for they will never stop chasing us, until our very memory is erased, like tracks in the sand... Or take matters back into our hands again. They think we're down, they think we're weak and powerless. Defenseless... Incapable. Will we prove them right? Years ago, when they conquered us, the Citadel, we were fools. We were overconfident. We knew they were powerful but we thought we were safe. Up until the end, when they breached our walls, we thought we would be safe. And that was our downfall. And now it's their mistake as well. Especially since they beat us once, they think they are safe. They think they have nothing to fear from us."

"Us?" Haseeb snorted. "Since when are you part of 'Us'?"

"I am one of you now. To the end. There's no turning back now. There's no escaping them. You all have this on you now," he added, pointing at the scar on his face. "My mark, you are all damned with me. Unless we remove them from power once and for all, you will run for the rest of your short, miserable lives."

"And you think you can lead us to victory?" one of the young lieutenants, named Arslan, asked with more curiosity than resentment.

"I think I have a good chance, yes. I'm not a leader, I'm a survivor. That's what we all are, survivors, and this is our greatest strength, this is the key to beating the soldiers of the Horde. Because each of us is their own master, each of us wants to survive... and live again. The Horde terrorizes and whips its soldiers into complete submission. They have no will of their own, no power of individuality. All they have is their fear of their leader, and their invincibility. Once one is removed, once it is proven they are not invincible, their confidence will shatter. The fear that keeps them disciplined can turn on them in a heartbeat!"

"I'm afraid," a man protested, which made everyone laugh.

"Good! You'd be a fool not to be afraid. But you know you are afraid, so you can master that fear, make it work for you and not against you. He who masters his fear becomes much more powerful than the one who denies its very existence."

"Nice words," Haseeb said with obvious disdain.

"We have less numbers than they do but we have a definite advantage. We are fighting for our lives. They are fighting for power, for thirst of blood, to keep their dominion. We are fighting to end their reign of terror-"

"Zahim's words didn't help him much," Haseeb countered.

"I'm not talking about words. I know a secret way into the Citadel that I am sure was never discovered," Madan revealed.

If his rousing speech had had some effect, very mitigated, on the men, the news of a real possible advantage over their enemies perked everyone's attention.

"How come? How can you know this?" Haseeb demanded, almost outraged.

"He was born in the Citadel, as I told you already," Raydr spoke up.

"Why didn't you say so before? Why did you let us be massacred? Raydr! You knew?" Haseeb said, definitely playing the outraged card.

"At the time we were abandoned and chased by the remainder of the HomeBasers. You didn't wait for us," Raydr retorted, a jibe to all those that had been left callously behind.

"So what are your plans with this secret way in?" Arslan asked what most men wanted to hear anyway.

They didn't want a fight for leadership, they wanted a surefire method to make their enemies pay.

He had made it up during the night, barely sleeping at all.

Like all battle plans, it rested on luck, bad decisions on their enemies' part, and risking it all for the cause.

But he was risking everything for the cause along with them, he was plunging straight into the melee with them.

The risks, the rewards, shared equally.

The Plan was simple. The bulk of the army, two thirds of it, would lead the Horde's army on a merry chase, leading them away from the Citadel, so that the remainder, led by Madan and Raydr, after having recuperated the weapons stolen from HomeBase, would have a clearer path to invade using the secret way in only Madan knew about.

A surefire plan, so full of holes and wishful thinking it was almost ridiculous to dub it a 'plan'.

But all the men's blood was boiling at the chance of getting back from their humiliating defeat. One advantage, imaginary or not, was enough to rekindle the fire that had pushed them to defy the Horde in the first place.

They had signed up, so to speak, for their own reasons, because the Horde's tyranny had to be stopped, and none wanted to crawl back home, or run forever because of their failure.

They wanted that chance to defeat the Horde once and for all.

Haseeb was the one who showed the most opposition, feeling as though the leadership of this bedraggled band was slipping from his fingers. But he was subdued when Madan named him leader of the biggest chunk of the Rebel Army, charged with the mission of leading the Horde away and keeping his men alive.

It was a risk to charge his biggest rival with this, but it was a calculated one. This ensured smooth communication and that he kept the people most loyal to him and Raydr for the attack on the Citadel.

The greatest problem was if Haseeb didn't uphold his end of the bargain, if the Horde army came back to the Citadel, but that was to be anticipated, expected even.

He didn't need much from Haseeb, just to get out of the way, and bring as much of the Horde as he could with him.

And so it came true that very day, the separation, each going their separate ways, the plan put into motion.

Getting back to the doomed city where they had defeated the last HomeBasers was long, each day a new risk to be caught, if the Horde had seen right through them and had split up themselves to hunt both parties down.

It was a risk they had to take, and each new day also meant a day more to heal for everyone, which was badly needed considering what everyone had had to suffer through in the past weeks and days.

Madan both wished for speed and dreaded the moment where they would actually reach the Citadel itself.

He had to prepare for it, mentally, physically, emotionally.

So many memories, hopes and dreams, had been shattered when the Horde had blasted through their fortress.

For the first time in his life, he was ready, or if not ready, willing to face them.

Win or lose, he would have to make peace with his past.

But he wanted to win.

It took them two weeks to reach the city where they had raged their final battle against the HomeBasers.

Time seemed to stand still: everything was exactly the same as when they had left, as though there had not been a wisp of wind during that time.

Their mechanic extraordinaire had survived the battle with the Horde and he was put to use immediately, reanimating the rovers so they would have a force to reckon with and vehicles to carry the weapons that the rest were sent to dig out from the sand.

Madan consulted with Raydr constantly to work out the details of the attack and make it as flawless as possible and while her support was invaluable, he thought she looked a little off her game, healing more slowly than he would have expected from her.

He found her dry-heaving in a corner of their tent when he came back from digging with the men to get their weapons back, and rushed to her immediately, fearing the worst.

"I'm okay, I'm okay," she retorted, pushing his hands away to rise on her own, a bit unsteadily.

"What's happening with you?" he asked.

"Must be the rads from HomeBase," she sighed tiredly.

"I'm not affected," he said, looking at her critically.

"Yay for you, want a medal?" she answered with her usual sarcasm, reassuring him somewhat. If her body was ailing, her spirit remained unbroken.

"Mayzin says he almost has everything back together; the rovers are almost ready for the road. Not a bad haul, weapons, ammo and all."

"But?" she prodded, recognizing the hesitation in the tone.

"Is it enough? Enough to beat the Horde?" he put to her, running a hand through his hair and letting a finger outline his scar unconsciously.

She gestured for him to come closer, and he settled down near her. She was a bit feverish maybe, but her warm embrace was exactly what he needed to settle his doubts - at least for a very few instants.

"We'll see," she said, caressing his forehead slowly. No one knows what the future holds. Your plan is good, feasible, at the very least. Everyone's confidence is heightened. They all think we have a good chance to avenge the fallen. Because of you. This is all because of you, so you have to be fearless. You can't show them your doubts."

"I don't agree, no point lying to them. It can work but I am not sure, so there is absolutely no reason to give them false hope."

Raydr sighed softly. "Well, is there a point to thrusting your doubts in their faces? They have enough to deal with right now. Work on yourself, and let them handle themselves. Sleep, and tomorrow everything might seem a bit clearer."

He nodded and grunted in agreement: it wasn't just the work but the tension that was fraying his nerves and making him completely exhausted. He was almost asleep in her arms when a thought woke him up completely. It had been nagging him for a long while and he had been trying to find the right words to tell her.

But now no more time for right words. They were about to get under way and march on the Citadel.

"Raydr... when we go against the Citadel, I want you to stay behind," he said, looking up at her.

Exactly what he feared happened: she stiffened at the order and breathed hard, as though containing a bitter diatribe.

But to him it was non-negotiable. He couldn't bear the thought of her in danger even though she was one of the most capable people he knew.

"I lost many more friends than you with the botched attack, people I have known for a long time," she retorted finally, with less bite than he had anticipated.

"You are wounded and weakened," he argued.

"So are you," she replied.

Nothing he could say there, as his shoulder was aching in that precise moment, but he wasn't about to let it go.

"Promise me, my heart, swear you will stay away," he whispered, looking her directly in the eyes.

Her breathing changed, obviously she was in turmoil of her own, and she finally let out a breath. "I can't do that, I'm sorry. I can't let you fight alone. If you need me, I will be there."

"I don't want you to fight," he admitted, trying hard to keep his voice even. "I want to know that you are safe."

"But there is no safe, not anywhere," she reminded under her breath. "If you do not need me, I won't fight, that is all I can promise," she finally conceded, after what must have been a terrible debate inside her.

He would have liked more but it was already a huge victory, as far as he was concerned. He didn't have the words to make her understand how important she was for him, how if she was harmed again, he would simply die from it… but the words were wrong, stuck in his throat.

He fell asleep to the sound of her beating heart, the one sound that mattered the most to him now.

Madan had never been a leader of anyone but himself.

Seeing a whole army at work, albeit a bedraggled one, under his command, his rule, had a profound impact on him.

The power, and the fear that came with it. He could lead them all to death, he could be condemning them to an early end, for his own revenge, his own wishes to see the Horde and its commander fall. And they were following his every word, enough to make anyone hungry for more power, to test that power, push the limits…

But he wanted nothing of it. He wanted to be one of the men, down doing the dirty work, where he had always been. This was his true place.

He was taking on the leader's mantle but only for a short while. But once the Horde was destroyed, he fully intended to leave this cursed job to, if not better people, someone who actually was crazy enough to want the job.

At the same time, it reminded him of the preparations, so long ago, at the Citadel, when they had learned the Horde was marching on them. Frantic, feverish, determined preparations, long days and nights he had spent sharpening weapons and oiling firearms... he hadn't been a leader then. Just a soldier, at the mercy of his enemies, and those he trusted, those who had sworn to protect them with the best of their knowledge.

He had never questioned the outcome before, he could have said they had been overconfident, but had that been his fault?

He remembered the terror he felt, the cold sweat as he worked to prepare, the fear in his wife's eyes... only their son noticed nothing.

That innocence, he had had it toward his leaders... had they callously thrown away so many lives?

Which was why he was adamant about saying the truth, not leaving anything out for his men. They were strong adults, they knew what they were getting into, there was no point hiding anything from them.

It was terrifying and humbling to think so much rested in his inadequate hands. He was the master of his own life and death, no one else would ever claim that title.

And he wanted the same for his men.

Every single one of them.

Even amidst those preparations, Raydr's ailing health was a source of constant worry for him.

He wanted to beat the Horde, triumph over his enemies, reclaim his city, his birthright, his home - but at the same time, he had had enough of this already.

Revenge carried to a point, and that point always hovered around the death of one or the other.

Raydr, on the other hand, represented something more, something he had not dared dream about, dared to wish for in so long. A chance for an actual life, a chance to recover everything he had lost in that doomed fight.

To juggle revenge and hope for more was a very tiring exercise on the mental front.

And Raydr kept denying she was feeling ill every time he confronted her with it, an attitude that was unlike her. She didn't want to bother him or she wanted her chance to fight and die?

He was pushed and prodded in every direction, it would seem, and to find a center of calm in this madness was almost impossible.

Finally their mechanic got every rover up and running and they started the voyage back, the march on the Citadel.

They were the invaders this time, two or so weeks away from their destiny.

Madan wondered idly if everyone else was feeling the same chills as he was.

Some days he was confident in their success.

Other days he wanted to hide in a hole and never crawl out.

He was plagued by dreams of the first attack, every moment relived in his mind with complete and utter intensity; he had forgotten nothing, it was all stored in his mind, ready to unfurl and make him doubt himself at precisely the wrong moment.

The thought of losing everything again... Was it better to have nothing to care about, nothing to lose?

What gave the most strength, really?

Raydr was asleep and so he got up without a sound, exiting his tent to take in the night air. It had been too long since he had gone into the night, the only time in which he had felt comfortable for so many years.

Taking in the desert landscape, he sighed tremulously. The moon was bright and made such shadows on the ground, was it enchanting or terrifying?

He tried to calm his racing heart but could not find a satisfying answer. Which was better? Which should he see, the beauty or the cruelty of the desert?

"Both," Raydr answered, making him jumpstart, not only because she had crept up on him, but because his mood had made him philosophy aloud.

She grinned tiredly. "When you are in that mood, we are all in trouble… What's wrong?"

"We're off, no turning back now," he whispered, his eyes unfocused on the barren land.

"Yeah," she agreed with a sigh.

"It's all hanging by a thread. Victory, defeat. The decisions we make right now, could condemn us all. What we're up against, can we really face it?"

"Your problem is that you have too much to think about. Overthinking can lead to disaster," Raydr admonished.

"So can underthinking," he retorted: this was not a mood to be dismissed as jitters.

There were so many details to consider, so many variables, he could not brush this aside and just focus on the 'now', the 'mission'. He was not Zahim, not a devout fanatic, not an idealist. Had it not been for him, those men would have run and lived. Perhaps a short life of misery and fear, but a life nonetheless. Like rats, not like men, but living was living.

He couldn't convince himself which was better; to die for something or live for nothing.

When he had taken over command, everything had seemed so crystal clear.

But now? Beauty or cruelty, and all the shades of gray in between. Nothing was clear any more.

He wished he could have told her as much, expressed it in such words, but everything stayed stuck in his throat, incapable of coming out.

"You are not responsible for the final outcome, don't put that pressure on yourself. If we fail, we fail. The men believe in you because your plan is sound. You know the enemy better than anyone. You bear their Mark, you were their slave; you should have died but you stayed alive. They failed at killing you once, twice, how many times already? This is the power you have over the Horde: You survived the worst they could throw your way."

"I am responsible for the final outcome. I held them back when they wanted to run, I gave them hope for a miracle, I-"

"No!" Raydr cut in. "You offered them a choice, you didn't force them into anything, you were powerless to stop them if they decided to say screw you. With your option, your knowledge, they wanted to fight. Madan, they wanted to fight a long time before you barged in. Now they have a chance to avenge their fallen brother. They were ready to die for the cause because with the Horde in power, they have no life to speak of, they have nothing to live for. Remember that they follow you because you gave them hope of recovering their freedom. Whatever the final outcome, they have a purpose now. And that is enough to carry on."

He snorted. "When they are running from the Horde,

branded or worse, all hope gone, they will curse my name and the day I barged in with my great plan."

She shook her head. "It won't happen."

"How can you be so sure?"

"I believe in you," she answered and surprising himself, this simple phrase struck him deep. Deeper than he could have explained or put into words.

"Now try to sleep. Heavy is the crown, that's how the saying goes? Then throw that stupid crown away. Don't be a leader, be the survivor you have always been. That man is who they all trust, because he survives."

"Go back to bed," he said softly, kissing her forehead. "I will come soon."

He had to think a bit more, think and remember…

Who he was and everything he had gone through already…

He couldn't say he knew what he wanted to do any more, what would come after. He knew there was no point to thinking ahead, to imagining if they won and reduced the Horde, but his mind wandered nonetheless.

What if they won? There would be survivors, there always were. What would he do to them? What if he recognized one of his old friends, those who had turned?

He wasn't surprised by his first impulse at the idea, the rage he would feel, the need to throw them off the walls, to see them splatter on the rocks as his parents had done.

The rage was overpowering, but was it the way?

Did he want to become like them, to give in to his darkest impulses?

Problems best left for when it would happen, if it did happen… but if he wasn't prepared for it, what would he become?

They were eating the kilometers separating them from the Citadel at such an accelerated pace that everyone began to feel a bit anxious, they were racing toward their deaths or renewed life and this duality was putting everyone on edge.

There was also a change in the atmosphere, something that made them all jittery, for their instincts were well-honed and they were all extra sensitive to any sign that something was off.

It became obvious after a few hours, what was coming their way could not be avoided. Or seen as inconsequential.

They had reached an area of plateaus with a few mountains and were heading at full speed toward one of the passes that would allow them to continue their journey... but they were not going fast enough.

At first they could only see a blur on the horizon, with the sky darkening progressively although it was only midday.

It wasn't just a sandstorm, it was a monster of one.

Encompassing the whole horizon, racing toward them at full available speed, it smothered the breath right out of their chests before it was even on them.

They pushed to go faster, hoping to cross the mountains and have that natural barrier to give them a modicum of protection, but their best speed was no match for the mastodon heading their way.

Tracking them, following them, targeting them: It truly felt as though they were the bull's eye, and the storm had a grudge against them.

The first swirling sands started to fall on them before the winds reached them; they would not cross the pass in time, they would be right against it, in the most precarious and dangerous situation to be in when faced with such a massive storm.

The air was becoming thick and so hard to breathe; it was

not normal. The closer the storm got, the more they could see a kaleidoscope of dancing colors inside it.

Not just a sandstorm but a rad storm with lightning that could fry all electric components in vehicles, simply the worst that Nature could throw their way.

Soon it became too dark or just too dangerous for the rovers to work; they powered down, leaving their owners stranded and at the mercy of an unfurling monster.

They felt the panic at that moment. This was worse than the Horde, worse than anything they could anticipate. The storm was so wide-spanning it could take days to pass, and if they set up their tents, they would be ripped away clean for sure.

The head doctor came to see Madan and Raydr as soon as the convoy was forced to stop.

"We cannot stay in the open, we cannot stay here. Can you feel it? Smell it? This will scour our lungs and kill us all. Once I found a party that had been stuck in something similar, their mouths and throats had been burned from the inside. We have to hide!"

"I believe you, we will," Madan said, putting a reassuring hand on the man's shoulder. Reassuring was not the proper word but he had managed not to shake - too much.

"What do we do?" Raydr put to him, at a loss herself.

Madan looked ahead, trying to see a sign, anything that would give them a chance to survive.

He wrapped a cloth over her nose and mouth and gave her a kiss on the forehead. "We walk, we don't stop until we reach the mountains"

"We're caught in the open," she said, trying hard to keep her voice even.

"We march right now, leaving everything non-essential

behind. I do mean everything!" Madan ordered his terrified army.

They did not protest, how could they? Digging a hole in the ground was akin to suicide, staying put was the same, their only very slim chance was to move, give everything they had in finding some kind of shelter, if they could have such luck.

But that slim chance was a wish more than anything else: caught in the open, they could not survive. And without their vehicles, they were not advancing quickly at all.

Fifteen more minutes of rover time and they could have had a real possibility to make it, but now they were running against a giant clock, a merciless hourglass.

Their time was up, there was no other way to describe it.

They had not even had the possibility to pit themselves against the Horde, that had been taken from them.

Why were they tested and rejected this way? Why, who, what Forces protected people as cruel and ruthless as the Horde?

They walked and ran as quickly as they could, looking back every other second, at what was coming their way, hurtling toward them at impossible speeds.

The fact that the storm had not reached them yet only added to their worry; this extra time they were given was not a stay of execution, it was a testament to the immensity, the unforgiving behemoth that was crashing on them.

So immense its tendrils reached the higher spheres of the atmosphere first, reducing visibility, making day seem like night, except for the lightning strikes already visible from the distance.

This was a storm that could literally last days, eating away everything, turning everything to charred dust.

There was no surviving it.

Some men became so exhausted, assaulted by the first wave of sand, that they fell and did not get up.

Madan himself felt the despair creeping on him, but Raydr was in his arms, he was helping her go faster, she was clenching her teeth against the pain and exhaustion.

There was no giving up, there was only trying to the end, however bitter it would be. They had reached the foot of the mountains and were desperately trying to climb up when the winds hit them; the most wary hunkered and hugged the ground, others were swept away for a few meters as the winds whooshed back around, the forewarning of what would soon overtake them.

They stayed prostrated on the ground a few seconds, afraid to lift their heads and face the obvious, that they could not and would not escape.

Many people coughed, including Raydr: the air inside that storm was foul, dangerous, deadly. They could not afford to get stuck in the open but what other choice did they have?

It was hopeless, there was no possibility of escape, no happy ending possible.

So what to do now? Sit down and die?

"Let's GO! Run! Find shelter, look for anything, any crevice, save yourself, but MOVE!" Madan yelled over the roar of the coming storm.

His screams galvanized the men out of their terror-caused daze: they wouldn't die on their knees. Not in front of the Horde, nor in front of the worst Nature could throw their way.

They started running, hoping to find some kind of shelter: Madan helped Raydr along in spite of the sand now stinging their eyes. If they had to die, they would together, he would have it no other way.

The sky was darker than ever, the storm front closing in on them: why was everything leaguing against them, was someone trying to tell them they were wrong? That their mission was pointless, that the oppressors would always win, that you could not even challenge evil without paying for it?

Even as the fear and despair took full possession of his heart, Madan rebelled against the very thought.

They had to be given a chance, he had to be given that chance.

To set right everything that had gone wrong in his life, to fight for his birthright, to get back the city that had seen him grow... To honor his parents and give them both a proper funeral, honor and protect their memory once more.

If there was any justice in this world... any justice at all.

Raydr coughed again and faltered in his arms, making him hold her up, then carry her completely as she had passed out.

What justice was there?

Who was watching, caring?

No one, no one at all.

If she died, no one at all...

They were alone in this vast, cruel, cold world... and they were about to die, their story, hopes and dreams lost forever, scoured clean by an unforgiving storm.

And no one would care in the least.

"Here! Here! HEEEEEEEEEERRRRRRRRRRRE!"

Over the roar of the wind, it was hard to focus on any sounds, to understand anything besides the drive to keep on in spite of everything that was going against them. Madan almost didn't even turn to the voice, determined to push on until he fell from exhaustion, but something, some awareness brought him back to reality. What if?

It was hard to spot anyone in the darkness of the storm, but a rush of people was going one way, and he followed them back to the voice, still beckoning them all.

Finally he reached it: Arslan was covering his mouth with a cloth, coughing, near vomiting as he had to uncover and breathe the foul air directly to scream.

Some kind of narrow opening, half-filled with rocks and sand, jagged metal as well, the unknown, but everyone was pouring in, pressing in, desperate to enter this strange cavern and have a modicum of protection from the storm.

"Okay?" Madan worried, setting Raydr down. He wouldn't be able to bring her in for some time, too many others were getting savage to go through.

Arslan coughed, looking gray. "Get her inside, it's weird but I think it will hold."

"How large is it, can everyone fit?" Madan questioned, just wishing he could push and prod and secure a place for Raydr, at the very least.

Arslan shook his head, eyes wide in fear. No guarantees. Nonetheless, the moment after, he got back up and screamed at the top of his lungs for everyone to come to safety.

Soon all visibility would be gone and the storm would be smack upon them, no reprieve. Those still outside would die without a doubt, the rads would kill them if the winds or lightning didn't.

Madan made sure Raydr was as protected as she could be and started herding the soldiers onward as well.

It was such a narrow opening but no one was coming out, no one was saying stop piling people, it's full, so there was a chance to stuff everyone in relative safety.

A slim chance of survival was better than none at all.

The winds picked up even more; it was difficult to stay upright and even more so to yell, their voices were lost in the ever-growing howls.

A final group of stragglers staggered in sight and both men went to help them along, pushing them into the narrow opening before exchanging a glance.

They had no time left, they had to think of themselves, the rest was out of their hands.

Raydr was half-buried by a newly formed dune and Madan fished her out as quickly as he could, fearing that she had suffocated while he helped others.

Arslan helped carry her inside and they plugged the hole as best they could, so the winds would not hurtle deadly sands inside.

The job was exhausting and they were already out of strength because of the race to the mountains; the air was not helping either, it was too thin and hurt the lungs just breathing it.

Finally they were able to crawl away from the opening and track deeper into the cavern, for lack of a better description.

Raydr's breathing was very hoarse but Madan had greater preoccupations, like trying to get away from the mountain flank to get deeper: soon they encountered the first of the escapees, pressed against one another.

"Is this it?" he asked, his voice barely above a whisper as his throat was raw with pain. "We can't go deeper?"

"Don't know," a man answered, "I don't know anything."

Near Stygian darkness, the echoes of moans and raspy breaths, the howls of the storm outside, it was hard to get past all these distractions to get to the bottom of things.

This was one of the moments where having royal authority would have been nice, everyone parting before him: all he wanted was a little more safety for Raydr!

But survival made everyone feral, there was no authority left when came the moment to choose between your own life and that of a leader's.

They were all survivors, and no one would accept a pointless sacrifice.

Still he did not settle down, although Raydr was getting very heavy; he wanted to get further in, to know what they could expect from this providential niche.

After a lot of prodding that made many protests, he and Arslan managed to get to an antechamber of sorts, completely dark save for a few torches that had been lit by the escapees.

They cleared a spot for Raydr and took a second to catch a breath.

Just a few minutes to clear their lungs and stop the spinning in their heads; Madan intended to go tell them to douse the torches, the air might get very bad and they needed all the oxygen they could keep within the cavern.

But exhaustion took over every other consideration and he woke up much later, to a howling and rumbling sound that made the hackles on his neck rise.

From asleep, dead to the world, he sprang on his feet, convinced the end had come.

The torches had waned and were flickering, everyone was cringing in fear, the whole cavern was shaking, their hideout was not so secure after all.

"Get down," Raydr said, her voice barely above a whisper. "Get down, some rocks have fallen."

He hunkered down to protect her, gathering her in his arms. "Are you all right?" he worried.

"I'm okay, I guess," she said weakly. "How are you? You don't look too good."

The darkness was everywhere, all they could really see was each other's eyes, so he couldn't help but chuckle. Trying to divert the attention away from her, as usual.

The laughter quickly became a wheezing cough: he was not in the best of shape. And neither was the whole army. Caught like rats, how long could they last?

"Tell them to spare the water we have," Raydr said when the coughing had calmed down. "I don't know how long we will stay here, how long this will last."

He looked up as more creaks and howls from the winds outside invaded their makeshift hideout. Most hugged the ground or whimpered.

"Getting stronger," Raydr said, answering his forming question.

"How long was I out?" he queried.

"I don't know, I woke up some hours ago, the winds keep getting stronger. The air smells worse and worse, I don't know how much longer we can hold here."

"Nowhere else to go," he said.

"Yeah I know that," she sighed, coughing weakly.

"Nothing to do but wait…" Madan said, looking up at the darkness and the shadows caused by the weak torches still burning in the middle of the antechamber.

How to describe being stuck, piled up one over the other, no place to breathe, crushed by a giant storm that wouldn't end. Hours of unstoppable tension and terror, where every rumble, every roar, made the heartrate jump faster to rhythms none could have thought possible, imaginable?

The air getting so foul they were all light-headed and every movement brought them close to fainting, yet they could not relax and sleep because the threat was there, they needed to be ready to move if the worse happened.

Not that they would be able to do much, but they were all

survivors, they all thought in terms of living another day.

Waiting for the storm to pass, trusting it would leave them battered but unscathed, was a great stretch for them. Hours upon hours, unable to sleep and relax, unable to get up and walk it off, too much darkness and people, unable to do anything more than stay in a state of terrified stupor.

Thirst became a factor as much as air, as they had only brought the minimal supplies with them and the water reserves were quickly running out.

Their lips turned cracked, their skin peeling from the indirect exposition to the scouring toxic winds, every second was a new hell waiting to implode on them, they could not hold a moment longer, they could not bear the wind pounding on them, the cascade of dust and sometimes rocks, how could they stay sane in these conditions?

How much longer could it last, how much time could they stay like this, everyone was feeling it, how intolerable it was becoming, how one spark could start an unstoppable flame.

They were at the end of their patience, resistance, what more would be asked of them, they were cooking and suffocating one horrible minute at a time, conscious through it all!

What had they done to deserve such a cruel fate?

Exhaustion or lack of air got the better of a few of them, the lucky few; Raydr oscillated between consciousness and dreamland constantly and Madan himself was more numb than awake, in spite of his resolve to keep her safe, whatever happened.

Because the others could go crazy, it was a very real possibility that some would turn rabid soon, vanquished by the trial they were imposed.

Human nature being what it was, he could not afford to trust anyone. Survival also brought out the worst in people, not just the best.

But he himself was not immune to the tension, the fatigue, the thirst... He woke up with a start, to the sound of screaming, the howling of a wind so powerful it sounded as though they were about to be crushed to a pulp, and an unearthly rumbling that could only mean their end had come.

Now the panic came and invaded everyone, and although they were all weakened and on the verge of exhaustion, some jumped on their feet, ready to do anything to escape this hell, even run outside to a more immediate death.

Shouts as men grappled, wanting to fight, to beat the fear and panic away, or reacting violently to the trampling, it was starting a chain reaction that would spread through all the survivors, as weary and beaten as they all were. They would turn on each and tear each other apart.

Madan himself got up, barely feeling Raydr's weak tug to keep him down, away from the others and their craziness, keep him with her if the end was really upon them.

He had a flashlight in his meager possessions and he switched it on, making many cringe as the light was blinding, and only showed the cascade of dust falling from the ceiling onto them. He quickly found the men who were fighting and using strength he didn't know he still had, pushed them apart.

Glaring at them but not saying a word.

The rumble hadn't stopped, it seemed to grow deeper, resonating in their bones, threatening to shatter them apart.

What would kill them first?

Madan drew all stares to him as he made his way over people to the middle of the 'antechamber'. No one understood what he was doing, what he wanted to do, but all shouts stopped for a moment, waiting for what would come next.

Perhaps they hoped for a miracle on his part, but he himself had no clue what to do, just a feeling.

What had to be done, the only thing left to do when one was powerless, in the hands of a giant force of nature with no heart whatsoever.

He set the flashlight upright, so the light would shine on the ceiling and nothing else.

He looked around at the terrified faces, the men looking at him for a solution... but he had none. Nothing at all.

He was just a man, he had no power.

He got down on his knees and closed his eyes, trying to remember the words, as though these sentences and syllables could somehow make the whole difference.

None can to his mind, he was so terrified he could barely form the words. "In the name of God, the All-Powerful, the Merciful-"

He didn't even know where the words came from, where or why the memory was returned to him, all he knew was that he had to keep speaking, even through his tears, pray until he couldn't any more, because there was nothing else he could do.

Pray for God's help for no one else could or would save them, no one cared, no one would shed a tear if they disappeared tonight or today, whatever the time was.

He had no strength left, no tricks, no providential saves.

This time he would die, they would all die, if Someone did not show them the mercy the world they lived in had always denied them.

It started as a murmur, barely audible over the rumble and the howl of the wind, and steadily grew, everyone following his lead, everyone forgetting about panic and fear to concentrate on prayer.

The harder the wind got, the louder they prayed, no longer caring about thirst or fear, only hoping their voices be heard, or that they would be ready for the next phase, whatever it was.

Leaving their earthly concerns behind, if they had to die, they would, but they would not go as terrified rats.

They would leave this doomed world as men, humbled by Nature, but men nonetheless.

None could say how long they lasted, if some did not fall from exhaustion to rise again when they regained their senses; Madan himself lost all track of time, and someone had to shake him, hard, to make him open his tear-crusted eyes.

He reacted with near panic until he saw it was Raydr, and, of all incongruous things, she was smiling.

A ray of sunlight illuminated her face, she almost looked like an angel, and that was when he realized what was different, what had changed. No rumble, no howl, light coming from all around; the storm was over, it had passed.

He tried to stand; his legs were completely numb, incapable of supporting his weight, and Raydr hurried to help him and hold him up while he was assaulted by incredibly painful pins and needles.

But he didn't cry out in pain, he did his best to walk out, he needed to get out of that cavern and see what they were up against now, see what the storm had left in its wake.

They were the last to come out, everyone else was already outside, some on their knees, praying in thanks, others lying down in relief.

The sight was glorious, a perfectly blue sky, not a wisp of cloud to be seen on the horizon. It felt as though the storm had scoured everything clean, ready not for death, but for a second chance.

"My God, look at that!" Raydr gasped, turning him around.

The mountain flank had been scrubbed away by the winds, revealing the vague outline of a huge metallic structure, what they had taken refuge in.

"A plane, my god, it was a crashed plane, that's insane," Raydr muttered under her breath.

Madan vaguely remembered those flying mastodons from his early youth but he had never seen one up close, or been in one, until now.

What twist of fate had made it possible for them to find this wrecked plane and take refuge in it during the greatest storm they had ever witnessed?

He felt like crying again; his lips were cracked and his skin was peeling, he was thirsty beyond belief, but all he felt like doing was thanking his luck, his God, to have allowed such a miracle.

"God is great," he whispered. "God is great."

He was finally steady on his legs again, able to walk without Raydr helping him, and went to join the rest of the army. He did not expect much from them, panic maybe, after all, they were alive but just barely, and they would not survive more than a few days if their vehicles had been scoured away, a very real possibility.

He felt so strange himself, like cleansed, his heart lighter. Weak but able to take on anything, he had no strength but he had belief. At least for a time, he felt an uncommon peace with himself.

As they saw both their leaders approach, the men started rising from the ground to come greet them.

Madan didn't quite feel up to convincing them to go on, try

harder; he was buoyed by his own experience but he was also on the verge of collapse from dehydration.

"Thank you," said the first man who reached them. Madan thought his name was Hassan but he wasn't completely sure. All he remembered about that man in particular was that he did not seem to like him very much, and mostly sided with Haseeb.

He had opted to come with them and Raydr had warned him Hassan could be a spy for Haseeb. She always envisioned the worst-case scenario.

Madan was so surprised he didn't react and Hassan grabbed his arm warmly. "Thank you, brother, you saved me."

"I didn't do anything," Madan replied, not knowing where this camaraderie came from.

"You did, you saved me, I was ready to... You gave me courage to endure, you saved me," Hassan assured.

Madan was about to protest some more: truth was, he had been about to go crazy himself, and he had done it for himself, not thinking about anyone else, but many others came to grip him with the same warmth, the same appreciation, telling him how his action had given them strength, fortitude and had allowed them to tough out the storm.

He caught Raydr's smile at his embarrassment, her slight mockery of his newfound 'spiritual' leader title, but she said nothing, waiting for the men to be done with their effusions.

"I did nothing," he insisted finally. "You endured with me, and this is our reward. One more chance to bring change, one chance to prove ourselves... and now it's time to find our supplies, before the Sun gets too hot."

The men's newfound respect for him had definite advantages, as they started off immediately without one moan or complaint.

Despite the dehydration, they seemed eager and determined to recover their supplies and gear and continue their mission.

"What happens when we find the rovers wrecked?" Raydr asked him in a whisper as they followed the men.

The scenery had changed but their sense of direction was good and they were going the right way, back to where they had been forced to stop.

"I hope we don't find out," he admitted.

The shock of the ordeal they had just lived was fading and with it seemed to go the confidence that had animated him, empowered him.

What if everything had been destroyed, what if they had nothing left? Survived one catastrophe just to be faced with another?

The newfound confidence would be shattered then, in a million tiny pieces.

He shook his head, chasing the doubts away.

Whatever would come their way, whatever trial they were imposed, they would face it. To live or die didn't matter, they would try to the best of their abilities.

They would not give up their belief, their faith, even in front of another speed bump.

He almost grinned.

Speed bump, their rovers wrecked and supplies gone? Had he turned into an optimist now?

He wasn't sure what had changed inside him while he prayed, if it was permanent or not, but the feeling of peace was still there.

If he focused on it, he could calm the unnecessary fluttering of his heart and focus on what would come next.

Every step soon became a torture for their water-deprived

bodies, the sun was shining brighter than ever and no one was sure how long they had been battered by the storm, how long they had had to combat dehydration already.

All they knew was that their future, or lack thereof, could only be found by crossing those kilometers and reaching the area where their rovers had stopped working due to the lack of adequate sunlight.

The storm had reshaped the desert, destroying landmarks, nothing was the same.

The Face of the Earth, remade. Madan could only feel awed by this colossal transformation. They were puny and unimportant in front of the forces of Nature, and yet, somehow, he felt it was a sign.

The world was about to be remade. All impurities cleansed.

The process would not be easy in any way, they would lose much… but they would gain much more.

If they still had their gear…

All rested on a near impossibility, that they had in fact survived this monstrous unfurling of deadly forces, unscathed.

The closer they got to the approximate area, the more his heart began to flutter and skip beats. If their future came to an end here, a dead end…

He couldn't see how it could not, he couldn't envision how another miracle had happened, and yet he wanted to believe, he knew… they had not been given the chance to survive the storm only to be abandoned now.

In spite of the pain and thirst, he walked faster, leaving Raydr behind finally, as she could not keep up with him. In the end he was running, and others, including Arslan and Hassan, were running with him.

Towards barrenness, there was nothing there, nothing at all.

The Sun glared over everything, almost overpowering them, rendering them blind and helpless… But there was nothing to see.

Only dunes, sand, death.

Was this their renewal, their new world?

Was this what they could look forward to, a meaningless death?

Exhaustion, or was it despair made by incomprehension, made Madan crash down on his knees, grunting in pain as he hit something hard and not just soft sand.

"It should be here, it should be," Hassan said hoarsely, as they were all almost completely dehydrated. "This is where we had to run, I remember from the distance to the mountains, they should be here, but nothing is the same, nothing!"

"Maybe it's further away," Arslan suggested while more and more men arrived, all flabbergasted by what they were seeing. Or rather, not seeing.

"Where are they? Where is our gear, where are our supplies, where is everything?" started fusing from everywhere, the men losing hope in front of this new bane.

Madan wasn't even paying attention: when Raydr arrived at their level, most men were panicking and she could not spot him anywhere, lost in the confusion of the shouts and laments.

Until she saw sand being thrown aside and heard the most incongruous sound in their situation: laughter.

She hadn't heard Madan laugh very often and certainly not in delight. She hurried to his side as most men were attracted by the noise as well: he had dug a hole, uncovering part of one rover.

He was still laughing when he saw her and with a near trembling hand showed her the solar panel of the rover, certainly one of the most fragile parts of the vehicle.

Completely intact.

"The first wave of sand duned over them, protecting them," Madan explained, still laughing but with tears in his eyes. "They're fine, just under the sand, I can't… believe it."

The men were just as dumbfounded by the news, by this sign. Not everything was given to them on a platter, far from, they had to give all they had, they had to fight, but somehow, they were protected, they were given a sort of promise that they were on the right path.

And they started to dig like madmen.

CHAPTER 9

The Eye of the Storm

They concentrated their efforts on one vehicle at a time, for they needed immediate supplies, they were in terrible need of water.

The problem with real miracles; there was a lot of work involved with surviving, nothing was handed out to them on a silver platter.

To have been granted such a chance was enough, they had to fight for the rest, prove their worth, survive.

After some hours, working in unison, they were able to unearth one of the rovers and recover their supplies, the water and food reserves.

The sun was close to setting, but they all had to take a break, they had to restore themselves as many had fallen prey to the stifling heat and lack of water.

After so many days, they could not handle so much water at a time, and those who had not dug took over, reviving the rest who had had heat strokes or worse.

Raydr distributed water for as long as she could before feeling too dizzy; she went to lie down next to him in a heap of piled-up sand that was warm from the pounding sun.

Already though, the chill of the night was coming; after all that heat, she felt cold with the slight drop in temperature.

She gave him more water; he was almost asleep.

"Hmmm," he grunted.

"You need it," she insisted.

"I need to sleep for a year or more, wake me up when it is all over please."

She laughed softly. "No such luck for you, you are now more popular than Zahim ever was. Did you hear the men talking? You saved us all."

"Some have the energy to talk?" Madan retorted. "Ah, well, I should put them to work, then."

She chuckled lightly. "You can do no wrong, now. Not one miracle, but two? You have them believing."

"In God, not me, I did nothing," Madan replied.

"You know how it goes," she shrugged.

"I won't use it, if that is what you are suggesting. The plan keeps on, we take the risks together, the rewards are ours as well. If they have faith, then good, nothing has changed," he argued.

She smiled. "Of course, what did you think I was going to say? Become a despot? We just survived a deadly storm and we still have a chance to live and attack the Horde... I was just saying the men have more courage and confidence than they should, and it is because of you."

He was dead tired but he opened an eye to glance at her. "Are you trying to say you believe?"

She lay down next to him for more heat against the coming cold. "Now I see the Sun has fried your brain," she retorted. "I was just making a constatation."

He felt like chuckling himself but he was too tired to go ahead with it. He was asleep the second after.

The night did become frigidly cold and they had to huddle and use whatever covers they could to protect themselves from it.

Their hardships were far from over but they had a newfound

confidence that could carry them over many obstacles.

That storm had been about renewal and change, and they felt that strength in their bones. They would be the agents of change.

Which didn't mean they had it easy in any way. There was a mountain of sand to remove to get their vehicles out and every day was constant and exhausting work; even performed by thousands, the task was near insurmountable, they had to move by hand what Nature had blown in using its most powerful agents.

Water became scarce rapidly and Raydr organized expeditions to find sources beyond the mountain range with the few rovers they had managed to free first.

They were going behind schedule, if such a term applied to their grand 'plan', they were putting Haseeb and the rest of the army at risk, and themselves in more danger, but this could not be avoided.

They worked themselves to exhaustion and could not go faster, they were numb by fatigue every time they took breaks.

The work was nonstop, their dreams were filled with the same images, they were lost in the moment, forgetting all about the future.

Nonetheless, the morale wasn't plummeting, on the contrary, they were redeeming themselves, proving their worth to the God that had allowed them to survive.

Madan knew Raydr wasn't convinced, that she was calculating what this forced stop and these hardships would cost them in the long run, but there was simply no way to avoid this time-eating task.

They had been hit hard, they had come out alive. Now they did need to prove themselves.

Thankfully the expeditions were able to find some untainted

sources of water which supplied the devout workers. They spent close to two weeks attacking the dunes and rescuing their vehicles and gear and at the end of it, there was some definite exhaustion.

However, they had not faced another storm, and if many had had side-effects from the rads they had inadvertently absorbed, most were on the mend, and ready for the next part of their mission.

After almost three weeks of forced stop, they started forward again and that speed at which they raced toward the inevitable confrontation was exhilarating and terrifying at the same time.

Madan sent runners to try and rally the rest of their army back to them if they could, but it was a fool's errand, as they had no clue where to run and look.

But no stone should be left unturned, no chance forgotten; they were trying to win, not just die at the hands of the Horde.

The storm that had nearly killed them had devastated everything in the region as well, which was a sort of advantage, as the Horde army and sentries were therefore weakened and less vigilant.

Although Raydr warned him to think the opposite: a wounded beast is always more dangerous than one in full possession of its means.

To get back to this area brought back a lot of memories, a flood of ghosts that demanded his attention and presence, screaming to be heard, his past life wanting to influence his chance at a new beginning.

Although a lot had changed in fifteen years, even more so considering the storm's passage, he still recognized it, felt it in his heart.

The call of home.

What could have been, what was, what could be...

If they failed against the Horde, that band of murderers would continue terrorizing the area, bringing pain and terror as they pleased.

If they vanquished the Horde... a big blank.

New possibilities opening up, a future they would shape themselves. In good or bad... but it would be theirs.

They were a day's march - on foot - when Madan called for a halt, and ordered to set up a camp with sentries at key points to warn them in case of imminent attack.

The Citadel was not yet in view, hidden by some mountains and wooded areas that had been badly battered by the storm but had somehow also survived, proving the resiliency of Nature.

They hadn't spotted any scouts but they had to assume the worst, that they were being tracked and followed and that their enemy was aware of their every move.

Everyone was on high alert, ready for anything, especially when Madan ordered a reunion of all the division leaders for a brief talk of the next steps they needed to take. "Thank you all for coming," Madan began, wondering idly if they could hear the pounding of his heart in his chest. Some fearless leader he was!

"We are closing in on the Citadel and I am sure the Horde is well aware of our presence. We want to attack as soon as possible, but we will have to wait a bit. First we must organize a recon team... and I will lead it."

Everyone looked surprised by this but none more than Raydr, who looked alarmed and ready to argue about his safety and importance for the army.

"I promised you a way in," Madan said, silencing all opposition with an imperative hand gesture before they could even be uttered. "A way to breach the walls and take the Horde by surprise without wasting lives needlessly. Before attacking on faith alone, I need to check if my secret way in is still intact and ready for use."

"You mean... you're not sure?" one man said in alarm.

"I was driven out, this scar fresh on my cheek, hands and feet bound in chains, more than fifteen years ago. Lots can happen in fifteen years ... this tunnel was a personal escape route of my family's, so I think it is still there and in good working condition."

"What if your family told the Horde about it?" one man worried.

"My whole family died, every single one of them," Madan said, his voice coming close to breaking, surprising himself.

But the ghosts were there, behind his eyes, made alive and stronger by the proximity of their resting place, demanding retribution...

"Will you go alone?" Raydr asked, almost scowling at him, apparently already fearing his answer.

"If there is a volunteer to come with me, I will be glad to have him with me. In case something happens to me, the knowledge that will unlock the Citadel won't die with me. They won't go without a fight. It will be the fight of our lives, gentlemen, let's not kid ourselves, many of us will not survive it. But I know none of us will have regrets, because we will give our everything, and the outcome of the battle is in God's hands, not ours."

"That and good preparation," Raydr added.

"Their reign of terror has lasted long enough. Order will be brought back to Chaos, or we will die trying to make this happen. We will do everything in our power to win but in the end, we don't decide. If our mission is right, just, true... This will be another storm we will have to weather… before our triumph."

"I'll come with you," Arslan said readily, and Madan could not hope for a better comrade.

Madan nodded in assent and looked at the assembly again. "When we get back we will plan our assault. In the meantime, stay alert and on your guards. If they are smart, they will stay within the Citadel walls and wait to break us on the walls again. But we don't know what they have had to face, if they were badly affected by the storm or other unpredictable events, or if they have grown more arrogant and they decide to take the fight to us. Remain on your guards at all times. Be ready for any eventuality. The fate of everyone, not just us, everyone… is in your hands. I know I can trust all of you. I know I can count on you, Raydr."

She looked a little feverish again - but he was happy she had not suggested going with him.

He had been worried she would, since she had so much trouble delegating work, and had she not been wounded, she would have been the finest ally to have with him.

"We will be ready for anything, I swear, whatever comes our way… Waiting for you to return with good news," she said quietly.

"We'll go now and come back as soon as possible," Madan decided. The night would be falling soon and he intended to use it to their advantage. The night, his old companion.

Once this reconnaissance was over, they would prepare for war.

Raydr caught up with him as he was packing a bag of supplies. Obviously she wanted to tell him something but she seemed to be lacking the words to do so; she only watched him without saying a word.

"I don't want you to fight," Madan said as she finally spoke up: "How sure are you that your secret way is still there?"

They both waited for the other to answer first and finally Madan sighed. "About ninety percent sure. My family built things to last."

"But never used them in times of crisis," Raydr criticized with her usual tact.

"I sent Maira toward it, told her to hide there, take Awan and my mother with her," Madan answered, stuffing the additional ammunition in his bag a bit ragefully, his hands trembling. I don't know what happened, why she didn't go, why she didn't-"

"Sorry, I'm sorry," she said with emotion.

"I don't know what happened," he continued. "Not enough time I guess, they broke through our defenses too quickly. Please don't fight, promise me."

She inhaled sharply, looking away. "If I told you, don't go, forget about your plan, stay with me, only me… Madan, what would you say?"

He looked at her, evaluating. "I would say, I am too far in now, I can't go back, only forward."

She nodded slowly, but he was shocked to see a touch of disappointment. She had actually been serious, or testing herself as much as him.

"Good luck, Madan. Come back safely," she said as she moved away.

He wanted to walk to her, do something, tell her how much she meant to him, consider her offer… But he was too far in, he could only follow his fate now.

"Dayan. My name is Dayan," he told her before she left the tent.

"Good luck, Dayan," she said, coming back to give him a kiss.

He hugged her as tightly as he dared given her wound. "I'm coming back, Raydr," he assured, whispering in her hair.

"Layla," she said, pulling away from him.

He could hear her stifling a sob as she moved off, and he had to fight the urge to catch up with her and forget about this whole mission.

He had this paralyzing feeling that he would never see her again, that something bad would happen. Something terrible, and her walking away from him would be the last image he would ever have of her.

But she left, the moment faded. They were in the middle of a war, they could not afford such weaknesses.

They were against the clock and all other considerations had to be put to the side. For later.

They had to make that later come true.

"My Layla, I will come back to you," he swore under his breath...

And went on his way. He was home.

In spite of all the time he had spent away from it, cursing it, wishing those memories away, gone forever, he felt the warmth of home as soon as he got closer to the Citadel.

Home had a beauty to it, a serenity, that inescapable feeling of protection and contentment... which made it all the more painful when home had been defiled, violated by murderers and profiteers, looters, rapists, monsters.

He had to fight and save his home.

Both were very careful in their insertion, Arslan just as cautious as he was, following Madan's lead to perfection.

Madan was glad to have a soldier such as him to watch his back, should the worst arrive. Arslan would stand his ground and fight to his last breath, there wasn't a doubt that he was loyal to the core.

The land had changed, it smelled and felt different, vilified somehow, and as they progressed deeper into 'enemy' territory, the thought of eradicating those usurpers forever became completely overpowering.

He wanted to see them disappear, out of sight, out of mind forever. He wanted his home back, the way it had been, not the way he saw it now.

The night was clear, the moon hung over the horizon, illuminating the landscape perfectly; it was almost as dangerous as a daytime trek but they were ready to face the risks. They couldn't afford to wait and let their enemy organize an assault against them.

They had to prove the insertion had a chance of working, they had to validate the plan, make it a reality.

They walked through a scraggly forest that became denser with each step; along with more trees came a lingering smell that soon became very unpleasant and Arslan looked at Madan questioningly.

"Sewers?" he queried, his impression confirmed when they reached a cleared area littered with foul-smelling ditches.

Very poorly kept as well, or maybe the storm had left lasting effects here as well?

The trees would have been uprooted and devastated, this was poor maintenance at work, and it angered him even more. The drainage field was a dangerous strip to cross, there should have been plenty of sentries here to watch the possible breach entrances that were the sewer pipes but he could detect none at first glance…

"Yeah," Madan answered, staring intensely at the field, wondering how they would make it through while avoiding detection. Was someone even looking for them?

He would have felt more reassured to see patrols out and about, did they have a secret way of guarding the field he didn't know about?

"Your super-secret tunnel into the Citadel is the… sewers?" Arslan put to him.

"Don't you wish," Madan replied almost gamely.

They had to stay alert and ready but Arslan's banter made some of the tension he was feeling dissipate and he was very thankful for that.

Alert, on the ready, but his heart rate needed to go down a bit, he needed to be focused.

"Option B, please," Arslan retorted, grimacing.

"Coming up," Madan said, putting a finger to his lips. Now was the time to move forward, no slip-ups allowed.

In spite of his best resolve to keep a cool head, it was difficult to keep the focus: he was so close to his home. Fifteen years ago he had been kicked out, dragged out in chains and had thought he would die long before seeing the Citadel again.

But now he was so close, so close! His heart would not keep calm and steady, he felt ready to scream. He was back and he was coming to take it back, away from the usurpers.

But he couldn't let revenge take over his better judgment, he had to think about his army, Raydr, everyone that depended on him to succeed.

Revenge wouldn't bring the Horde to its figurative knees; careful planning and near flawless execution… plus luck, would get them the prize they wanted.

There were a few trees and mounds of sand and rocks that blocked the way in some places and they raced over those obstacles as quickly as they could, wanting to get to the other side of the drainage field, to another wooded area, to some kind of cover.

There was a sort of fever to being in someone's scope, evading detection, a sort of tense elation that could make one feel invincible, invisible, and Madan fought that false feeling of security to stay as alert as he could… He made Arslan duck in the nick of time, just before the well-hidden sentry turned toward them.

They were not alone after all, their enemy wasn't dumb or nonexistent, they were in the bullseye, the hunt was on.

The two men were used to such split-second changes, thinking on their feet, without losing a single second.

In spite of his vigilance, they made short work of the sentry, stripped his weapons and dumped him in one of the ditches filled with the smelly sludge that flowed from the Citadel.

Now the gloves were off, they had launched the attack, drawn first blood. Pure adrenaline pumped in their veins, their breaths were quick pants that barely fed them enough air but they were flying through the drainage field as though the Devil was on their heels, which wasn't so far from the truth.

A devil they couldn't see yet, but was around, just ready to pounce…

Clouds had gathered around the moon, blocking most of its light and Madan had to draw on his memory rather than what his eyes could see as far as general direction was concerned.

After so long a time, could he really find his way back to the escape tunnel, recognize the markers?

Everything had changed, of course, but he was home, he still knew it like the back of his hand, and he did not stop once to look around, trusting that his instinct would guide him to destination.

To his credit, Arslan matched his pace and determination, not once doubting, moving forward with a confidence that could almost be qualified as zealous.

All other considerations were barred from their minds, and now they could see the tower guard of the Citadel in the distance, because of the fires lit there for the guards. Those walls had never seemed as hostile as in that moment, those walls from which his parents had met their death…

Madan had to push those thoughts away and aside; only there to distract him, put him off his game. He would complete the mission and get back to his army… and together they would bring the Horde to its knees.

The drainage field was behind them and they were back in the brush and growing forest, sprinting as quickly as they could without stumbling or making too much noise.

The brush was thick and prickly in some areas and their fast jog through it left them scratched and bloodied, as they could not find the time to avoid these unpleasant thickets. Speed was of the essence and they both felt they were overcoming their welcome, drawing the attention of too many invisible eyes.

A ray of moonshine illuminated the path before them and for a split second, Madan saw a reflection, a slight glitter that had no place being there. He hunkered down to cut his speed before hitting the tripwire and Arslan plowed into him, almost making the both of them fall into the trap set by the Horde soldiers.

Madan's nose was less than a centimeter from the tripwire when he managed to push Arslan off.

His heart had literally stopped beating for a second or two and they exchanged a glance. From now on, no more speed, only caution. They could not afford to be caught in a trap. They didn't need to exchange words: from now on, their every step had to be measured. It was very despairing as the time factor was at the very least quadrupled, and the thought of having to bring a squadron through this mess was even more discouraging. It was difficult to believe they could mount an effective assault in such conditions but it was just a speed bump, nothing else.

They had to keep up the faith. If the passageway was there, no obstacle would stop them. And now wasn't the time to despair; they were in a more deeply wooded area and closing in on the mountain that flanked the north side of the Citadel, and Madan definitely recognized the terrain. Nothing much had changed, including the entrance to the secret passageway.

Both men pushed away rocks and brush; to Arslan it looked like nothing more than a rock facade, but he waited as Madan closed his eyes and dug deep into his memories, the one time his father had shown him the trigger mechanisms.

"Burn this in fire in your soul, my son," he had told him then. "Never forget this, for it could be your salvation one day." Madan muttered those words as his fingers locked in on the lever that activated the counterweights that lifted the mountain wall with a creak and rumble that could have raised the dead…

Perhaps because the dead would be raised now. Raised and avenged. The secret passageway into the Citadel was opened, a stygian dark tunnel that led into the bowels of the Earth.

Arslan was almost overcome with emotion as they stepped into the musty smelling tunnel, praying under his breath for all his lost comrades that had met their deaths against the Citadel's walls… when they could have had a way to take the city without shedding unnecessary blood.

Now they had a chance for victory, for revenge… if the tunnel wasn't obstructed in some way.

They went at it slowly, having no torch to guide them in the total darkness, their eyes were completely useless in the bowels of the earth. They went by touch only, sometimes having to backtrack, as they met dead ends or partial cave-ins - as a result, the distance they traveled seemed to quadruple, time seemed endless, as though they had voyaged for untold kilometers, their own private road to hell...

Sweat dripped from their foreheads, the tension became near unbearable as they had to push away rocks to move forward, the tension was even harder than the actual work, the fear of failure, of coming back empty-handed, of having to clash against the Horde head on was wreaking havoc with their frayed nerves.

Once they crawled through the last cave-in and arrived in a bigger part of the tunnel, they felt the change. The air was different, the city stench was reaching their nostrils, warning them of what they would soon encounter.

People living in close quarters, the stench of unwashed bodies and dirty souls. A far cry from the glory of the Citadel he had known in his youth.

This angered Madan beyond belief, to think that they had used and abused and corrupted everything his forebears had worked for, sweated for, bled for. He wasn't sure why he was so affected, it was no surprise, after all.

Conquerors never respected and improved what was there, they pillaged and wasted, as they had no consideration whatsoever for those they had vanquished.

But to see it in front of his eyes, to feel it made him all the more determined to put the Horde's reign of terror to an end. If there had been any kind of hesitation in his mind, it was now completely gone.

Soon they could not go further any more. Still in darkness, but they knew the city lay just beyond that rock facade. They were so close, the wall so thin that they could hear the footsteps of soldiers or city folks from beyond the wall.

They didn't need to test the opening as it was obvious a few well-placed ram-ins would make it crumble and give them access to the inner sanctum of the Citadel.

Their mission was a success; they could come back with good news. All they had to do was get back safely to their camp.

The journey back was much faster and lighter than the other way around and they almost sprinted the last few meters, eager for fresh air and freedom from the gloom.

Madan was already going through the preparations in his mind, what needed to be done, how he would need to convince Raydr to stay away, when Arslan plowed into him and made him stagger to the ground.

Far from protesting this rough treatment, Madan bit his lower lip in anger. How could he have missed that patrol, coming their way? How could worry over the next step have blotted out all common sense?

Live the moment, not the future, or there would be no future to speak of.

Six men, coming their way, but Arslan's quick thinking had made them stay unseen for now, and thank God for small favors.

They were not out of trouble for so little. The Horde patrol was alert, looking for their fallen compatriot; they knew the Rebels had come back for another shot at them and they were ready to do anything to keep their stronghold over the Citadel.

A missing sentry was not something they dismissed as benign.

The two intruders crawled away slowly, trying their best to stay out of the patrolmen's line of sight.

They backed up in the opposite direction they wanted to take, going back toward the forest and its deadly booby traps as it offered cover whereas the sewer drainage field was too bare, impossible to hide from the soldiers there.

They were almost stuck for the trek inside the tunnel had indeed taken time and the moon was setting, dawn was already well under way.

With the sun shining, they would be spotted in a matter of minutes, they had to get back to the forest to hide until nighttime came again.

"We have to move," Arslan whispered as Madan pushed him against a boulder for some inadequate cover.

"They'll see us," Madan retorted, raking his mind to find a solution.

"They'll see us anyway," Arslan muttered urgently. "We should take them head-on, be done with them!"

It was hard to think sanely and rationally with the stench of the sewers and the tension caused by the risk of detection when they were so close to their goal.

If they couldn't get back, the knowledge of the secret passageway would die with them. Disappear forever.

Should they separate? One drawing the Horde soldiers' attention, allowing the other to escape? Sacrifice, waste one life to preserve the rest?

It was so easy to fall into those thought patterns, put the greater good over the individual, the quick way to solve a dilemma. But that was not what Madan wanted to do, who he wanted to be.

Share the risks equally, and the rewards as well.

No one was more valuable than the other, they were all as expandable or important.

Enough of these 'tough' decisions leaders complained about having to make all the time. Consider the alternative, value the lives of your men and your own… and perhaps then you would see a different way to defeat your enemy.

Whatever the cost, he would not take the easy way out.

"I'll draw them away," Arslan decided. "While they're after me you can escape and get everyone ready. If I don't make it, you will avenge me, I will be forever grateful."

Madan held him back before the young man could waste his life away for nothing. Instead, he made him - and himself by the same token - roll into the foul-smelling ditch. They barely made a splash going in as it was not water in the ditches but rather a sort of mud with a thick crust because of the torrid temperatures of the past few days.

Arslan almost let out a cry of outrage - he seemed to think a pointless glorious death was much better than this alternative, the cowards' way out in the worst smelling sewer sludge this planet had ever produced.

Madan put an imperative hand on his mouth: neck-deep in the sewer, there wasn't much they could do now but wait, trying to wade their way forward while keeping an eye and ear out for the patrol.

In the dawn's early light, Madan could see Arslan's betrayed expression. He almost felt like laughing and saying: You will thank me when you will come out of this alive, but the time was not right for such banter, nor did he have that confidence to think somehow, his alternative would yield the right results.

Would they survive this, would they come out as winners?

Only time would tell.

Of course, the patrol came closer, advancing right on them and at Madan's imperative order (made through gestures only) - Arslan really seemed hurt by it - they both dove under the sludge, immersing themselves completely to try and avoid detection.

Holding their breaths while being surrounded by such foul liquid seemed even harder than in normal water. Both were desert-raised and so hadn't had much chance to practice swimming skills, let alone holding their breaths for so long, but the emergency of the situation made them hang on much longer than they would have thought possible, until all danger of detection was passed.

The Horde soldiers did not detect anything out of the ordinary and continued their patrol; perhaps they did not want to spend too much time near the ditch.

Both men tried not to gasp too hard, but they were both gagging after what they had had to endure, bile coming up their throats without them being able to stop it.

After they managed to make it pass, swallowing it back down or vomiting in the mud, they started to move forward, wading in the liquid as quickly and silently as they could to put as much distance as they could between the patrol and them.

Progression was extremely difficult and punctuated by many other dives in the mud as they spotted signs that the patrol was coming back their way.

Dawn had come and gone, midday had passed and still they were stuck in the sewer ditch. The smell was so overpowering they had trouble thinking straight, there were so many flies buzzing around and over them it seemed impossible to imagine another sound actually existing.

Beyond the ditch now seemed so inaccessible, how would they ever get back to camp?

In the distance, they could see where the drainage field reached the forest, which would allow them to look for a longer way around back to their army.

This was their salvation and gave them the strength to

continue, pushing themselves far beyond what they could believe possible.

Just a few dozen kilometers away, what was Raydr doing? Had they seen patrols, were they worried? Sending people after them? Was she going out of her mind?

What if the Horde had decided to take the fight to them, then what would happen, what was happening now?

Worrying about her fate wasn't helping Madan focus, but he was reminded of his feeling, that he wouldn't see her again… and somehow that made him even more determined to get out of this mess.

He was going to prove that feeling wrong.

They got to the forest and started climbing out of the sludge, their clothes dripping wet. Somehow it seemed more exhausting now to get out of the ditch than to stay in, but it was just the jitters of screwing up their one chance at making it back to their camp.

The chance to screw everything up when victory was in their hands. Jitters often had a basis in reality. Was it fate? As they were trying to empty some of the sludge that had seeped into their clothes, they heard some movement.

Madan was not as far up as Arslan and he reacted with an instinct borne of decades of survival in precarious situations. He plunged back into the sewer ditch without a second thought, just as the Horde soldier discovered their position.

Arslan was caught red-handed, so to speak, almost unable to defend himself, uncertain of the next course of action. Should he protect his leader, fight to his death?

As long as it got the job done, he was ready to sacrifice himself, but would it help Madan to get away from the Horde patrol?

A split second of indecision was enough to turn the tide, start or end battles and Arslan was staring down the barrel of a pistol – and held at spear-point – before he could make up his mind.

"You alone? You alone here!" the Horde soldier said with a bad accent.

Arslan put his hands up at mid-level, not even knowing how to answer, what to answer. Had Madan swum away, letting him deal with this mess?

He was able to deal with most situations but having the future of the Rebel Army on his shoulders, on this very decision, was enough to make him lose all common sense.

It seemed better to die quickly than be faced with such indecision.

"Don't kill me, please, don't kill me, I'll tell you everything, everything," Arslan begged; he disgusted himself, he almost sounded serious, believable.

"Are you alone? Are you alone here!" the soldier insisted; he didn't seem like the brightest kind.

"I am-"

Arslan saw Madan rising out of the mud and he rolled on himself to be out of the soldier's line of fire in case he let an involuntary shot out.

The Horde man received a well-aimed ball of mud in the face and Madan pounced on him while the element of surprise lasted, throwing him down on the rocks to crush his skull.

Unfortunately, while this plan worked to perfection, the soldier did yelp very loudly in fear, and, worse still, fired a shot that sounded like thunder in the buzzing of flies.

Now there was no chance for stealth any more, they were hunted, the patrols rallying to find the intruders.

They didn't bother to sink the sentry in the sludge, they just ran.

Towards the forest at full speed, they were out of time and luck, and they had to give their all to survive the next few minutes.

Even if all seemed pointless, doomed already, they could not give up.

They managed to reach the forest just as a few bullets shot past them; the Horde patrol had spotted them without a doubt and was now closing in on them full charge.

They were exhausted, all nervous energy spent, too much time running on adrenaline that it could not help them stay in top shape any more. The images were blurred by sweat, and no matter how hard they tried, they knew they would be caught, it was simply inevitable.

They needed a plan of action, but how to make one on the run, how to regain an advantage they had never had?

They were in enemy territory, nothing was going their way, how to change the tide, turn the scales around?

Prove beyond a doubt that the Horde soldiers were just usurpers, this was his home, not theirs?

Arslan tripped and Madan went to pick him up, stopping in mid-motion as he saw one of the trip wires on the surface of the forest.

How to turn it around? By using their own devices against them, by being smarter rather than stronger.

The patrol was hurrying, so close, they could hear their vengeful breaths, their curses, their threats, their promises of horrible torture…

Madan looked at Arslan intensely and without words, the plan became obvious to the younger man.

The bait, the trap, everything rested on chance, on timing their actions perfectly, on the Horde soldiers being too bloodthirsty to realize the obvious.

They did not hesitate to put it into motion, they had no choice in the matter.

Arslan tried to hide as best he could, rolling up in a ball to be as small and invisible as possible, while Madan rose to his tallest, putting all his defiance in the gesture, all his scorn for his enemies, all his hatred.

Whatever happened, they would not break his spirit. They had never managed to break him, not defeated, not enslaved… and certainly not now.

"Come and get me!" he yelled, a roar of pure loathing, and sprinted away to lead them on.

The soldiers focused on the visible enemy, forgetting about caution. Not that they tripped the boobytrap wire as they ran past, but they did not see Arslan and so could not stop him from tripping it, activating the trap.

Neither Rebel knew what the trap was all about, what they would unleash, and they were both blown away.

Literally, as the bomb they had triggered lay the forest to waste, producing such a powerful explosion that Madan and Arslan were both half knocked out by it.

The disorientation and dizziness was bad but they both got back on their feet as quickly as they could, in case some of their enemies had survived.

The explosion had been bad, heard from a distance without a doubt, although their own ears were ringing so loudly they could barely hear each other shouting at the other.

The soldiers were hard to even identify from their remains, even their weapons were useless.

Nothing left to do but run back to camp as quickly as they could, to get the news back and prepare for the assault.

They were extra-careful around the forest and its tripwires given what they had experienced, but speed was still of the essence; that noise would not have gone unnoticed and would attract the thunders of the Horde Army on them.

Precipitate an attack?

Madan was going over possible scenarios as they ran; maybe the Citadel had been his home and he still felt linked to it but every step he took toward his camp made him feel much better.

His home, his people… he was coming back to them after all.

The Rebel sentries were of course in high alert after the explosion and they were nearly caught in friendly fire: their smell soon became the center of attention as they hurried to get back to the main camp to prepare the attack.

Night was coming and with it some cover: in spite of their fatigue, both men thought now was the time to strike, before the Horde could reorganize and expect a direct assault.

Maybe it was too late for a completely surprise attack but they would make the most of it.

The news that the plan was on, the secret passageway was indeed there, made the tension reach a paroxysm in the men. Their wait was over, the sacrifice they had made could be repaid, their warrior spirit was rekindled and set afire.

They were ready to face the war, in good or bad.

Which was exactly what Madan expected from them.

The preparations began immediately and Madan tried to clean up a bit, if only to have a little more grip on weapons, if not dignity, but his appearance was far from his mind.

One person hadn't come to greet them and he noticed her absence with a little anxiety.

"Has anyone seen Raydr?" he asked. As no one answered,

he grabbed a passerby carrying weapons. "Raydr, where is she?"

"Your tent, last I heard," he shrugged.

He had to tell her the news himself, and also urge her to stay away, not participate, not risk her life. The battle would be merciless, she had to agree to stay far from it, or he would never be able to focus on what needed to be done.

"Raydr, don't mind the smell, I'm all right, we just got back and everything is ready and we will launch the attack tonight-"

He stopped in mid-step and sentence. Their tent was in no way large and luxurious; if he couldn't see Raydr, it meant she was not inside.

Madan went out and circled around it, looking around to see her. She could be anywhere, he was well aware of that, as she was fond of overseeing preparations all over the camp but… this ominous feeling had invaded his heart.

Something had happened, he would not find her, she was nowhere to be found.

He could have gone to find another soldier, asked him, asked whoever he found in his way, start a whole manhunt for her, yet somehow he knew this would not yield any results.

He rushed back into the tent instead, and tried to see what he had missed, clues to her presence or lack thereof.

He was exhausted from the chase through the drainage field and frantic but he immediately saw what he had missed the first time.

Both he and Raydr only carried minimal gear with them, but everything of hers was gone.

He wasn't sure how to interpret this and felt a bit dizzy, nearly crashing on their 'bed', a few cushions and blankets strewn about in the middle of the tent.

There was a piece of paper lying atop one of the cushions,

paper worn out from many uses in battle planification; Raydr's handwriting was sketchy at best, as was his own recollection of the written language but he was able to piece it together, whispering the words under his breath. As he read, it almost seemed to him he wasn't reading at all, but rather she was whispering in his ear, her voice soft and strong, close to breaking at the same time. Her farewell.

"When you will come back I will have left. I can't stay and not fight. I can't stay and watch you die, thinking I could have prevented it if only I'd been there for you. And I can't stay and fight either. My time of fighting died with the last HomeBasers, I have nothing left in me. Nothing at all. I know you will triumph, Dayan, I know you won't let anything happen to you. And I also know in time, you will come to find me. And when you do find me, I won't be alone, you will find us, and we will welcome you home."

Tears sprang in his eyes as he read the message again; he was overcome by fear, of losing her, but also relief, that she was thinking of both of them and the mission, his revenge, knowing how important it was to get rid of the Horde.

He saw every word with extreme clarity and everything became so self-evident. He would find 'them', not just her. The reason why she looked ill, why she wasn't recuperating as quickly as she should have… Not the rads at all, something much more beautiful, perhaps the one sign he needed to give him more courage. The courage to see this battle through, at all costs.

For he wouldn't be fighting for strangers or brothers-in-arms or revenge. He was fighting to keep his family safe again.

He stifled the sob that still threatened from his lips and took a moment to calm down. A few deep breaths to get his focus back. Raydr was safe, his child-to-be was safe as well. All he had to do was keep them this way.

He carefully folded the letter and wrapped it in a cord, to wear as a makeshift necklace. His pledge, his protection, his future.

Now all he had to do was deal his wretched past a crippling blow.

CHAPTER 10

The Charge

A diversion within a diversion.

They intended to distract the Horde soldiers by launching an attack on the Citadel's walls with the bulk of the army while a small squad went into the secret tunnel to eliminate key guards and open the gates, allowing everyone inside.

Once that was done, they would fight with all their might. Good or bad, victory or defeat, everything would end with this charge.

None of them were even considering retreat as an option. To the bitter end, this time; they had made their peace with their God.

But Madan still intended to win.

The fatigue was gone from their limbs, most of the smell had been scrubbed off, in fear that it could give their position away… Madan almost felt as though he had rested all day, the adrenaline rush was so strong he could not feel any pain, or so it seemed at the moment.

Invincibility had a tendency to disappear in the blink of an eye.

Madan left command to the army to Hassan while he and Arslan led two squads into the drainage fields and booby-trapped forest.

All good and fine, but they had to make it happen, get this

plan moving.

Time to die or live again.

Madan thought his soldiers looked more serene than he was; Arslan looked so focused and determined, but maybe he was a master at hiding his emotions... or maybe Madan himself didn't realize the confidence he exuded as he led the charge.

Of course, their run-in with the patrols and the explosion had made the Horde double up the guards in the drainage field.

Madan and Arslan's squads had to move forward carefully, waiting for the other part of the army to apply pressure and divide the Horde soldiers' focus.

Of course, at the same time, they could not wait too long and risk exposing their comrades to too much enemy fire. A question of hairline balance that could tip one way or the other.

When they heard distant explosions, Madan gave the signal to move forward. He didn't know what kind of means of communication the Horde had but he would not risk his men unnecessarily.

He preferred risking himself.

They crossed the drainage field without meeting any resistance, those patrols had been called back to face the attack, but the forest was booby-trapped in more ways than one. The Horde knew all about the patrol it had lost and they had doubled up the guards there, perhaps fearing another attack that would decimate their ranks.

If the squadrons were able to avoid the tripwires with careful observation, they were caught by an ambush and pinned down by enemy fire.

Using trees and rocks to protect themselves worked to a point but they were running out of time, they could not afford to lose any more minutes trying to get around the dug-in Horde soldiers.

Their men were dying around the Citadel walls, providing them with cover, they had to move now!

But Madan could not see that happening anytime soon, they were in a gauntlet, what bad luck had made the Horde lay an ambush there, they could not make a detour to get to the tunnel, not with the way the hills were protecting their enemy.

He had ordered a small team to try and flank the Horde's position but from the gunfire they heard in the distance, things were not going well there either.

How to rout them out, give them a clear way into the tunnel, they had no time to waste!

How to get this attack moving?

Madan was going insane, heroics wouldn't do the trick, he didn't want to lose his men, he had to get into the city, why was he stuck here of all places?

He almost wished he could have banged his head on the trunk of the tree he was hiding behind, but Raydr had had a point, he couldn't show indecision and fear in the middle of a battle for their lives.

He couldn't freeze up either, he had to move forward, not back, come up with something!

"Tripwire," he muttered under his breath.

His ears were still ringing a bit from the explosion he had lived through earlier on. Those bombs were powerful, more than enough to devastate a hideout, if properly delivered.

He didn't even think of telling his men what he was doing. years of fighting alone had bred him to be independent and to act quickly when an idea popped into his mind.

He ran off, looking for the last boobytrap they had avoided, following the trigger wire back to the explosives set to destroy the unwary invaders. He wasn't an expert with bombs but it looked particularly nasty to him, the charges set around containers full of metal pebbles to cause maximal damage.

He was puffing out his breath slowly, trying to remove the explosives wrapped around those containers when the sound of boots on the forest ground made him whirl around, throwing the knife he was using with deadly precision.

Arslan was saved only because it hit his weapon, which he had slung on his shoulder. "What are you doing?" he accused.

Madan didn't even bother saying sorry, there was no time for apologies.

"Help me get this off!" he ordered.

Arslan quickly understood what he was up to. After giving him his knife back, he did his best to dislodge the explosives from their niche without setting them off.

They were both sweating heavily, anything could trigger the bomb, they were not experts on the subjects, and they were pressed by time.

Finally Madan held a hellish looking device, weighing about thirty pounds, and he had no idea what to do with it.

How to deliver it to the enemy, how to bring it to the optimal spot to wipe them out? He had just traded one impossibility for another, some leader he was!

But overthinking also led to disaster, so he ran back to the front lines, which had shifted a bit, the men getting worried with both their leaders' disappearance.

There was no way he could throw it far enough, and the stand-off was continuing, their way forward was blocked, and retreat was out of the question.

But the second Mayvin, their resident genius, saw the device, he looked ready to kiss Madan for giving him the way to destroy the enemy nest.

The wonder of working with motivated, intelligent men.

Within seconds, the mechanic extraordinaire had rigged three of their harpoon launchers to fire simultaneously and send the deadly device over their enemies' heads.

They engaged the enemy to distract them, wasting bullets but it was for the good cause, or so they hoped.

There was always a sort of poetic justice to dealing a crippling blow to their oppressors by using their own weapons against them.

The explosion was devastating, flattening the whole area, making their ears ring and bleed from the force of the detonation. Still the second they could stand on their feet they charged, before the dust could settle, in case some of their enemies were still entrenched. They needed to eradicate them once and for all to move forward, this was the first leg of their journey, not the last, they could not afford any more lost time.

As they ran past the area, they heard a few moans or muffled screams that they quickly silenced; within minutes they were in front of the secret tunnel, sprinting in to catch up and come to their comrades' rescue.

The distance seemed so little compared to the day before, the cave-ins were plowed through as though they weren't even there, no hesitation, no fear, only pure determination.

As they were closing in on the thin wall that separated them from the inner Citadel, Arslan began to laugh under his breath, becoming almost hysterical.

"First we get massacred, the whole army against the Horde. Now we split up once, twice, and we will bring them to their knees!"

Madan envied his confidence. All he could say was that they

had a good chance if they didn't screw it up.

All he could say was that he was about to step back in his city, his Home, after more than fifteen years of running.

His every sense was heightened by the adrenaline, to a point where he felt almost invincible… but he knew better than to trust this impression.

Extreme caution and vigilance, as well as luck, was what they needed right now.

Once enough of them were piled in front of the wall, they started to ram it in to destroy it and expose the city within.

A part of Madan's mind half expected to find a firing squad ready to send them all to Hell, the fitting end for such a risky, crazy enterprise.

But in spite of the ruckus they made punching the wall in, they were met with deserted streets, not a sign of the inhabitants of the Citadel.

They could hear shouts, clamors, gunshots from the outer walls, where the battle was taking place, and after a few seconds of stupor, as though they did all expect death for their transgression, they pushed forward, going for the kill.

Madan wasn't sure how he was still breathing, thinking, moving, acting. It was as though he was a puppet and someone else was pulling his strings, making him move when all he felt like doing was running away from this deathtrap.

But his will was stronger than the irrational - or rather very rational - fear, and they invaded the city methodically, going for the points he had identified as strategic to open the way for their comrades in arms.

If they secured those locations, the battle would be won.

If they invaded the Citadel, the element of surprise would do half the work for them.

He knew that from experience.

When the veneer of invincibility fell, the panic made one do crazy and completely unproductive things.

And this time, the Horde soldiers would feel that panic, not him.

Death or victory, no in-betweens.

They reached a few key places, one of the defenses for a side entrance that was being pounded by their comrades, as it was one of the most likely insertion points.

The distraction worked perfectly and they were able to cut down those soldiers with minimal noise and attention, having been identified as reinforcements before the truth became obvious.

"Let them in!" Madan ordered gruffly. Now wasn't the time to celebrate a tiny victory, now was the time to push as they never had before.

No mercy, no quarters given or expected. A fight to the death to rid his city of the rats that had taken residence.

With the breach point, the Rebel army changed its strategy almost immediately, as they had been eagerly waiting for that light at the end of the tunnel.

Of course, it attracted a lot of attention, brought in more guards on them, and started the real battle for survival.

Madan had already moved off with a few handfuls of soldiers, to open up new breaches, to let everyone in, to kill as many guards as they could before it became obvious the Citadel was breached.

They needed more noise, more fight points, to confuse the enemy, to give themselves more time.

But mostly they needed to eliminate as many people as they could.

The plan was going right on track, perhaps even better than Madan could have expected. He kept thinking it would end, their advance would be halted, they would meet resistance they couldn't handle.

But nothing of the sort happened. The Horde soldiers did not retreat much but they were not invincible, and unlike the HomeBasers, they were not as fond of using the old technology to their advantage. As such, the Rebels quickly conquered key spots on the Citadel wall, which allowed them to invest the city.

They could not be dislodged now, they were in, and would not leave without getting what they wanted.

Total surrender and eradication of the squatters.

They met sparse pockets of resistance, but as they pushed forward, it became clear that the Horde members had in fact retreated, leaving only a few diehard fanatics to cover them and distract the invaders long enough to make their escape and prepare their last stand.

Madan had a good idea where they would be entrenched, where they would be waiting for the Rebels, where they hoped to turn the tide in their favor.

And he was determined not to let them get away with it.

None of them were letting their apparent victory get to their heads, but with less resistance to deal with, they were able to assess the state of the city, and they discovered another reason why they had been able to breach the Citadel with relative ease.

Without the secret passageway, none of this would have been possible, but the defenders were not in a great state.

Madan had to plunge into a side room through a wooden door that had seen much better days and he was confronted to a roomful of corpses, already beginning to stink, proving the city folks were overwhelmed and hadn't had the time to bury their dead properly or at the very least burn them.

Disease had struck and spread, weakening their enemy. While they faced a storm, the Horde was being incapacitated from within.

Divine intervention, just deserts, whatever they were witness to now was nothing short of miraculous and they had to make the most of it.

Because desperate men could become the worst opponents and do something insane just to keep control and dominion.

With the way they had used those explosives to rig the forest to be deadly, he wouldn't have been surprised if the Citadel hadn't been prepared in the same lethal and destructive way.

Never let anyone conquer them, destroy it themselves instead.

He became convinced this was the case. Not that he had the time to tell the others, but he pushed them onwards with ever increasing determination, going for the tallest building of the city.

That hadn't changed in fifteen years, although the Horde had changed its outer appearance, making it appear a tower of blood and death instead of the Tower of light and justice it had been before, having been their temple, hall of justice and governing council chamber all at once.

Now it was a monstrous palace and unfortunately they would have to discover what kind of debauchery and moral degrading had happened there.

And as quickly as possible.

Madan felt the panic, he knew his intuition wasn't wrong.

The Horde would fight for the city, but the second it seemed they were losing, they would destroy everything rather than yield.

He had to stop it: there was no fear apart from that one, the fear of having his victory stolen by this coward's way out.

When he recalled the Horde Commander spitting on them, treating them like worms… and this man would rather die than yield.

Madan was animated by a fury he had rarely felt before; he needed to show that commander who was in charge.

No one could pretend to the role of Master of Destiny except one Being. They were mere mortals, they had to yield to His judgment.

The tower was heavily defended and a direct attack on the steps and easy entrances would be too long and risky.

Nonetheless, to make his plan happen, he needed noise and distraction, so Madan left his men to attack it while he, Arslan, Mayzin and a handful of others rounded up the tower to the north side, where there were more windows.

There were bars but from the distance, it seemed a man could slip in without problem.

Which was exactly what they would have to do, and that was where the harpoon launchers they had carried with them came handy again.

They would be exposed and the climb would be dangerous, if not deadly, but they had to try. They had to get up there.

Madan didn't hesitate an instant; he went first as soon as the harpoons found something to hang on to, climbing as quickly as he could. He focused only on himself, shutting out everything else, trusting the others to cover him, trusting them to protect him if he climbed up fast enough.

He was a little dizzy and out of breath when he arrived at the window, but no one had dropped boiling oil on him, no one had even peeked out, as though their attack had gone unnoticed for now.

Good sign, bad sign?

He plunged into the window, into the tower, without even taking the time to catch his breath, ready for anything…

But not the heavy scent of perfume that came from the room he had crashed into.

The room was dark as it had heavy drapes over the windows, plenty of beds and cushions, the smell…

The Horde commanders obviously kept a harem and good fortune had allowed him to choose that window out of all the choices. The women had probably been evacuated elsewhere or were cowering in fear somewhere…

This was the perfect insertion point.

He was moving to the window to tell the others to hurry - he fully intended to run off on his own as soon as he had given the signal - when a slight rustle made him duck. Thus avoiding a knife, expertly thrown, meant for his neck.

He rolled and dodged as more pieces of furniture were thrown his way, as well as spears and whatever else came handy.

The women hadn't been evacuated, they were inside the room, and ready to defend their lives with everything they had.

One of them ignited a vial of perfume and threw it on him: the fire spread on his clothes, forcing him to remove his outer clothes and exposing his armor underneath, and his face, no longer shrouded by his burnous.

He didn't know how many enemies he had in the room, but he let out a salvo to calm their ardors and make them hide again.

He took cover behind a bed, trying to see where they were. His flaming clothes had made some draperies and cushions catch fire and this brought some light in the room but also obnoxious-smelling smoke. How could they hide in here, where were they hiding?

"It's over!" he cried out. He had bigger fish to fry than women and he could not afford to lose time over their zeal. "The Horde is over, you're free now, get out of here!"

Even as he said those words, he realized the problem. Harems were made to keep the women in, they probably couldn't escape the room, which was the reason why they had attacked.

If only the others would climb up already!

But it would somehow be embarrassing to need help in front of a group of women.

So he spotted the main door and sprinted toward it, shooting it down as he went to force the women to cower and give him the time to show them the way out.

Once the locks and hinges were destroyed, the doors fell down with a loud clank.

Madan moved off, trying to see the women in the light of the spreading fire, wanting them to leave and be done with them.

He had trouble believing they would be ready to defend the Horde given the 'place' they had been given, but he didn't want to be caught unawares a second time.

He wanted to get back to the window. Putting out the fire would have been a great idea because he didn't want to attract any unnecessary attention.

But he had to eliminate the threat the women posed first.

He skulked in the room, hiding behind a column, keeping his ears pricked for any kind of noise coming from his opponents.

He did hear some desperate whispers, and light coughs because of the growing fire.

In spite of all his caution, he was attracted by a clang coming from his right, and so lost focus of what was happening behind him before it was too late.

The women were throwing whatever they had on him, in this

case vases used for potted plants, made heavy by the earth and sand they were filled with.

He let go of his gun but still managed to roll on himself and pull out his knife, closer to a scimitar than anything else.

As he did this, he heard imperative whispers, someone telling others to run and padded feet scampering off.

The dizziness was short-lived; it wasn't the embarrassment pushing him to act, but plain old survival.

Women were just as vicious as men, just as merciless and dangerous, he never made the mistake of underestimating them.

Now most of them were fleeing, acting on their instinct of survival as well, but when he got up on slightly shaky legs, one of them attacked him, hissing at the others to run.

She was using a chair, waving it around like a bat, and one swing connected painfully, making him plow to the floor before he could gain control of the fight.

He saw her in the light of the growing fire, silk gowns hindering her from swift movement, diving to recuperate his fallen weapon.

She might not have known how to use it, but he could not take that chance, since she was obviously resourceful and determined…

He rushed on her and they grappled: she just managed to squeeze away from and get back up, wielding the firearm with unease but enough assurance to know that she was aware of its basic use.

Still Madan barely moved and just stayed in a half crouch, stunned.

When his hand had come into contact with her skin, the strangest feeling of familiarity…

Long ago, the image in his head overcoming his best

judgment, his survival instinct, that tingle on his skin, every time he touched her. The girl of his dreams, the way she smiled had always enchanted him…

And he looked at her now and his heart almost broke apart, shattering at what she had become, at the pain and torture she had had to suffer through.

One eye was white and blue, having been burnt through. Scars on her face, missing teeth, one finger cut off, signs that her arms had been broken more than once, her expression, the folly, the pain, he let out an involuntary whimper of disbelief.

"Maira?"

She gasped in panic, her useless eye growing wider as though she was trying to see through it, as though she could not believe what the other was seeing.

Her eye was moving so quickly, trying to detail and recognize him visually, where it was obvious her heart had already told her the answer.

"Dayan." She could not even hold the weapon up any more, it was as though all her strength left her broken, abused body.

He could not find the words to speak, he only extended a hand toward her.

The weapon clattered on the floor, she was under the shock, a hand going to her mouth unconsciously, as much to express her dismay and disbelief as to stifle the uncontrollable sob that was rising from the depths of her being.

"Maira, you're alive," he said, incapable of saying anything else, of speaking the words rushing in his mind, how he had mourned her, cried for her, wished only to be dead with her. How the years between then and now had seemed empty and pointless without her, how tortured he was to think of all she had had to go through, all the hardships he saw written on her body, on her broken soul.

But nothing would come out right, and she coiled back from his hand, hiding her scarred eye, looking ashamed and devastated, incapable of uttering anything other than whimpers herself.

"Alive?" she sobbed in disbelief.

"A... Awan?" Madan asked, although he was almost sure of the answer. But he had to know. To find her again in these circumstances was unimaginable, but if their son...

The groan of pain that escaped her trembling lips made the threatening tears spill down. Of course, he was dead, and perhaps it was better this way. Who knows what he would have become raised in this hell?

But the pain did not think in such terms, the pain only thought of the smiling baby torn from his mother's arms, an innocent life destroyed for no purpose whatsoever.

Maira shook her head, her heavily applied makeup running down her cheeks; words were unnecessary, words were too painful to utter.

"I'm so sorry, I'm so sorry, I"- Madan wanted to hold her but she pulled away from him.

"Don't look at me, don't - please don't. You were dead, everyone was dead," she whimpered; there was such shame in her voice, such torment.

Madan put an appeasing hand up so she would stop trying to run; she was backing up toward the window unconsciously.

"You were alone, you had no choice, you did what you had to do to survive," he muttered, his voice close to breaking. "None of it is your fault, Maira."

"Don't look at me, please, don't look at me."

"It's not your fault, they made you this way," Madan argued.

"Maira is dead," she said finally, sobbing. "She died so long ago, all she left is a husk. I'm not Maira, I'm no one, don't look at me like that, please, don't look at me!"

"We do what we must to survive," Madan said. "You survived."

She shook her head, incapable of looking at him in the eye. "The things I did," she barely had the strength to speak the words.

"The things I did, Maira, to survive… It's not your fault, it's not mine, you are here now, I found you again," he said, almost catching her hand; but the missing finger allowed her to escape his grasp.

She was crying and shaking her head, having tracked to the window now. In the light of the fire, she looked like a ghost, an apparition, the gleam in her dead eye defiant. No longer torn by indecision and torment, her choice was made.

"Maira is dead, she died long ago, she was always dead."

He tried to run to her but it was already too late. He could have sworn he heard her say 'goodbye' but by the time he reached the window, she was so far down, plunging to her death, that he could not even see her any more.

He didn't know what happened next, he was plunged into darkness, remembering moments he had thoughts were gone from his mind forever, happiness that had been stolen and ripped from him.

He wasn't sure if he was sobbing, or howling out, but when Arslan put a worried hand on his shoulder, he got up, red-eyed but steady, more determined than ever to end this.

Destroy those who had created and spread such pointless pain, uncaring of the lives and spirits they destroyed, those they corrupted beyond redemption, even in their own minds.

For every death, they would pay tenfold. Revenge is a fire

that consumes everything in its path, outwardly and inwardly, a destroyer like no other, that burns away sense, reason, fear: Madan was animated, possessed by revenge as he ran forward, pursuing the Horde soldiers that were trying to defend the Tower, defend their leader, and in his personal opinion, allow their leader to set demolish the whole city, in an effort to undermine their victory.

Standard mentality: If I can't have it, then no one will.

Madan was so focused that he felt nothing except his unleashed hatred; caution, moderation, strategic work, all those concepts were gone from his head.

All that mattered was finding them and eradicating them, every single one of them, all those who had imposed such pain, such misery. Masters of the world and destinies, condemning others to a fate worse than death, so much so that death was the release everyone wished for, death was the only freedom they were left with.

His parents, Awan, Maira, everyone who had ever been in their scope…

He didn't feel invincible, he was simply out of his mind. He wasn't sure he could feel pain, it seemed he was afire with a pain greater than any bodily woe.

He was the instrument of vengeance of all those who had been killed, abused, tortured; their strength was his now, and it was completely overwhelming because there was so many of them, so many souls aching for retribution.

Only Arslan was able to keep up with him, trusting him implicitly to lead them to victory, not once doubting his abilities or sanity.

Their rush seemed to give them an advantage; the Horde soldiers expected a coordinated, careful attack, not two madmen running and shooting everything in sight, not even bothering to secure the rooms and hallways they were 'conquering', just plowing forward, even at the risk of getting engulfed inside enemy territory.

As such, they reached deep, causing panic, as many Horde soldiers took this as the proof they were being overwhelmed, and the fear they were already feeling, the fear that told them all the signs were coming true, their time was at an end, grew to an exponential point.

Madan and Arslan were Angels of Death, untouchable, unkillable: myths were formed in seconds, that was the power of the mind.

Granting them power they did not have; but by granting them this power, they made it happen.

Behind them echoed the sounds of a terrible battle, the rest of the Rebels having to deal with the destabilized Horde defenders.

But Madan did not care, he could not care about any individual fate, not when the whole was screaming through him for justice. He and Arslan reached deep in the tower, climbing storeys and leaving their enemy panting in their wake. If they stopped and thought about it, they probably would have been paralyzed by fear at their own gall: how could they expect to come out of it unscathed?

But that was the whole point, they weren't looking to make it out, only make those who had created this situation pay.

Eventually though, whatever form of communication the Horde possessed warned those higher up the Tower who was coming their way and what to expect, and they reacted with a fanaticism that was to be expected, detonating the hallways, endangering the whole stability of the building.

The Tower had ten storeys, the tallest building of the Citadel and most imposing building he had ever seen, save for those who stood in the old cities.

They had attacked the third storey and now they had climbed up to the seventh. The explosion knocked them out, the concussion coming from the enclosed quarters making them even more dizzy, their ears ringing so loudly they could barely hear anything other than the blood pumping in their veins.

They were not immortal, they were not invincible, but they were unstoppable.

As soon as he was steady enough on his legs, Madan pushed forward, met by a barrage of debris they could not get across without losing an incredible amount of time they did not have.

They heard noise and prepared to fight and defend their lives, but they quickly realized their comrades had caught up with them.

"What happened here?" Mayzin worried.

"Blew out the corridor and the stairs," Arslan answered while Madan went to a nearby wall that was still standing.

Arslan glanced at his leader: Madan seemed in turmoil, ready to break through with his fists, but nothing could have been further from the truth.

He was actually raking his mind, every memory he had cast away for so long, his time as a child, his father having been part of the ruling council of the Citadel.

He had been in those walls before, bored to death sometimes while his father and the other councilmen talked and talked about what the future of the city should be…

Had they only known…

But he had had friends then, and they found their own ways to play, much to the dismay of the Tower's maintenance personnel.

Their playtime had earned them more than a few reprimands.

"We secured the lower levels, they're ours, but not much fighting, what's up, what are they doing? Hassan says the City has fallen under our control, still pockets of resistance, but we will get rid of them soon enough," Mayzin said. "What are they doing up there?"

"No idea, they just ran for it and now they've cut us off," Arslan answered, but he was watching Madan, hoping for a solution, another miracle.

"Let's find out," Madan muttered, tracking backwards, finding one of the small interstices in the wall that served as an air vent to allow good air circulation.

What he and his friends had discovered long ago was that the hole looked very small, but that was just an illusion. The vents were much larger, but when he made the cover slide out, he discovered just how much time had passed since those days.

Not quite as spacious as he remembered it to be.

But that wouldn't stop him.

He didn't even utter another word, he was still possessed by the same urgency as before.

He knew why the Horde was retreating, why they weren't fighting down to the last man.

They fully intended to make the Rebels pay for their victory, by snatching it from them in Hell.

Arslan was attuned to his mood and started following him immediately, trusting him completely. The others looked at each other in confusion, but their blood was boiling from the battle and all they wanted was to end it, knowing that the city was secure, they had won without a doubt.

The climb up wasn't exactly easy. There were a few

outcroppings to help but it was mostly through determination that they managed to get to the next level, especially carrying their weapons and gear to continue the battle.

Once they reached the next level, Madan looked back and put a finger to his lips. No point going back, exposed in the hallway. They would skulk on in the vents and reach their destination unseen and unheard.

Stealth was particularly difficult for the bigger men so Madan, Arslan and Mayzin took the lead, wanting to discover where their enemy was holed up and what they were up to.

The others followed as quickly as they could with their bulkier weapons.

They began to hear angry shouts and hisses, obviously people who were on the edge and panicking at the thought of losing their power.

One voice roared over the others and Madan had an involuntary gagging reflex as well as a shudder. He knew that voice all too well, it had haunted him for so many years, kept him awake in his jail, slave to the Horde soldiers, for months of torture.

The commander.

Of course, he would still be alive, of course he would still be at the head of this madness… ready to destroy them all.

Madan accelerated his crawl through the vent: now or never, this was their last chance! They reached the vent opening that connected to the room the Horde top men were holed up in. From what they could see as they peered in carefully, there were three dozen men in there, all looking nervous, save for the biggest of them all, shrouded by a mask, almost completely covered by his battle armor. The Horde Commander was at work on some sort of column, unfathomable actions for Arslan but Madan was sure of himself, he was preparing the end of the Citadel.

How much time did they have left, how to know, how to be sure?

They had to attack as quickly as possible, before the commander finished his work.

The element of surprise could give them a tiny advantage but to attack so many men was akin to suicide.

They would quickly overrun them or destroy their sole means of entrance into the room. What they needed was a good diversion to divide and conquer, for that tactic never failed.

Madan sent Arslan to warn the others, still struggling to catch up with them. They would exit the vents from another opening and attack the room directly to give Mayzin and Madan the chance to eliminate the threat from within.

The wait had to be the worst part, gnawing at his nerves, rendering him completely insane.

"What is he doing?" Mayzin whispered in low tones. "You know what he's doing, what is he doing?"

"Making sure we all lose," Madan answered, keeping a close look on the commander's actions.

Perhaps, the Horde was not the most technologically advanced faction around, but they knew how to destroy, they had a particular talent for it.

Reports of gunfire made everyone jump to the ceiling, Madan included. So focused had he been on the commander, trying to pierce his sick mind and identify his secrets, that he had forgotten about the imminent attack.

It only took him a second to recover his wits and while the top men of the Horde rushed to the door to make their stand and push back the invaders, he rolled into the room and started shooting.

No time to be precise and methodical; despite the danger of hurting himself as much as the rest of them, he attacked with his strongest explosives, grenades and rounds that could cut an ageless boulder in two.

The concussion from the grenades was bad, stunning, but he was getting used to that kind of reeling assault on his senses, if bleeding from the ears could be considered a normal occurrence in a day.

Parts of the ceiling tumbled down as well, showering them with dust and chunks of rock and cement, reducing visibility greatly.

Creating cover for both the attackers and the defenders.

But Madan simply did not care. For someone who had always been careful at surviving, he was throwing away his every cautious habit. It wasn't time to be careful any more, everything was in the balance, survival wasn't enough any more.

Time to step up or step out, but he would no longer tolerate anything other than eradication.

He wasn't sure if he had cut down everybody but the lieutenants were of little import, what mattered was the commander and somehow Madan knew he was still alive and preparing havoc and mayhem and death.

Mayzin had gone directly for the commander while Madan attacked the rest, knowing instinctively that something was afoot, but the boy did not have what it took to face such a monster.

When Madan reached that part of the room, the commander was choking the young man, having raised him up in the air by the neck.

Mayzin was suffocating, turning blue, incapable of defending himself. Madan could have shot the commander and been done with it, done with everything, but he would have killed

Mayzin at the same time, the bullets being too powerful from so close.

He didn't even hesitate, even though he should have considered the greater good.

Instead of using his weapon, he rammed into both men, making the commander plow to the floor, letting go of the young man through the surprise.

Madan was ready to grapple and fight and end it now, if he could by blowing the other's head off, but the commander was a strong man, used to quick actions in battle.

He didn't want to waste his time fighting a soldier when he could destroy the whole movement. He pushed Madan off, kicking him away so powerfully that the breath was knocked out of him.

But he wasn't too dizzy to notice what the commander left as a parting gift as he ran away from the room.

Madan rolled away as quickly as he could to get away from the epicenter of the explosion.

Even curled up in a ball, it felt as though he had been rolled over by ten heavily loaded trucks and all he heard was ringing that seemed to tear right through his mind.

He wanted to get back on his feet but he simply could not find his balance, he could not feel the floor any more.

He was gripped and barely had enough strength to push back his attacker: someone was screaming in his ear but he couldn't understand the words, too much noise, too much pain, he was nauseous just when it was time to be strong.

Find the nexus of calm, he could not change the past, but the future was his to shape.

It was not out of his hands. So many things were beyond his reach, impossible to take or give back, but not that.

One more effort, push himself far over his limits, what did it matter? Death awaited them if he could not face his demon.

"His medallion!" Mayzin was coughing out as loudly as he could. "His medallion is a trigger, don't let him use it, don't let him-"

Sounds were confused and confusing in his damaged ears but the message was received loud and clear, and spurred him to push himself again, uncaring of his poor state of being.

The commander hadn't just wrecked the room, he had destroyed the exit, trapping them inside.

Or so he thought. Madan went directly for the vents, knowing instinctively that the commander was going for the roof, that whatever he intended to do needed a clear transmit window.

He was alone in the fight; this did not deter or bother him in any way. The fight was to the death, and he wanted to be the one to end that monster's life.

Poisoning his world for far too long, polluting his thoughts, dominating his fear, the Horde leader was a cancer that needed to be eradicated once and for all.

The climb helped Madan get control of his body back and by the time he emerged on the roof, his hearing was the only thing that was still impaired by a continuous ringing. Apart from that, he was ready for anything… although he realized with some panic that in his haste, he had forgotten his firearm and only had his knife left to attack and defend himself.

The commander was near the ledge, looking over the Citadel, as though to appreciate the view one last time before destroying it all.

Even with a weapon, Madan would have had to get nearer, to steal the medallion from him: The Horde Commander was holding it at arm's length, as though admiring its power and the destruction it would bring. Savoring it in advance.

The Citadel's state was dismal. Even as he approached the commander, Madan's eyes tracked down, at the destruction that had already swept the city.

Inside the Tower, they hadn't felt, heard or seen the extent of the damage, but no one had been spared.

The Citadel was already in ruins, the fight had been deadly, and the commander seemed to relish this violence and pointless death.

The medallion was the trigger, but how did it work, how could it bring the final destruction, what should he do?

Smash it? Tempting but that could not be the solution, it could not be so simple. Smashing it would probably trigger the doomsday device they had rigged.

One solution, he had to steal it.

More than killing the commander, he had to remove the medallion from him.

It would have been so much simpler to just pounce and kill, only have that in mind; to have a secondary purpose was wreaking havoc with his concentration.

How long before that blasted monster would turn around or finish his appreciation of the deaths he had caused?

How much time did he have to act?

One miscalculation and they could all die. Now wasn't the time to feel dizzy or overwhelmed and Madan chased those useless emotions away. His enemy was right in front of him.

After all those years of waiting, of running, he could finally take back the power that had been taken from him.

With one swift movement, he made the medallion jump from the commander's hand, but the man was no fool, having been a soldier and warrior, as well as a madman for most, if not all of his life.

Instead of bringing the medallion to him, the commander jerked at precisely the wrong moment, reacting to the threat, and that made Madan lose his tenuous hold on the necklace, which fell a few meters away from them, making a dull clank on the rock floor as it landed.

The two men glanced at each other, at the medallion; both were armed with long knives, nothing else, both were capable of delivering death in one stroke with those weapons, and both knew the real challenge would be to steal the trigger away from the other.

Run for it or attack for it?

Madan was sick of running. Uncaring of the risk, he plowed into the Horde commander, managing to surprise him, as the Horde leader expected him to go straight for the medallion instead.

It was like hitting a boulder. The man was so strong, so powerful that it seemed impossible to overcome him.

He was disbalanced by surprise and recuperated immediately, grabbing Madan and throwing him against the Tower ledge as though he weighed nothing at all.

The breath was forcefully knocked out of him but he did not stop moving. He did not feel the bruised, protesting muscles and bones in his back, all that mattered was fighting back.

The Horde Commander presumed too much of his strength or put too little value on the resistance of others.

He thought Madan was out of the fight and was going to recuperate his medallion to finish his task.

Madan ran and slid, jostling the bigger man out of the way and grabbing the medallion as he scraped past it. His leg was bloody for this but he held it in his hand, he could see a hint of worry in the only part of the commander he could see, his eyes.

And that was the greatest victory, for once fear was instilled in the other, that seed of doubt would grow and fester and give you the advantage…

Or maybe he was underestimating the viciousness and ruthlessness of the beastly man that had terrorized the whole region for two decades.

With a growl that seemed to resonate right through Madan's bones, the Horde Commander attacked with a speed and determination that seemed unstoppable.

Madan wanted to kill him himself, no doubt about it, for all the pain he had caused, the torment he had imposed, the dead screaming at him to take revenge… but he had the medallion; if he gave in to revenge, if he fought, he could give that monster the advantage, the chance to blow it all to hell. And he couldn't let that happen either.

Against every fighting fiber of his being, he ran. He ran to find strength in numbers, he ran to preserve the whole and keep everyone alive.

The Tower top was not immense, he didn't have so far to go to scurry back down the air vent.

However, the surface of the roof was littered with debris, ropes, abandoned weapons, as this was the perfect vantage to survey the city and protect it from certain threats.

The defenders had been called back because of the last desperate and deadly act of their commander, but their gear was all around, and the second he ran, the Horde Leader grabbed a medium sized piece of wood and threw it with incredible accuracy and force, straight on Madan's legs, making him plummet to the ground.

He hadn't let go of the medallion, his fingers were curled

around it so hard he thought he would break it before letting it go, but he was now on the ground, no breath left, and the commander pulled on a rope that ran underneath him, pulling him closer to his enemy.

He was losing focus, everything was happening too quickly, he couldn't let fear overrule his better judgment, he had to fight!

Running was over, he had to get back on his feet and risk it all, because only madness could win over that oversized, over strengthened fool.

Just as he pushed back on his feet to face the threat, the commander used a length of rope to wrap it around his upper body: the neck was almost caught but Madan was able to put an arm up just in time to avoid being choked to death in a matter of seconds despite his poor position and this allowed Madan to free his neck.

The commander wielded his weight as though it was nothing, jerking him forward to meet a vicious kick to the upper body.

Madan managed to squeeze past and avoid most of that destructive kick but his ribs still screamed in protest - and the Horde leader was just getting started.

That monster had trained in the arts of war for decades, becoming a machine, unrelenting and unrelentless, destroying everything in his wake.

His folly was his strength, his confidence a weapon like no other. He knew no fear, only the thrill of the fight, the excitation of breaking others, the pleasure of shattering families and dreams.

Evil incarnate, but how to vanquish evil?

Fear was his enemy and he had to banish it, stand up, stand tall, for all those who had been broken and stepped over.

The commander jerked him forward again, fully intending to smash his chest apart, but this time Madan was ready.

Instead of fighting the pull and trying to stand his ground, he went with it, he let it carry him, using the strength of the other against him.

His body became a weapon, a driving ram that crashed right into the commander's chest, making him plummet backwards.

He hadn't seen that one coming.

They were close enough to the ledge that the unthinkable happened. The commander actually flew over the rock railing and fell into the void.

Madan didn't even have the time to be relieved as the rope dragged him forward, almost making him tumble over the edge himself.

The commander was holding on, already beginning to climb back up; this time he was enraged, having been humiliated by an unworthy adversary.

Who was now the only thing keeping him from plunging to his death.

Madan had no qualms about letting that monster die this way, this was the way he should die, like he had killed so many, including Madan's parents, but the rope was so tight around him he could not extricate himself from it.

He was pressed against the railing, the rock outcropping digging into his stomach, robbing him of what little breath he was able to get in; he had to cut it off before that killing machine climbed back up, he could not waste this opportunity!

One hand still gripped the medallion, it seemed he could not control those fingers any more, they had decided to stay curled around that object forever, and the other was pushing back against the railing to try and regain control of the weight dragging him down but that was only benefitting his enemy, not him.

He let go of that hold and found himself even more smashed against the rock railing, chest compressed, the Horde leader growling as he climbed back so quickly, so damn quickly...

Madan's hand tracked to the sheath on his thigh and freed a small knife. He was slow, so slow, almost incapable of coordinated movement. He needed to attack that rope and cut it off before it was too late.

The knife was very sharp and the movement caused by the commander scampering up was enough to start to cut through for the rope pressure on his shoulder made Madan almost incapable of controlling his hand in that position.

But the rope was failing, strands breaking at an accelerated pace, just a few seconds from total collapse when the commander leapt up to grab him by the neck instead.

The pressure was off the rope now but he had to fight not to tip over. He wasn't sure what the commander's goal was, climb up and kill him, or bring them both down in death, but he tried with all his might to push him back, using both hands to beat him away.

The moment he caught a glimpse of the medallion, the commander tried to grab it, one hand curled around his shoulder, the man's nails, blackened sharp things, digging into Madan's flesh even with the cloth to protect him, as the Horde leader slipped down slowly, his other hand flailing to catch the necklace's chain and clasp to steal it from his enemy.

At the same time, the commander caught the chain and jerked on the rope still around Madan's shoulder.

He slipped, the weight too much to bear, he slipped and fell forward as the commander tried to grab the medallion for himself.

The clasp gave way and the Horde leader was destabilized as well, his eyes growing wide as he realized they were going down, both of them, with nothing to hold onto any more.

He tried to slash at Madan again, catching the makeshift necklace that held Raydr's precious letter and the flayed rope. Given the man's weight, both snapped off almost immediately, falling with him while Madan tried to fight gravity as much as he could while losing the battle.

One second's difference, maybe, between his fall and the commander's, but it was enough to see the monster of a man screaming in rage and fear as he went down.

Madan didn't even have the time to feel fear. He didn't know what would happen, he still clutched the medallion-trigger and hadn't a clue what would happen when he would hit the ground.

Total and complete failure, but... he never reached the ground.

Somehow the rope had twisted around him and its other end was tied to a very solid post.

It felt as though he had been snapped in two, as though his limbs were simple twigs, nothing else. The pain was overwhelming, blinding, consciousness-wrecking.

But his fingers never let go of the medallion.

He didn't feel when his men pulled him up, having spotted him hanging from the side of the Tower. He was also unconscious when the doctors worked on him to put him back together, dislocated shoulders, broken leg, shattered elbow.

But he never let go of that deadly trigger.

EPILOGUE

The morning sun streamed into the room, warming the bed he lay in.

Madan grunted in annoyance, as he was barely capable of moving out of the way and the sun was right in his eyes.

How many days had passed since they had secured the Citadel, won against the Horde?

He wasn't sure, it was lost in a fog of pain, but despite his sullenness at being thus incapacitated, he couldn't say he was angry. Because he was still alive to feel that pain.

Mayzin had deactivated the doomsday device that had been activated by the Horde Commander, and the dismantling of the bombs spread across the city had begun.

It would have leveled the Citadel three times over.

He could be proud that he had held on, that he had given his all and that it had proven to be enough.

Or just about.

There were always new problems and he had to address them today.

Namely all the prisoners they had captured, those who had given up and begged for mercy.

Some had been killed but the number of them had been a bit too overwhelming for his lieutenants to execute in cold blood.

Also, they wanted some kind of public show, to demonstrate without a doubt that the Horde was beaten, shattered, demolished for good.

And as leader of the Rebel Army, he had to officiate, even broken up as he was, his leg and elbow in a splint, his shoulders aching with every movement. He wanted to be there, he had to be there.

Arslan came to help him up; he had to use all his self-control not to cry out in pain.

He managed to keep it down to a grunt; the cane helped him walk but it was mostly Arslan's help that allowed him to move forward and face the assembly.

A beautiful morning, smelling fresh, the renewal of spring, and all those men on their knees before him.

He was reminded of when he had been one of them, wounded and shattered, the turmoil so strong all he wanted was to die.

What to do with them, hundreds of them, all on their knees, weeping or stoical, knowing what their fate would be.

He looked at the faces of his men, the revenge, the glee, the anger, they were hoping for an execution.

"We all did things we are not proud of to survive," he began, his voice much louder than he expected, considering how weak he felt.

Arslan looked at him in surprise; all his lieutenants had been expecting something else.

"You are beaten, your leader is dead, the whole world hates you. You come from conquered nations, from thieves, from murderers, you did unspeakable things to survive. Like we all did.

"Today I say the murders stop. Today I say it ends here. We will not repeat the mistakes of the past, we will build a new world, unlike the old one. The old one poisoned our land, poisoned our hearts… It's time to let it go and form our own nation. I can't judge you. I wish I could judge you and put you all to death, blame you all for every bad thing that has happened and that will happen in the future, but I can't. You did what you thought you had to, to survive. So now survive with what you did."

"Madan!" Hassan intervened in a hissing tone.

"Enough death, enough revenge, enough falling into the same traps. Your conscience will be your judge. You are free to go."

Everyone was stunned, the victors and prisoners alike. Both were incapable of moving, of thinking, there was only one language on this cursed Earth and it was the language of death and retribution. Only that made sense. Kill or be killed.

Everything and anything else was heresy.

"You are free to go and survive with what you did to survive," Madan insisted, nodding (as much as he could nod) for the guards to remove the chains.

"But they're monsters, they're-" Hassan protested.

"And we will not lower ourselves to their level simply because we won. They are free to go," Madan ordered.

Arslan looked at him with a mixture of fear, amazement and respect. "Now you sound like Zahim,"

Madan couldn't explain it to himself completely. It would be so easy to perpetuate the same old, fall in the same patterns, deliver death and expect it in return. But if no one took the step, if no one tried to change, then they were all falling to oblivion, falling to their ultimate doom.

He was going to have faith in something new.

The men were so awkward and uncomfortable, incapable of believing what they were doing, freeing their enemy when they thought they would be putting them to death, in a shameful public execution.

The prisoners were just as disoriented, having expected nothing other than what they had always given.

Death and more death.

No one was ever given a reprieve, no one was ever given a second chance.

They weren't sure this wasn't a joke, something was wrong, but the Rebels obeyed their leader, for he had given them hope, he had been martyrized to protect them, he had defied a storm and always led them to victory.

"What are you doing?" Hassan worried, as Madan tried to get away from the assembly, wanting to get back to his bed for this 'stunt' had asked a lot out of him.

"It's better this way," Madan said in a pained mutter.

"Sir, please, sir."

One of the prisoners was trying to get closer to them, to Madan, and the soldiers reacted with great caution, threatening to beat him, making him fall on his knees again.

"Please, please, I want to talk to your leader, please, I beg you," the man sobbed.

"Let him," Madan said, but he couldn't claim his heart hadn't done a somersault in his chest.

Doing the 'right' thing was harder than it looked.

"Dayan, it's me," the man said and Madan was stunned by the use of his real name.

He studied the man more carefully but couldn't say he recognized him.

"I remember, I remember… when they branded you," the man started, his voice breaking. I was so scared, I told them I would do anything, anything…"

He started sobbing in shame and Madan felt tears threatening to spill from his own eyes, that pain, that pain was everywhere.

The man crawled forward to reach his feet. "Please forgive me, please forgive me," he whimpered.

Madan didn't know what to answer to this. It brought back bad memories, the brand on his cheek, the boy next to him crying in fear.

"Zaid," he said softly, remembering the long-forgotten name. "Zaid, I have nothing to forgive you. Nothing to forgive you."

"I left you, I left you, I was a coward, you were brave, I am a monster, please forgive me, forgive me." Zaid was showering his feet with tears.

Madan somehow managed to get down on his less damaged leg and he put a hand on his long-ago friend's head. "I have nothing to forgive you. You survived, you bear that weight. Forgive yourself, brother. Forgive. Yourself."

He gave him a kiss on the head and Arslan helped him up, to walk away while Zaid kept sobbing, incapable of doing anything else.

The display had affected everyone, impressing both his men and the ex-Horde soldiers.

He was serious, he really intended to let everyone go freely and face their own demons.

"Today they weep at your feet, tomorrow they stab you in the back," Hassan said bitterly

"Maybe," Madan agreed. "Everyone betrays the others, this is how it always ends. Unless we stop it."

He served Hassan an eloquent look; betrayal could come from friend as much as from foe.

And that was enough to silence his opposition; Hassan left, looking disgusted.

Arslan glanced at Madan as they walked back to the building that had been transformed into a hospital for the wounded.

"What will happen now?" the younger man put to him.

Madan sighed deeply. "Tomorrow… Tomorrow, the sun will rise. And with it will come… Problems and solutions. Troubles and rest. Fear and happiness. Despair and hope. What do we do, Arslan? We face it, every new day, we live it. We start living it. This is what we do from now on."

This was the only answer he could find for himself.

This was living free, as far as he could tell.

THE END